Gussy

Also by Jimmy Cajoleas

Goldeline
The Rambling

JIMMY CAJOLEAS

Gussy

Quill Tree Books
An Imprint of HarperCollinsPublishers

Quill Tree Books is an imprint of HarperCollins Publishers.

Gussy

Copyright © 2021 by Jimmy Cajoleas

All rights reserved. Printed in the United States of America.

No part of this book may be used or reproduced in any manner whatsoever without written permission except in the case of brief quotations embodied in critical articles and reviews. For information address HarperCollins Children's Books, a division of HarperCollins Publishers, 195 Broadway, New York, NY 10007.

www.harpercollinschildrens.com

ISBN 978-0-06-300877-9

Typography by Katie Fitch
21 22 23 24 25   PC/LSCH   10 9 8 7 6 5 4 3 2 1
❖
First Edition

Gussy

1

MY FAVORITE TIME IS WHEN ME AND
Cricket finish Last Lights, the final Rite of the day, when the
work is all done and the protections are up. The wolf and
the star are drawn in the dust, the cardinal feathers dangle
in threes like little flames at the four corners of the town,
and the chicken foot is buried in the desert dirt just outside the gates. It's a between time, that gloaming hour after
sunset when the daylight is still hanging on, pushing back
against the night. It's the first moment that I truly get to rest,
and it's the most perfect time of all, me and Cricket sitting
there satisfied on the front porch while Grandpa Widow
smokes a pipe and tells us stories. It's the safest I ever feel.
At night, when the Great Doom is on the roam, the wind
can howl and roar, the stars can blacken themselves, and the

moon can run off and hide, but I know our village will be safe because the Rites were performed perfectly. I saw to it myself, me and Grandpa Widow and Cricket too.

Cricket's my dog, by the way, has been for years. He wandered up all scruffy and half-starved out of the desert one day, and Grandpa Widow let me keep him. I don't know why I named him Cricket, it's just what he wanted to be called, I knew it the moment I saw him. You can tell by the way he sticks his tongue out every time I say his name. He's a happy fellow usually, likes to bark and fetch and sniff everything, but he takes the Rites serious, same as I do. Because the whole village depends on us.

Just the thought of the Great Doom out there at night, beyond the walls, past the gates, hovering over that whole stretch of dirt and rock all windblown and wild . . . I can't help it, it gives me the shivers. The Great Doom is always trying to creep in on the winds, and it'll sneak inside any way it can, through the smallest error in the Rites, the slightest rule broken. So once the gates are shut, they stay that way. And if you think I'm being some kind of scared little kid about the whole thing, well, you've got a lot to learn.

Trust me. When nighttime comes, you don't want to be out there, past those gates.

But this day, just after Last Lights, it all went a little different. This was how the troubles started, the very things that would change me and Cricket and Grandpa Widow and our whole village altogether. Yep, just as the final daylight glimmers were nearly dead and it was time for Big Gordo to draw the gates shut, I spied a speck on the horizon, small and tiny as a desert bat coming up over the hill, flitting through the glimmer. A rider, solo it looked like, some poor bedraggled messenger fleeing the dark.

"You see that?" I said.

Grandpa Widow just grunted. You could tell he liked it about as much as I did. A rider coming at twilight never brings good news. Truth was, I don't know how we missed him, as normally you can see for miles and miles everywhere and it's plumb impossible to sneak up on a body. That's a trick of the desert, a mystery of the light around here.

"I tell you one thing," said Grandpa Widow. "That rider best hurry, because we shut these gates when the light goes, no matter what."

Our village sits in a valley of desert, the Darkling Valley, bare dusty hills surrounding us for miles away on either side. It's a hidden little spot, an oasis in the long endless stretch of nothing. I say "nothing," but I just mean there aren't any people in it. There's all kinds of other critters out there in the desert, snakes and spiders and lizards and wildcats and night birds and vultures and hawks and eagles and just about everything else you can imagine. They're smart enough to eke a living out of dust, which is more than I can say for humankind, let me tell you. If we were half of what critters are, we wouldn't have a care in the world.

Travelers through the desert aren't uncommon—we have a dozen different folks dropping in and out day to day, messengers and peddlers and outlaws and hunters and just about any other type of person you could think of passing through on their way to elsewhere—but most folks don't cut it so close to nightfall, when the Great Doom is on the roam. Still, sometimes I wake at night and I see lights crossing the valley, wagon trains led by torches. I hear little snippets of singing, folks hollering hymns and prayers, protections against the Great Doom. I see them and I say a prayer myself, the winds roaring and howling out there, and I'm grateful to be safe here in the village, protected.

"You wouldn't close the gates on the rider, would you?" I said, because the nearest town is a three-day journey from here at best. "You wouldn't leave him out there all night?"

Grandpa Widow spat in the dust.

"I'd do what was best for the village," he said. "You know good and well that is our first priority."

Grandpa Widow is twig-frail and about a hundred years old, but he's still the toughest person I've ever seen in my life. I bet he could whoop half the village with a hand behind his back. Not that he would, mind you. Grandpa Widow isn't much for violence.

"Listen here, Gussy. . . ." That's what Grandpa Widow calls me, Gussy or just plain Gus, even though my whole name is Gustavina Mithridates Pearl, which is a mouthful and a half.

He'll say, "Violence is always a mistake. Even when it's necessary."

I don't much know what that means, because in what world would mistakes sometimes be necessary? But that's the way Grandpa Widow is. He likes to say something and let you chew on it awhile. Says the act of figuring out what something means is more important than the meaning itself. Drives me crazy sometimes, I'll be honest with you.

But it's hard to hold anything against Grandpa Widow. He's the one who raised me up, who taught me how to keep us safe. He's the one in charge of keeping the Great Doom from creeping in and infecting everything by performing the Rites. Years and years of Protectors have come and gone to pass down these rituals to Grandpa Widow. He brought them here to the village more than fifty years ago. Because when the Great Doom gets in—from a hole in the gates, or an ill-tied cardinal feather, or if some desert dog digs up the chicken foot, if anything at all goes wrong—then it sets about infecting things. And if a house gets sick, that's trouble, because that's the sort of sickness that spreads faster than a fire. Grandpa Widow can cure a house—he can cure anything, so far as I'm concerned—but it takes a lot of work, and that's hard on a fellow as ancient as Grandpa Widow.

That's why he is training me and Cricket. We are supposed to take over when he gets too old.

It made me nervous, watching that rider, still so far out from the gates. I wished he'd hustle up. Things take so long to arrive anywhere in the desert, even when you can see them coming with your own eyes. I didn't want him getting shut out, the Great Doom having its way with him.

Big Gordo was getting antsy too, you could tell. His name is no joke. He's near seven feet tall and bald-headed as the moon, his voice rumbles like faraway thunder, and he's the only person in town strong enough to swing the gates all on his own. His biceps are twice the size of my whole skull. But Big Gordo's no brute, not when you get to know him. He spends most of the day reading, for one. I'm always sliding him books from Grandpa Widow's library on the sly, so he can have something to do instead of stare out at nothing, hoping for some kind of fancy mirage all day. He has the gentlest blue eyes the shimmer of hailstones, and he can whistle like a blackbird. Also he's a poet, but that's another thing I'm not supposed to tell anybody. He writes poems about exotic flowers, mostly, and about snowstorms and great big slabs of ice he calls glaciers. He says they move slow over the earth like ancient beasts, scraping the ground dry.

"But why don't you ever write about stuff you see every day?" I asked him once. "Like why don't you scribble an ode to scrub grass or turkey vultures or a cow skull with a flower in it or something like that?"

He shrugged at me. "I write to travel, little buddy."

I thought that was a pretty good answer.

The rider was coming closer and closer, that horse galloping with all its might. I wished we were in the Rectory eating Grandpa Widow's unnamable stew. I'd play Grandpa Widow all the fiddle songs he wanted. He likes the ballads, the one about ships sinking and all the young men drowning and the maidens building boats out of their bodies to sail home, crying all the way.

Me, I like the adventure songs, the ones about sea monsters, anything having to do with the ocean, which I'd never seen before, seeing as how we're all surrounded by the desert every which way. It's a sea of sand and rocks and weird little scrub plants, that's for sure, and sand is plenty interesting. I mean, there are critters hidden in every nook and cranny, camouflaged spiders scurrying sand-colored across the dunes, snakes sliding in deadly curlicues across the beige. Even toads, believe it or not, who only wake up when it rains out. I love it when it rains in the desert—not a big storm, mind you, which can be awful dangerous for us— but just a fierce gush of water come and gone so quick you hardly notice it, the kind that leaves the sand awash with purple blossoms, flowers hidden deep beneath the dust, waiting for their chance to bloom. Me and Cricket were like that, I thought. One day we'd get our chance, and we'd show everybody what we could do. I hummed a worried quiet song to help the rider hurry, that sun sinking and sinking, that galloping horse drawing ever closer. I clenched my fists and prayed to the One Who Listens, that it would hasten that rider up. Big Gordo bit his lip, and Cricket whimpered. But Grandpa Widow was stalwart and still as one of those big desert rocks that sprout up like stone churches out of nowhere, showing not a bit of feeling on that face of his.

The rider made it through the gates just as the light snuffed itself out and our world fell into darkness. Big Gordo pulled the gates shut, locking them good and tight, and me and Grandpa Widow chanted our little blessing over them, the quiet one we did come every nightfall, as the moon rises and the stars unleash themselves. Cricket let loose a long lonesome howl, and that's how I knew we were safe for the night. The winds could holler all they wanted, but they couldn't blow the Great Doom into our town, not no way, not no how. It felt good, knowing the village slept safe for what we had done.

This rider was a woman with long brown hair and a dust-covered face. Other than that, I couldn't tell a thing about her. She lay panting across her horse, facedown and drenched in sweat, like she'd just popped out of a river

8

somewhere. The horse was panting too, both of them worn flat out, riding all day just to escape the dark. Grandpa Widow helped her from her horse, and I ran and fetched a cup of water. Big Gordo led the rider's horse away to the stables for some grub and some rest. Lord knows that poor horse was twice as tired as the rider ever will be.

Grandpa Widow leaned there against his cane waiting while the rider guzzled about ten straight cups of water. I almost told her to slow down, that if she drank any more her bladder would burst and she'd keel right over, but I figured a person who just rode a horse through all that desert ought to know her own business well enough. She drank until she was finished, and finally she raised her eyes up to us.

"Which one of you is Grandpa Widow?" she said.

Grandpa Widow gave me a look, and it was all I could do not to bust out laughing.

"That'd be me," he said.

"Should've figured," she said, "only the whole widow part threw me. I mean, who ever heard of a widow man?"

"When you've lived as long as I have," said Grandpa Widow, "you learn to hear about near everything."

It was true, I didn't know the mystery of Grandpa Widow's name. He said somebody gave it to him a long time ago, and that I shouldn't dig too deep into the past unless I wanted it to rise up and bite me on the butt. He was always saying things like that when I wanted to know what happened before I came around. Heck, I don't even know where I came from. I wasn't born in the village, that's all I know. Sometimes in my dreams I heard this loud crashing sound, and I could smell salt in the air.

"Dreaming of the ocean," Grandpa Widow always said, his eyes all bright with knowing.

"But how can I know about the ocean if I've never been there?" I'd say.

"Knowing is in the blood," he'd say. "Your body's born knowing all kinds of stuff. Your brain too. If we had to learn every last thing we knew, we wouldn't make it past our first day on earth."

I guessed he was right, but I wished he'd just spill it already about how I came here, or if I came here at all. Sometimes I pretended that Grandpa Widow spat in the dust and formed me out of the mud himself. To be honest, that wouldn't bother me none, because then I'd just be a walking talking miracle, wouldn't I, a piece of magic let loose on this earth to baffle and confound. I was a natural-born Protector, and this village was my home. I was proud to guard it with my life.

Sorry, I got distracted a little bit in the telling there. It happens sometimes. I'll just drift off in my own mind like a tumbleweed down a dried-out dead ditch if I'm not careful.

"This is for you," said the rider, handing a rolled-up piece of parchment to Grandpa Widow.

"Did you read it first?" said Grandpa Widow.

"No, I didn't read it," said the rider. "You think I don't have more sense than that? You ask me, this letter's all sealed up with magic, and if I'd opened it, my tongue might have gone furry in my mouth. The letter itself might have burst into flames right in my hands and the Great Doom would've gobbled me up forever."

Grandpa Widow gave her the slightest little grin. "You'd be right about that."

"Shoot, it was hard enough getting here by sunset. Had to ride two weeks' worth of days and nights just to make it. I can camp out fine under the starlight with my horse, Darla, and have me a time. Maybe the best times in my life, to be honest with you, just me and Darla and the starlight. Might bust out my kazoo and play a ditty or two, just to ward off the snakes. But I wouldn't be caught dead in this valley at night, no sir. It's about the least safe place in the entire desert lands."

"Wise woman," said Grandpa Widow.

"Well, I wouldn't go that far," she said.

"Got a name?" said Grandpa Widow.

"'The Rider' will do just fine, thank you," she said. "Folks get to know your name and then they got a hold on you. I don't want anybody ever getting a hold on me."

Grandpa Widow grinned. "Wise woman indeed."

"You got an inn around here?" said the Rider. "Somewhere a body might get some grub and entertainment? Maybe a card game or three?"

"Down the block is Old Esmerelda's," I said. "The food is pretty good, and you can get jasmine tea, which is more or less the best thing you ever tasted in your life. It would be my favorite place on earth if only I was allowed to go there more, which I'm not, of course, being a Protector and all. Just wouldn't be proper."

The Rider looked at me like I'd lost my wits. "Old Esmerelda's, you say?"

"Best inn in town," said Grandpa Widow.

"It's the only inn in town," I said, and his eyes just sparkled at me. It's an old joke, and an obvious one, but it always makes Grandpa Widow laugh.

"That'll do for me then," said the Rider, rising to her feet. "Might just stay a few days, take the troubles off my mind. Give myself a little vacation here. A body can't risk her life riding through the desert with that Great Doom fast on her tail and just take off again come morning. A body takes a risk like that, she's earned a warm bath at least. And if my boss at the messengers' office can't take that, well, he can just plumb find a new Rider, for all I care."

After she was all watered up, the Rider sauntered off

toward the town square, where Old Esmerelda's was. I wanted to follow her, maybe sneak in the window of the inn's kitchen and poke around awhile, but Grandpa Widow didn't like it when I went there. He said it was a corruptible place for a young person like myself, but of course that just made me want to go all the more. "We are people of discipline," he always said, "people of order and rules. People who follow the Rites."

And Grandpa Widow was correct about that. It was a lot of responsibility, what we did at the gates. The whole village depended on us. It was no use for me to go exploring the nighttime if all it did was put everybody else in danger.

When we were back inside our Rectory, Grandpa Widow sat by the fire, just holding that parchment. He hadn't unsealed it or unscrolled it or anything yet. He stared deep into the fire and didn't speak a word. I wanted to take up my fiddle, maybe play a dirge or something slow and sad like that, but I could tell Grandpa Widow wouldn't like it. Cricket did his three circle spins and wound himself down into a curl at my feet all cozy like. I picked up a book about how to heal a poison house and I read over the steps, and then I read over them again. There was nothing worse than a poison house, especially in an isolated little hamlet like ours. Well, except for an infected person, but that hasn't happened in ages and ages, not since Grandpa Widow first got here. (They still tell stories about that incident sometimes, to scare kids.) No, there'd be nothing worse than that. You got to drive all that Great Doom away, seep the poison out into the night same as you would suck a snakebite. It was all very tricky and very technical and my mind kept wandering and wandering, wondering when Grandpa Widow was going to read his letter.

"Not until long after you're sleep, I'm telling you that right now," said Grandpa Widow.

"How'd you know that's what I was thinking?" I said.

"Because it's been about fifteen minutes since you turned an actual page of that book."

And he was right. That was the thing about Grandpa Widow. He knew just about everything there was to know, about people, about magic, about the Rites that protect us. He was the wisest man in all the earth. At least I thought so anyway. Slept with both eyes open too. I used to test him sometimes when I thought he might be napping. His eyes followed you clear across the room, even as the snores were pouring out of his nose. If you thought about it too much, it would scare the dickens out of you. I hoped one day I would grow up to be half the Protector he was, strange as he may be.

"Come on now," said Grandpa Widow. "Get yourself in bed. The night's turning late, and we got work to do tomorrow."

"I'm going to read just a little bit longer," I said.

"Suit yourself."

But the fire was warm, and Cricket was snoring these little dog snores at my feet, probably dreaming of endless prairie dogs to chase, and pretty soon I was all tuckered out and sleeping in my chair.

2

I AWOKE TO THE ROOSTERS CROWING dawn, but there wasn't any sunrise yet. The light through the window was a gray smear, an evening kind of light. I heard the faraway growl of thunder, the soft wind whispering up the dust. A storm was coming, I knew that good and well. Cricket was up with me, his tail wagging, a worried look in his puppy-dog eyes. My back ached a little from sleeping in that chair all night. Serves me right, I suppose.

"It's okay, pup dog," I said. I scratched his noggin and gave his back skin a good tug. "We'll get the Rites over with quick today and be safe and sound before rainfall."

I said it like I meant it, but really it was more of a hope. Odds were, we were going to get soaked today. And rain can be a dangerous thing in a valley like ours. Sure, a good rain shower gets all the desert flowers brief and blooming, and the whole world can look like a rainbow sprung a leak and spilled itself all over the valley. But storms can mean flooding too, quick walls of water that gush their way through with a fury. And don't even get me started on twisters. Nothing's worse than seeing the snarling black of the clouds fling themselves to earth, spinning ramshackle and wild over the desert, sucking up everything they can. We have Rites to protect us from those, but sometimes nature's just too powerful, even for Rites as strong as ours. Sometimes nature just up and does whatever it wants, and there's not a thing any of us can do about it.

Grandpa Widow came bustling through the room, his traveling robes on, a knapsack slung over his shoulder. He was gathering up books, little leather volumes about herbs and rituals, filling the sack with them.

"What's going on?" I said.

"Going to have to make a little trip," said Grandpa Widow. "A month's journey at least."

"This about the letter?" I said.

Grandpa Widow nodded, riffling through books, plucking one and then squinting at the cover only to return it for another.

"It's a summons from the Council of Protectors," he said.

This was a huge deal. The Council of Protectors was the last vestige of the Order of Protectors, of whom even

Grandpa Widow was still not an elder. These folks were descended from the Protectors of old—mighty Protectors like Saint Petunia the Bold, or Sir Ulalee of Longbow—trained in the great Clypstone Cathedral itself. No one could refuse a summons of the council, not even if they were on their deathbed. Far as I was concerned, a council summons was a great honor.

So why did Grandpa Widow look so dismal about it? Sure, the order wasn't what it once was, back in the grand days of the Protectors I'd read about in Hieronymus's *Splendors of a Glorious Age*, my favorite history book. It was all about how the Rites were formed thousands of years ago, in the darkest of times, and the Protectors practiced their art to fight back. It led all the way to the building of the Clypstone Cathedral, the establishment of the order. Since then, well, it's like Grandpa Widow always says. History is a wheel, not a straight line. The good times come, the bad times come. The light beats the darkness, but the darkness always has its time to come back around. And right now, times were awfully dark. There wasn't a safe village other than ours in three weeks' ride at least. The Darkling Valley, and beyond, was menaced by all kinds of terrible creatures, from roving rotten-hearted witches to furious demiurges to poltergeists and beasts from the abyss to your run-of-the-mill swindlers and hoodwinkers. Even a sorceress so terrible as Lucinda Withern was allowed to roam free, causing destruction anywhere she went. Not to mention the worst darkness in all the land, the Great Doom, a force so fearsome I bet even the Council of Protectors—all safe in their cathedral anointed with saints' bones and under which a stream of blessed water always flowed—quaked alone in their beds at night with just the thought of it.

Maybe that was why Grandpa Widow was worried. Maybe they were going to make him go banish the Wailing Winds from Bilgewater Hollow or something like that, as I'd heard the Protectors over there were having an awful tough time of it. I remember hearing one story about how the ferocious witch Lucinda Withern kept a whole mining settlement in her thrall while she stole every last thing from the ground, leaving all the townsfolk stupefied and memory-lost for months, all because Protectors couldn't do their jobs. I bet expertise like Grandpa Widow's was sought all over the land, even by the Council of Protectors. No wonder Grandpa Widow didn't want to bother with any foolishness like that when he had his own village to protect. Still, I was excited. I'd never been to a real city before. I'd hardly even left the village, except for little excursions here and there. Lord knows I'd wanted to see the Clypstone Cathedral all my life, with its grand Ossuary of Dreams. I wanted to see everything.

"I'll pack my bags in just a second," I said.

Grandpa Widow cut a fierce eye at me.

"You will do no such thing," he said.

That stopped me cold in my tracks. Of course I was going with him. I had to be going with him.

"There are bad winds blowing up from the east," said Grandpa Widow. "I think you can feel that in the air. The Great Doom is on the move, it surely is, and I can't be leaving the town unprotected."

"So what are you saying?"

"What I'm saying, you hardheaded lunk, is I need you to stay here and perform the Rites," he said. "Protect the town. Make sure the Great Doom stays where it belongs. Which is on the other side of these walls, lest I remind you."

I couldn't believe it. There was no way.

"You want me to do the Rites all by myself?" I hollered.

"Precisely," said Grandpa Widow. "I've trained you since you were an infant for just this purpose. Surely you can handle a few weeks on your own, can't you? And you're not alone. You have Big Gordo, and you have Cricket here to help."

Cricket yelped. He was so happy it made me mad.

"But what do I do if there's a problem?" I said. "Like if the village folk have a grievance or some such?"

"Do what I do," said Grandpa Widow. "Give it your best. Be wise and kind, and above all merciful. Consider others' needs above your own. Perform the Rites precisely as I taught you, and be exact about it. No shortcuts, no laziness, no variation. They only work if you perform them diligently, with your best heart and intention. And above all else, keep those gates shut at night."

Grandpa Widow placed a hand on my shoulder and looked deep into my eyes. When he spoke, his breath was hot with coffee and pipe smoke, the sleepless night behind him and the long road ahead.

"The Great Doom will try to sneak in," he said. "Don't you doubt that. It'll take advantage of any rule break, any mistake or laxity or looseness with the rituals. If you make even the tiniest error—if you relax your intention for just one split second—it will worm its way inside. And then you'll have a whole mess on your hands, rest assured."

"What do I do if it gets in?" I said.

"It won't," said Grandpa Widow. "Not if you do exactly as I taught you."

"But what if it does?"

Grandpa Widow looked at me and sighed, his shoulders slumped low, all the concern in the world a gray fog in his eyes, and for just one second he looked so very old and tired, like he hadn't slept in a million years, like he could keel over and nap in the dust for the next half decade or so.

"You have the books, and you have the training. You'll know what to do when the time comes. Your heart and your brain and your spirit will all work together to spell it out for you. The universe is always talking, if only you'll unstop your ears long enough to hear."

And then—and maybe this was the weirdest thing that ever happened to me—Grandpa Widow pulled me in close and hugged me so tight it near squeezed the breath out of me. I was plain shocked. The old fellow wasn't much for displays of affection and never had been. It scared me a little.

"Promise you'll come back?" I said.

He looked up at me, and I saw a quick glimmer of fear there. Then he gave me his customary grimace.

"What are you so concerned about, girl? I'll be back in no time. It'll probably be hours of meetings, a bunch of old folks arguing about some obscure passage in a language no one can quite remember anymore. That's all it ever is."

But something in me doubted him, just a little bit. I felt worry caterpillar-creep over my skin.

Me and Cricket followed Grandpa Widow outside, to where Big Gordo sat studying a book of maps.

"You headed out, Mr. Widow?" said Big Gordo, and Grandpa just nodded.

He brought his old horse, Miss Ribbit, out, a dust-colored mare with a bad left eye. She huffed and clomped around, clearly furious about having to do much of anything other than eat hay and nap. Thunder boomed in the far-off, and Miss Ribbit whinnied and kicked.

"Quiet down now," said Grandpa Widow, and Miss Ribbit obeyed. That horse surely did seem to love him, ornery as she was. I watched Grandpa Widow stare into her one good eye and talk sweet to her, telling her they were about to head off on a journey and it wouldn't be an easy trip but it was a necessary one, and I'd be a liar if I said the horse didn't understand every word. Grandpa Widow always had a way with animals. He's less secretive with them, tells them more than he'll ever tell a human. I watched as the horse steeled herself for the hard ride to come. She seemed to blink alive, a little light come into her good eye at the prospect of a challenge.

I wasn't happy about it, though. It was bad enough not getting to see the city, to have Grandpa Widow go on a journey without me. But how in the heck was I supposed to keep this town safe, just me and Cricket and Big Gordo? Sure, I could perform all the Rites in my sleep, but what would happen if the Great Doom did creep in? What would happen if a house got sick, or worse, a person? What would I do then?

The real truth of the matter was this: what if I wasn't good enough? What if I messed up so bad Grandpa Widow didn't want me to be a Protector anymore? What if he banished me out to the desert, to seek my fortune on the roam with all the other vagabonds and ne'er-do-wells, my whole life destroyed because I wasn't up to the task? I couldn't imagine anything more fearful than that, getting booted from the village because I wasn't good enough.

I said a quiet little prayer to the morning hour to help me.

Maybe that's dumb, praying to a time of day, but that's what I did. And whatever it is up there that keeps things moving—we just call it the One Who Listens—I knew it heard me. I knew it saw the Rites and smiled down at me and Cricket, all the work we were doing. I knew that it listened, whatever it was, just the same as if it were one giant invisible ear dangling up there in the cosmos. Heck, I figured it even liked me, that it was happy when I spoke up to it. I don't know why, but I always have. Is that such a strange thing to believe, that you were created with love, that whatever made you delights in you too?

Just as Grandpa Widow was mounting his horse and about to take off, who should come ambling up but Mayor Benningsley, that no-good busybody who fancies himself the mayor of the whole village? Nobody even voted for him or anything, he just started calling himself that one day, and the name stuck. He was from the oldest, richest family with the biggest house in the village. It was so big, in fact, if he stood on his front porch he could see over the walls, out into the desert, though he never once volunteered for guard duty. It was said his daddy found a treasure out in one of those desert caverns south of us, something called the Valley's Heart, that he kept locked up in a safe deep inside their house. Rumor has it the Benningsleys shave a bit off the Valley's Heart and sell it far off in the city, and that's how they live so extravagant.

Personally, I never liked the man. He didn't care for me and Cricket, it didn't seem like, the way moneyed people always fear mystic folks, deep in their hearts. He gave even Grandpa Widow a wide berth except for when he was riding him about something, a little request he wanted done right then and there. Which drove me plain nuts, if you want to know how it really is. Nobody worked harder to keep the village safe, and not even Mayor Benningsley could deny such a thing.

Yet here he came, huffling on toward us, waving his arms like a fright witch.

"What is the meaning of this?" he hollered.

"The meaning of what?" said Grandpa Widow, who cared for Mayor Benningsley about as much as I did.

Mayor Benningsley gestured at the horse. "You appear to be leaving us."

"Just for a spell," said Grandpa Widow. "I received a summons from the Council of Protectors, and goodness knows I can't ignore that."

"A summons?" cried Mayor Benningsley. "On a day like today, when so much is at stake?"

He was so angry he was spitting everywhere. I'd never seen a person so worked up before.

"A storm day, you mean?" said Grandpa Widow, an eyebrow raised.

The Mayor looked confused a moment, then nodded

furiously. "Yes, yes, a storm day. That's exactly what I mean. There's a storm coming, right out there on the horizon!"

"A bad one, by the looks of it," said Grandpa Widow.

"Yes sir, indeed, a bad one. And you know what happens in storms, right?"

"It rains," said Grandpa Widow.

We need protection on a night like tonight. We need protection in the days to come. It is critical for the safety of the village that you not leave us alone at a time like this!"

"Gus here can take care of you," he said. "You'll be in good hands."

"Good hands? She's a child, if you haven't noticed."

"She's a Protector, is what she is," said Grandpa Widow. "Trained by me. She can take care of anything the Great Doom throws at her, don't you worry."

I couldn't believe it. Grandpa Widow giving Mayor Benningsley guff on my behalf? You could have named the brightest nighttime star after me and I wouldn't have been happier. Even Cricket gave a yip and hung his tongue out, all pink and happy.

"This is preposterous," said Mayor Benningsley. "Absurd."

"And yet it is the truth. Good day to you, sir." Grandpa Widow tipped his hat. With that he galloped off into the valley, an evil black mountain of clouds looming before him, lightning flickering all around, a low rumble on the horizon. I watched him until he was gone.

For just a moment my heart was overwhelmed with chaos and fear, with the dread that I couldn't do this, that I wouldn't be enough, that I would lose everything I loved. Worry hung on my shoulders like a wounded calf I had to carry back home. That flickering lightning in the distance, the fog of rain like a gray shroud over the horizon.

Fine, fine. Worry all you want. But there's work to be done, and no one else to do it.

I clomped myself back to the Rectory and took up my fiddle.

"Come on, Cricket," I said. "We got us a village to protect."

And we set out through the gates, into the valley, the desert outside, to keep the dark in check, while Mayor Benningsley slouched there watching, arms crossed, like he was just going to stand around waiting on us to fail.

3

I'VE BEEN TALKING A LOT ABOUT THE Rites, about how important they are, about how they protect us from the Great Doom, how the safety of the entire village depends on them being performed just exactly precisely correct. And yet I have neglected to tell you what the Rites even are. This is an oversight, and I'm real sorry about it.

How about I just take you through what we did that day Grandpa Widow left, which was the same as what we did every day? Except of course Grandpa Widow was always with us, leading the chants, belting out the Mysteries, making sure I didn't fudge even the tiniest syllable or note of a hymn.

First thing this morning most dark and dreary, me and

Cricket made our way outside the gates and walked three times widdershins (that's counterclockwise, if you don't know) around the village, both of us single file, keeping our eyes focused on the ground before us, our hearts filled with gratitude for the dust of the earth. That's a real important part of the Rites, what our hearts are doing, what our minds are thinking. Grandpa Widow calls this our intentions, and we must always keep them correct. Like he says, "For where your intentions are, that's where your heart lies also." So we got to hold pure intentions of gratitude in our hearts while we take this walk. Some days it's right difficult, near impossible to do this, like trying to run while holding water cupped in your hands, all my gratitude and good intention slipping right through my fingers. But this day wasn't so hard, not with the storm approaching, not with Grandpa Widow gone. I was focused, my heart and mind and body about as intentional as they get. And you know what? It felt good, each step full of purpose winding widdershins around the village. It usually takes me about two hours, but that day I hustled so I came in at about an hour and a half.

That made me pretty nervous, to be honest with you. What if I'd done them too fast? Did I need to start over?

Calm down, Gussy, I said to myself. *There's no rule that governs the speed of the Rites. Just slow it down a little next time, watch your breathing, and you'll be fine.*

Next we sang the "Hymn of the Morning." It's a song for

the sunrise, high and full of color and light. Well, I didn't sing it. Grandpa Widow sings it. I just play it on the fiddle, that bright and shining melody lifting the sun up in the sky, even if today there wasn't much of a sun to lift up. Trust me, it's better that way. I sound like a warthog wheezing when I sing. Disrupts the sanctity of the occasion. Grandpa Widow is always telling me to suck it up, to let my voice sing.

"The One Who Listens don't care what you sound like," he says. "The One Who Listens only cares about your intentions."

That might be true, but I still didn't like to sing out loud if I could help it. I'll be honest, I was worried a little that maybe the words needed to be sung to work right, but anyone can tell you the melody of a song is about ten thousand times more important than the words ever could be, and besides, Cricket was howling along, barking the selfsame words in dog-speak, of that I was sure. I hoped in my heart that would be good enough.

And then I'd done it. The first of the Rites were performed, and it wasn't hardly ten in the morning.

I took a break on Grandpa Widow's porch and watched the storm ever on its creep toward us. Lightning came down in blue jags, slicing the air. I tried to do the thing where you count the number of seconds between the flash and the thunder boom, but there was so much lightning and so many crashes I couldn't tell which boom belonged to which flash. All I knew was that this storm was nasty, and it was headed right toward us. I don't have to tell you how rare a desert storm is, do I? We have only half a dozen a year, and they don't usually come in the autumn like this. What I'm saying is, there was something unnatural about this storm—the black-lipped clouds, the snarl of the thunder, the lightning falling down like flaming swords from Heaven—something strange and menacing about it. Maybe Mayor Benningsley was right. Maybe Grandpa Widow should have stayed here. Maybe I wasn't good enough.

But that kind of thinking wasn't going to save the village, no way no how. I had to be good enough, no matter what. That was the only way.

So I hauled my butt off the porch and got down to the Midday Salutations, which was when I picked up a handful of dust and let it slip through my fingers, the winds whipping it away in a long yellow-colored slash, dissolving out to become a dust devil somewhere else probably. I tried to do it exactly perfect, just like Grandpa Widow would have, even trying to mimic that faraway look he gets in his eyes when the wind takes the dust. Then I touched my little finger to my lips and to my heart and repeated that three times, because three times is the only way to make sure it gets really done. I grabbed my fiddle and played a kind of jaunty little work jig called the "Hymn to the Noonday Sun," something to keep you moving in the hot of the day. The words are all about the sun and the rain, the wind and the stars, how the whole world came together to make this place and to put us right here too, and that's really something, isn't it? I took a risk and muttered the words under my breath along with the fiddle melody, just in case that made the Rites stronger. I liked the "Hymn to the Noonday Sun," which can brighten up even the crummiest day.

Well, not exactly. This day wasn't getting any brighter. In fact, it was darkening, and quick, like someone was pulling an ugly black rug over the sky. It's like the old song says, "Storms a-creeping closer, and the rains come lassoing down." I hoped maybe we'd get a nice desert bloom out of this one. I'd only seen a few in my lifetime, and they were truly something, I tell you.

Midday Salutations is the shortest and the easiest of the Rites, so as not to interfere with the workday. It only takes about an hour. But I still hadn't done the most important part. That's when I go to visit the Book of Names. I was actually dreading it a little bit.

See, the Book of Names is the village registry, with the name of every person living here written in it. We don't cross anything out or add to it either. No, we just make a new book. If somebody dies, well, you got to make a new Book of

Names, same if somebody's born, or if some wayward traveler takes a shine to the place and makes it their own. Takes me all day to make a Book of Names, even though there are only six hundred and forty-two folks living in the Darkling Valley at the current moment. After I make the new book and fill in all the names, me and Grandpa Widow take the old one out of the village gates and into the desert, whisper a mystery over it, and set it on fire, burn it right up. Then we take the new Book of Names and nail it with a single six-inch spike to the meeting pole, right in the center of the village. Book of Names days are actually my favorite, even if somebody died and everyone's sad about it. It's a big ceremony, with music and dancing and singing that takes all day, and sometimes half the night. The whole village comes out, even the other kids my age. They just stand there and stare at me like I'm some scary mystic creature who could zap them like lightning with some obscure Rite. And truth is, I probably could. Maybe they're right to be a little scared of me, even if it does make things lonesome sometimes. It's hard to have a friend when you're a Protector. But that's part of it, you know? I'm proud of who I am and what I do. Loneliness just comes with the territory.

But there were no new names today, no births or deaths, and just a handful of travelers staying up at the inn, which is too temporary to chuck out a whole Book of Names for.

So this day my task was just to march the four hundred and sixty-seven steps exactly from the gates to the middle of the village square, stand before the meeting pole, and say the Mysteries. Normally Grandpa Widow does this, or I do it while he watches, nodding along, while for the most part the villagers ignore us. Today was different, with the storm coming and all, and I knew folks would be anxious about Grandpa Widow being gone. I didn't want all those eyes on me, all that pressure, when the only thing I wanted was to keep everybody safe.

I marched myself right up there, trying to get Grandpa Widow's exact stride down, which was hard because he's got a lot longer legs than me. Cricket followed all solemn behind me. On the way, Connor Carnivolly came running up to me. He was a skinny, scruffy, dark-haired kid with a front tooth missing. He was scrappy but kept his black shoes perfectly polished and maybe was the closest thing I had to a friend.

"Pick a card," he said, "any card."

I grinned at him, because that's what Connor always said. He's trying to be a magician. I picked a four of goblins and put it back in the deck. Connor shuffled and flipped the first faceup card. It was a two of moons.

"Sorry, buddy," I said. "That one's not mine."

Connor shrugged. "Someday I'll get it right."

"That a fact?" I said.

"I don't have any other choice. Magic's my ticket out of this place. I'll get my act so good I can travel the whole world, see lands I never even dreamed of. The traveling life, hitting the old dusty road, that's the life for me."

"You going to start pulling jackrabbits out of your hat?" I said.

He frowned.

"Not likely," he said. "I'm not even sure how you get a jackrabbit into a hat. Those guys are awful feisty."

"That's the magic of it, isn't it?" I said, and Connor laughed.

Cricket yelped, and Connor scratched him behind his ears. I liked Connor, even if he wasn't much of a magician. At least he talked to me. At least he thought I was a person worth being around. Not like I was ever going to let him know it, of course.

"Maybe you could be my assistant," he said. "I might learn how to saw you in half."

"I'm fine in one piece, thank you very much," I said. "But I'll holler if I ever change my mind."

I wished I could stay and chat, watch Connor do some tricks, but I couldn't afford any distractions right now, not with all the Rites still left to do. I hardly ever have time for anything except the Rites. Some days I wish I could just run around and play like all the other kids, work an act up with Connor Carnivolly, maybe set up around the meeting pole and play my fiddle while he does his magic tricks for coin. That sure would be something.

But not now, and not for me. My life is one of responsibility, and it is a great and terrible honor.

"Well," I said, "I best be off. See you around, Connor."

He grinned that missing tooth at me.

"Be seeing you, Gussy," and he scampered off, leaving me to my work.

I'd be a liar if I said I wasn't a little sad about it.

When I got to the meeting pole, I kissed the Book of Names, and then I raised my arms and shouted loud as I could, "Blessed be all whose names are inscribed in this book, and may they be kept safe from the Great Doom. May no misfortune befall them. May the sun rise tomorrow and bless their endeavors. May we all walk in light."

Bartleby Bonnard the baker hollered out to me, "Where's the old man today?"

But I pretended not to hear him.

"Think he'll be back soon?" asked the baker.

I stared straight forward. No good telling folks what I don't actually know.

Mr. Jilly the tailor asked me in his high crackly voice, "How's about that storm coming?"

This one I had an answer for. It was right there in the

Book of Common Rites, what I was supposed to say back to a question like that.

"Storms come and storms go," I said. "But the Rites are eternal, and the One Who Listens smiles down upon us."

That seemed to satisfy him a little bit.

I caught the eye of that good-for-nothing so-called Mayor Benningsley flittering around, whispering at folks, making a nuisance of himself. Why can't folks just let a body mind his own business? I swear, gossipers will be the undoing of everything, and that I guarantee you. He seemed to be trying to clear a path around the meeting pole, the street that led to his house.

A voice rose up from the dusty meeting pole square.

"A reckoning is coming, friends!" it said. "It could be this very night!"

Oh, great, I thought. *It's Lazlo Dunes.*

There he was, a bent-backed ramshackle old man with a beard down to his knees. He had a big wooden spoon and he banged it against a tin plate, yelping up a racket enough to drown out my fiddle.

"The Rites won't keep the Great Doom at bay, no sir!" he yelled. "Not forever, they won't. Change is coming! Yes, it is, friends, and it won't be pretty. Not for the likes of you all, anyhow. A reckoning is at hand. Friends, it will not come from without, but within, inside these very walls, this I know to be true. The Great Doom is on the way, and it will burn us all clean. Yes, it will, right down to our bones."

Lazlo Dunes was always talking all that noise. It was driving me crazy, day and night, his hollering and banging at all hours of the day. Who in their right mind would want the Great Doom sneaking into the village, infecting everything? Nobody, that's who. And yet Lazlo Dunes was starting to garner a bit of a following. It wasn't uncommon to see a crowd gathered around, people even hollering along with him, praying for the Great Doom to come. Some folks pick the most useless ways to spend their day.

Right about then, I heard a commotion from down the street. A black carriage came bounding into the village, moving way too fast. Folks scrambled to get out of the way as it passed the meeting pole on the way to the Benningsley mansion.

Lazlo Dunes cursed the carriage and spat.

"Greed!" he hollered. "Screaming, shameless greed! It'll be the end of us all!"

Then he wandered off, muttering. I was glad to be quit of him, but I wondered about that carriage. I followed it as it pulled to a stop in front of the Benningsley mansion. The door swung open, and a tiny man in a tweed suit stepped out of the carriage carrying a metal box in his hands. Two sets of guards walked out after him. Together they walked into the Benningsley mansion, the front door held open by Mayor Benningsley, who slammed it shut behind them.

Was this what the Mayor was so nervous about earlier today? I supposed it wasn't the storm at all. But why be so secretive about it? Fancy-dressed folks were always coming in carriages to the mansion, conducting some weird kind of secret business no one knew a thing about, except for maybe Grandpa Widow. But there was something different about this carriage, something slightly sinister about that little man in the tweed suit. Lord only knew what was in that metal box. I'd be a liar if I said I wasn't dead curious about it, but Grandpa Widow always told me curiosity has no place in the life of a Protector.

"We don't question who we protect, or why," he said. "We just do our duty, and our duty is enough."

Still, it was hard not to wonder. You could lose whole nights wondering and wondering, if you aren't careful. Some people spend their whole lives wondering. There are books and books and books about that very subject in Grandpa Widow's library.

I had turned myself away to go finish up the rest of the Rites when I caught a face staring out at me from the window. Little Chappie Benningsley, not more than nine years old. When was the last time I'd seen him? He used to be out and about with his father all the time, getting bragged on and strutting around the way rich kids always do. Strange, how people can vanish for long stretches of time, even in a little village like ours.

Strange indeed.

Chappie shut the curtain, and I headed back to the Rectory.

I took a break to eat lunch with Cricket, some fatback bacon and biscuits with a tiny bit of strawberry preserves Grandpa Widow gave me for my tenth birthday. I've been saving them, just a slim knife blade of red per biscuit, once a week. This rate, they might last me until my next birthday. I tended to the horses and animals, swept the Rectory up good, and reorganized my bookshelf, the one Grandpa Widow let me have for myself. There's only about thirty books on that shelf, but they're mine, and I try to keep them tidy. I decided this time I'd organize my shelf by mood—happy books, then books that make me sad in a happy way, easy-going books that didn't bother me any, then interesting-informative books, boring-informative books, and finally books that make me sad in a miserable way. I figured that was a pretty good way to do it.

The rest of the day I just took extra protections about the storm. I burned some dried snakeweed in my little bowl to help Grandpa Widow on his journey. I sure hoped he came back quick. I didn't want to have to deal with a storm and Mayor Benningsley both. I checked the four corners of the town where we hang the bundles of cardinal feathers—three in each bunch, fresh and clean, plucked from cardinals that weird Mr. Mayella raises in his hatchery. I chanted my little chant over the feathers (fire of Heaven, fire of earth, fire of Heaven, fire of earth) and made sure the knot would hold tight, hoping not to lose one in the storm. Toward evening I decided to take a lap around the village, just to make sure everything was okay. The sky was already darkening, and the clouds were creeping up, just like someone drawing a black curtain over the sky.

When I passed Old Esmerelda's, I saw Lulu Benningsley—Mayor Benningsley's daughter, two years older than me—near the side alley of the building. Lulu stood scowling in her little powder-blue dress, pigtails, and her grandma's famous opal ring she always wore, the one that sparkled and glimmered like a meteor shower. Everyone said it had a little bit of magic to it and that was why Lulu got away with being such a brat all the time. Lulu was awful proud of that ring, handed down in her family for generations. I supposed I would be too, if I had something so valuable and fancy to show off. But today Lulu looked like she was in some kind of distress, all worried like.

Lulu never liked me much. In fact, it would be safe to say she hated my guts, though I didn't really have a clue why. Most of the village kids treated me strange, except for Connor Carnivolly, of course. Maybe it was the robes, or the solemn way I performed the rituals, I wasn't really sure. Grandpa Widow said the robes were essential to the Rites, that in the eyes of other folks, the robes set us apart, gave us authority. Regardless, most kids kept their distance, and I was fine with that. Even though I knew better, I decided to be a good Protector and walk on over to her.

"Can I help you with anything?" I said.

"How about you mind your own business?"

"Glad to."

I nodded at her and kept going. Well, that went about as well as I figured it would.

But a few paces down the road, I looked back. Lulu was staring in the window of Old Esmerelda's, as if she was spying on somebody. What would she want in there anyhow? Benningsleys don't frequent Old Esmerelda's. They're too high-class for something like that, milling about with the rest of us. No sir, never would we see any of them—not Lulu or the Mayor or little Chappie, and certainly not Mrs. Lucretia herself—set a dainty little foot onto the warped wooden floors of Old Esmerelda's. Thank goodness. The rest of us all need a Benningsley-free space every once in a while.

Lulu caught me staring at her.

She cast a fierce eye at me. "Oh, go away, you creepy little toad!"

I'll be honest, that made me real mad. Nobody talks to me like that. I had a mind to bash her right over the noggin with my fiddle, see how she'd like that. Beside me, Cricket let out a growl.

But I remembered Grandpa Widow's words: "We keep folks from harm, always. We don't ever cause it." So I took a deep breath, nodded at her, and walked myself away. I'd chant a Mystery for her later, see if the One Who Listens could nicen Lulu up a bit. It's always a good thing to holler up prayers for people who are mean to you. Helps you forgive them.

Sometimes it does, anyhow.

As I walked away, this peculiar feeling crept on over me, one I'd been having a lot lately. It was the notion that something was wrong in the village, a tingling in my bones. I don't know. It's hard to explain. It's like there's this ill feeling, you know? A taint to the air. The way people walk through the streets, hands thrust deep in their pockets, kind of side-eyeing each other. How the corners of everyone's smiles are turned down a little. The way a neighborly "How're you today?" rings out a little sour in the noontime heat. Something odd was going on in this place, that's for sure, and I did not like it. In fact, it seemed worse today than ever before.

Of all the times for Grandpa Widow to leave.

Still. I couldn't worry about that right now. I had a job to do, and a village to protect. Besides, by then it was coming up time for Last Lights, the best Rite of them all.

I walked myself to the entrance of the village. I stood in

front of the gates and drew the wolf and the star in the dust with Grandpa Widow's ceremonial knife—the one with all kinds of charms and spells cut into the blade—while I chanted the Mysteries. I have to hold the words bright and sparkly in my heart always, so they never go out, so the light of them never so much as flickers. I walked clockwise around the village three times, with an intention of peace and comfort, wishing well on everybody's hearts. I dug up and reburied the sacred chicken foot exactly seventeen paces from the city gates, just as I was supposed to. The foot has to come from a chicken that dies of natural causes, of course, and we give it a good three-day ceremonial washing. It's a Mystery all its own, the sanctifying of the dead chicken foot, and of all the Rites it is by far my least favorite (chicken feet are gross), so I was glad this little guy was still there, buried where he ought to be.

Finally I played "Last Lights Wonder," the evening hymn. It's a mournful goodbye to the day, with the quiet hope of stars and moon to guide us through the terror of night. It's the sweetness that keeps the Great Doom away, that's what Grandpa Widow always says. Again, I wished he was here to sing the words, but I was glad for Cricket, and I whisper-sang them to myself while I made my fiddle hum and twitter and moan. It was the best I'd ever played, I knew that, and I hoped the One Who Listens was hearing it right and good.

Just as I was losing myself in the song, a voice hollered up from the dusk light.

"A change is coming! A reckoning is at hand! The Great Doom will have its day!"

It was Lalzo Dunes, banging his plate again. I'd had it up to here with Lazlo Dunes, I'll tell you that right now.

I shut my eyes and played harder, ignoring him, and Cricket flung his wolfish howl far above Lazlo's racket. No lowdown charlatan was going to interrupt us.

I felt a hand grab my shoulder, and it made me flinch a little, sending a bad note wafting out into the air.

I opened my eyes. It was Lazlo Dunes, his yellow-cloudy eyes staring deep into mine.

"You won't escape either, Gussy," he said.

We stayed a moment like that, his hand on my shoulder, a look in his eyes not of anger, but of concern. Lazlo Dunes was worried about me.

"Yes, even you," he said. "You'll be changed too."

And he straggled off, worn and exhausted like, his banged-up tin plate hanging uselessly in his hand.

I didn't quite know what to do with that, to be honest.

Just as Big Gordo pulled the gates closed, I saw a long sliver of lightning seem to rise up from the ground and strike the clouds, and thunder boomed so loud it made me jump. In the far off, I saw a twister dip its dusky ink to the ground, dirt rising to meet it as it swirled and scoured the desert floor. I said a quick prayer that nothing would come near us and sang a quiet hymn in my heart. I don't mind singing in my heart; my voice sounds just fine in my brain. I could feel the Great Doom creeping in with that storm, I could feel it lapping at the edges of the wind, I could feel it whinny and whine and growl, trying to slip its way past all our protections, trying to shadow its way into our village. Well, I wouldn't let it, even if there was a storm like none we'd ever seen before.

All through the village windows were latched, doors double locked, fires lit in every hearth. The Great Doom was on the prowl, everyone could feel it.

I walked to where Big Gordo huddled in his little outpost by the gates, the light seeping out the doorway. I hoped he'd be safe and warm in there. I hoped he knew he could come to the Rectory with us if ever he needed to. Maybe I ought to have told him that, just in case. Ah well. It was too late now.

"Peace and blessings, brother Gordo," I whispered.

I made my way back to the Rectory and lit a fire. We needed all the warmth we could get, all the light the fire would allow.

The sky roared, lightning blistering the clouds. The air had grown cold suddenly, the chill of an ill wind sneaking its way between the gaps in our little Rectory's boards. The storm was here. The Great Doom was on the move.

Right as I was closing the Rectory window, I saw scuffling through the streets a black-cloaked figure clutching a hat down on his head, trying to keep the wind from blowing it off, like a gangly ghost slinking his way toward the walls.

Was that Mr. Mayella, the man who ran the cardinal hatchery? It had to be.

I was always a bit in awe of Mr. Mayella, him and his office room all full of ritual objects pilfered from who knows where, little talismans I wouldn't touch with a ten-foot pole. Just sitting in his waiting room was enough to raise your hairs on end. I kind of liked it though, to be honest. I liked it even better when he'd give me a glimpse of the hatchery, all those red-plumed birds in their splendor standing on golden perches like royalty.

"Mr. Mayella!" I hollered out the window. "What in tarnation are you doing out there?"

But lightning boomed, and the wind roared like a flock of devils, and there was no way Mr. Mayella could hear me. The rain began to fall harder, and I knew I had to shut the window now. I took one last look at Mr. Mayella as he vanished in the shadows.

What could he be doing out there at night, in this storm, lingering so near the gates?

It made me uneasy, and I had half a notion to go after

him. Cricket, as if he were reading my mind, gave a little whimper, and I felt bad about it.

"Don't you worry," I said, giving his back a tug. "I'm not dragging you out there in all that mess. If Mr. Mayella wants a good soaking—well, that's his business, I suppose."

And I shut the window to the night, the storm raging all around us.

4

A BANGING SOUNDED AT THE DOOR. I had been asleep for hours, somehow, the fire died down to a pile of embers, gold as treasure. I could barely hear it on account of the wind and the rain, the thunder a constant booming overhead like the One Who Listens was knocking over all the chairs in its house, flipping the furniture. Cricket was up and howling.

I unlatched the door and it flew open, the storm exploding into our Rectory, the wind hurling rain so hard against my face it stung.

There stood Big Gordo, a black-shadowed giant, lightning falling down behind him in big gleaming arcs.

"What is it?" I hollered over the tumult.

"Come see," he said.

"What's out there?" I said.

But Big Gordo just shook his head, motioning me onward.

I sighed real deep, flung on my coat and boots, and trudged out into the storm. I'd never seen one like it before. The clouds above churned and swirled like something in a witch's cauldron, black tendrils of twisters snaking down and vanishing back up again, the protections strong on our village. I prayed they would hold. The lightning shot the sky brighter than day in enormous flashes, explosions of light and sound and power. All the hairs on my arms stood on end, the rain lashing my face, the wind in gusts so strong I had to lean all the way forward not to be blown over.

Big Gordo led me through the muck over to his little station, where a gap was cut into the wall, a peephole you could reveal by sliding a wooden slat out of the way, a secret lookout.

"You see it?" he said.

I looked.

In the wind and rain stood a small figure, a little shorter than me. At first I thought it was some kind of animal, all black silhouetted and hunched over in the storm. But no, it was on two legs, and it was walking toward us, head down, hair blowing wild all around it like black flames.

The lightning flashed, and I saw the creature's face. It was a girl, her dress soaked and torn, the wind ripping around her. How could she stand being out there in a storm like this? She struggled toward us, fighting the wind, her body bent over almost in half. She banged a fist against the gates. She seemed to know we could see her, to know someone was there, watching.

"Help me," she hollered, her voice a rasp in the darkness. "Please."

I didn't know what to do. Grandpa Widow had specifically told me not to open the gates after dark. That if I did so, it would endanger the whole village. It was my duty as a Protector to keep the gates shut, no matter what. Besides, she might be the Great Doom in disguise. Hadn't Grandpa Widow warned me of this very thing?

Cricket looked up at me and whined. I scratched his head. *I know, I know,* I thought to him, and he nodded at me like he understood.

"Should I open the gates?" said Big Gordo.

"We can't," I said. "It's against the rules."

"But she's just a girl."

"That's true," I said. "But it's not up to me. You remember what Grandpa Widow told us. We can't open the gates after dark. Not no way, not no how. Those are the rules, and it's my job as Protector to uphold them."

"But you can't just leave her out there," said Big Gordo.

He was right. It began to hail, drops of rock-hard ice flung down from the sky, pelting everything. They lay glowing on the desert floor like jewels. The girl cowered from them, covering her head. I wished there was some way we could build a shelter for her out there, anything we could do to help her without opening the gates and breaking the Rites. But of course there wasn't a thing we could do, not from in here.

"Please," she begged. "Please let me in."

I knew that if she stayed out there, she would surely die. But I had made a promise. I had responsibilities. The whole village counting on me. What if I opened the gates, breaking the Rites, and the Great Doom slipped on in after her? What if a house got infected because of me or, powers forbid, a person? I didn't know what to do. Nobody tells you this stuff about responsibility, about how maybe sometimes the right thing to do will get you in all kinds of trouble, how maybe sometimes there isn't exactly a one hundred percent perfect right thing to do at all. I put my head in my hands and clenched my eyes shut and shouted a silent prayer to the One Who Listens, hoping it would do more than listen this time, that for once in my life it would show me for sure what I was supposed to do.

That was when Cricket bolted out of the hut. He ran over to where the girl was huddled against the gates, and he began to dig.

"No, Cricket!" I hollered over the storm. "Stop it!"

But he wouldn't. He just dug and dug, like he was going to tunnel his way out there and get the girl himself.

I grabbed Cricket and tried to haul him away, but he growled at me.

I couldn't believe it. Never in my whole life had my own dog growled at me before. And then he went back to digging.

Well, that settled it. Me and Cricket were a team. And if he thought that was the right thing to do, then I trusted him.

"Fine," I hollered to Big Gordo. "Open the gates!"

A big piece of hail pelted me in the arm. It stung like the dickens, but I guessed I deserved it. When we got the gates open, the girl was slumped in the mud, like she was dead or passed out.

I couldn't help but notice that the wolf and the star protections I'd carved hours earlier had disappeared, swallowed up in the mud.

I dragged the girl inside (Big Gordo wouldn't set foot outside, even if he had opened the gates), and then Big Gordo shut the gates tight. Together we picked her up and carried her to our Rectory. She wasn't talking or moving, and she had a big gash on the side of her head from where a hailstone had struck her. I wondered if we'd been too late, if we'd made her stay out there too long and now she was going to die. We swaddled her in blankets and laid her by the fire. I saw in the flames that her wet hair was a deep crimson.

I sat and watched her, chanting quiet to myself a little prayer that would bring her back, that would heal her and help her to get whole. But what if even a shadow or a tendril of the Great Doom had come sneaking in while we were busy saving her?

Big Gordo looked at me, his eyes full of fear and wonder, and I knew he was thinking the exact same thing I was. Cricket whined, and I gave his back a little pat to calm him down.

"Whatever happens," I told them both, "we can't say a word of this to anybody. If she survives, we tell them she walked in first thing in the morning. No one can know we opened the gates at night. Especially not Mayor Benningsley."

Big Gordo nodded at me and Cricket dangled his tongue out, and I knew our secret was safe right here in this hut. I sure hoped we'd done the right thing. I sure hoped Grandpa Widow wouldn't be mad at me.

Who was this girl anyhow? Just one more lonesome traveler entering a village full of them? What manner of person wandered the desert alone at night, much less in a storm like this? One more weirdness in a day full of them. I didn't know what to make out of any of it. Lazlo Dunes's warning. That strange carriage at the Benningsley mansion. Lulu outside Old Esmerelda's. Mr. Mayella out in the storm. What was going on in the village? How was I ever going to protect it in a way that would make Grandpa Widow proud? Had I already lost control?

The thunder growled above us, and in the firelight I thought I saw the girl smile.

That night I dreamed. I was on a rock, but not like the desert kind of rocks, the big dead ones craggy as the bones of old gods left gleaming in the sand. This was a wild place, loud and wet and mossy, and all about me crashed the waters. Spray whisked the air, the taste of it thick and salty, soaking me. The ocean beneath (because that's what it was, what it must be) roared and churned, white foaming and angry, the way clouds do during a twister. I felt a pull out to those waters, something calling me in the blackness of the sky around. It was as if the waters thrashed and boomed against the rocks to call me, to summon me back.

To warn me.

5

I AWOKE TO CRICKET'S NOSE ALL UP IN my face. When I opened my eyes, he gave my cheek a good lick, to finish the job of annoying me awake, I suppose. I started to laugh and tell him to cut it out, but I remembered we weren't alone in there. I took a look over at the girl, curled up and quiet as a cat, that crimson hair fallen over her face, a little shadow of a girl. I hoped she'd be okay. I hoped that we'd gotten her out of the storm in time.

Well, I wouldn't wake her. Not after a night like she'd had. I pulled on my robes and ate some cold cornbread, leaving half the pan for her, should she wake and be hungry. The storm had quit during the night, and from the light seeping in I figured it was going to be a bright hot clear day, same as most days out here in the desert. I stretched and grabbed my fiddle, and me and Cricket set out for work. Just before I shut the door, I took a glance back at the girl. She hadn't hardly stirred. I said a little prayer for her.

The sun was just an orange wink on the horizon, but it was coming sure enough. Roosters crowed, and Big Gordo stood drowsily at the gates, waiting on me.

"How is she?" he whispered.

"Sleeping," I said.

"Does she seem okay?"

"Well, she doesn't seem to be hurt too bad, if that's what you mean."

"That's a relief," he said, but I could tell he was worried, that even though it had been the right thing to do, there would still be some kind of consequence for us breaking the rules, if maybe we had rendered the Rites useless for a night. But I couldn't think about that right now. I'd already made my decision to break the rules, and whatever came next was on me. I made a fist and shut my eyes and took three deep breaths, in and out real slow, just like Grandpa Widow had taught me, until I was calm. It was time to start the Rites.

I walked widdershins with my intention focused hard on the village, on keeping everyone safe, my mind not drifting even one teeny tiny bit. Cricket loped along behind me, stepping in my footprints, like he was my very own dog-colored shadow. The morning was hot already and I was sweating something fierce in my robes.

As we walked, the rising sunlight spilled over the desert, turning each speck of dust to gold. I wanted to run out and scoop up handfuls, to hold them close to me, the desert's own wealth in my hands, to clutch it to my heart like a miser. Boy, what I'd do with money. I'd live in a castle twice the size of the Benningsley mansion, and I'd have my very own piano and maybe a washboard too, and I'd play music all day and night, singing and hollering, eating whatever I wanted, with fresh T-bones for Cricket anytime he wanted them. I'd kick back and watch the clouds all day and the stars all night. My days would be one long dream of good living, and that's a fact.

I stopped myself right then and there in the dust. Sometimes I had inklings like that, these greedy grasping little thoughts. They disturbed me, that I could want something so profane as riches. I was a Protector, through and through, and one of the main tenets of our position is that we do not bask in worldly delights, nor do we take payment for our services beyond what is needed. I was not walking with my best intention. *Stupid, Gus,* I thought. *Getting yourself distracted at this moment when the village needs you most.* I was going to have to do a heck of a lot better than that if I was going to be the sole Protector for the next few weeks. Nope, cloudy intentions wouldn't do this valley a lick of good. I made a fist and shut my eyes and spoke a Mystery (this world is not mine, nor the riches therein, my wealth is the Rites, and the true intention of my heart) and waited for the clouds in my mind to clear, for all the distractions to scatter and fade, like a handful of dust tossed up to the wind.

Once I told Grandpa Widow I had greedy thoughts. He looked at me all sad like, a whole past and future of hurt in his eyes. I was real distraught about the whole thing. I figured maybe he'd give me a whooping, or perhaps send me out to the desert to walk and roam and pay my penance in sweat. But you know what he did?

Grandpa Widow put his hand on my shoulder and looked me dead in the eyes and said, "There isn't a person alive who's not at war with their own thoughts." He shook his head. "It's the fighting that counts, little Gussy. It's the fight you can't ever quit."

And that was what I resolved myself right then and there to do. I'd fight every bad temptation and impulse I ever had with all my heart, and I'd never quit until my last dying breath.

I felt better then, my intention secure. Me and Cricket set off again, walking in our rhythm. I was so glad to be walking widdershins not alone. I sure missed Grandpa Widow, but without Cricket I would have been lost.

The sun had risen by now, a bright burning beacon for the workday, and I was all done with the walking. I stood in front of the gates and looked into the village, my home. Everyone was up and abustling, scurrying about their daily tasks. It made me happy to see it, this whole community of which I was such an important part. I kept them all safe, and I smiled to think on it. Now was time for the "Hymn of the Morning." I put my fiddle up against my neck and drew my bow across the strings.

Snap.

My E string broke, the note run squirrelly and weird off into the sky. Bartleby Bonnard stopped right where he was and cast an eye at me.

I gulped and nodded at him, trying to show that everything was okay.

But everything wasn't okay. I'd never broken a string before, not during an actual Rite.

Cricket whimpered in the dust.

It was okay, it didn't mean anything. Strings break sometimes, that's just how life goes. It wasn't an omen. Absolutely not. I took a deep breath and let it out slow, that string just dangling down like Fate itself had snipped it.

Fine, fine. I didn't need a measly old string. I had three others, didn't I? But when I dragged the bow across them, everything came out warbly and out of tune. I was going to have to *sing* this "Hymn of the Morning." No, I didn't like that one bit.

But who says I had to like it? I was a Protector, wasn't I? My job wasn't to like things, it was to keep the village safe.

I cleared my throat and began the song.

Yeah, I knew it didn't sound as good as when Grandpa Widow sang, his voice all high and lovely and quivering, a slow sky-grazing eagle of a voice that cut through the air with a regal grace, but I did my best. Cricket howled along with all his might. It wasn't great, but I sure hoped it was good enough.

"You have to be kidding me."

I turned to see Lulu Benningsley standing there, a look of disgust on her face. I gritted my teeth and balled up my fists and tried to keep my voice calm.

"Do you need anything, Lulu?" I said.

"Only to never hear you sing again in my life," she said. "You have a voice like a kicked mule, you know that?"

"I am your Protector," I said, as quietly and calmly as I could. "And I may not be the best singer, but I hit the notes okay, and I didn't bungle the words, so the Rites are in place, and you are safe. That's my only job."

Lulu laughed.

"Yeah, my life is safe, sure," she said. "But my ears aren't. Good lord, I can't believe I have to listen to you croaking along three times a day until Grandpa Widow comes back."

You don't have to listen to anything, I thought. *You can just sit inside and be a brat all by yourself, can't you?*

But I didn't say that. Grandpa Widow always told me fighting back was beneath me when all I was dealing with was some rich girl's insults. That didn't stop them from stinging, of course. To be honest, I was about two seconds from crying, and there was no way I was going to let Lulu see that.

"See you around, Lulu," I said.

"Let's hope not," she said.

"As you wish."

I turned my back to her and headed to the Rectory to grab some grub and check on the mystery girl, tears burning in my eyes.

When I got back, the girl was awake, sitting up in the bed, reading one of Grandpa Widow's books—*Most Solemn Rites of the Starless Night*. It was a weird book, real esoteric, one I'd only skimmed a few times myself. All kinds of Rites for odd stuff, like how to fight off infestations of grasshoppers, and the best way to keep the bones of plague victims from working their way out of the dirt like worms, because everybody knows plague bones just won't sit still. Nothing practical, you know? Not for us in the desert anyhow.

"Hi there," I said.

The girl lowered the book and blinked at me.

"I'm Gussy," I said, "and this is Cricket."

Cricket barked a howdy.

The girl took a long, slow look around the room before settling her eyes back on me.

"I'm Angeline," she said. "Where am I?"

"You're in the Rectory. It's where me and Grandpa Widow live, only he isn't here right now."

"This book is fascinating," said Angeline. "This one too."

She pointed to another one of Grandpa Widow's books on esoteric Rites. This one was about something called air burial, which is what they do in the mountains. See, the ground is too rocky to dig graves in, so folks just leave the bodies out on a high peak to decompose and get eaten up by birds. They wait until the bones are picked clean, and whatever's left they pound into dust with hammers. It's interesting stuff, sure, but that book is grisly. The illustrations alone are enough to give you nightmares.

"You're the one who carried me inside, right?" She touched her head and winced. "I think I remember that."

"Yeah, I helped, but it was mostly Big Gordo who did the carrying. He's outside guarding the gates."

"I shall have to thank him later," said Angeline. She coughed. "May I have something to drink, please?"

"I can heat up some coffee for you," I said.

Angeline made a face, which I thought was pretty rude,

considering how I'd broken my most sacred rule just to let her in here.

"I mean, you don't have to have coffee," I said. "It's just, you know, what we got."

Angeline lifted a hand to her mouth, like she was embarrassed.

"Gosh. How rude of me. My head's still a bit throbby. I can't quite control my emotions." She set her hands back in her lap and smiled. "Coffee would be delightful, please."

I lit the stove and waited for the water to boil.

"I've got a little leftover cornbread with butter if you want it," I said. "Some ham too."

"I'd be most grateful."

Angeline was still sitting there in the bed, the blanket wrapped around her like some kind of a gown, her long red hair tangled past her shoulders, my bandage wrap a sad crown on her head. Grandpa Widow left for one night, and now there was a stranger in the Rectory. What a world. I set to work restringing my fiddle.

"So what happened?" I said. "How did you end up in the desert at night?"

"My family and I were seeking sanctuary after our old village was destroyed. Ransacked by bandits, and then a rogue warlock made the earth open up and swallow city hall. We had a Protector, but he wasn't very good. May he rest in peace."

I gulped. "Yes. May he rest in peace."

"That's why we risked crossing the desert. There aren't many safe places left out there, and we thought we might find refuge here, in your village. But we got lost in the storm." Angeline's eyes got real big, and she blinked away tears. "I had a kitty cat named Chester. A little gray thing with a nubbin tail. Have you seen him anywhere?"

"Can't say I have."

"I didn't figure you would. Anyway, when he leaped from the wagon, I went after him. I ran and ran, but he was gone. It was raining so hard it began to flood. I've never seen anything like it. It was like a river sprang up from the ground and nearly carried me off. Then that twister hit, and I couldn't find my family or Chester. I wandered until I saw the lights of your village."

"Strange, a cat leaping out in the rain," I said.

She nodded. "Chester isn't your typical kitten. He's awfully adventurous. Back home he used to go swimming in the lake just to catch fish for his dinner."

"Got any plans for finding your family?" I said.

"Oh, I'm sure they'll be here soon, looking for me. Don't you think so?"

I hoped so. It was a miracle this girl here had survived a night out in the valley like that, especially with the Great Doom on the prowl. Heaven help her if she'd come across a desert witch, somebody like Lucinda Withern and her ilk. It was said Lucinda could peel the skin off a person with her fingernail just the same as she'd peel an apple. A storm is nothing compared to a witch like that. I said a silent prayer just thinking about it. But if Angeline's family had made it through, they were bound to show up at the gates sooner or later. That was a big if, by the way, but I wasn't going to tell Angeline that.

"I'm sure they'll turn up any minute," I said.

Cricket padded over to her and gave her a sniff.

"Oh, hello!" she said. "Cricket, right? I'm Angeline."

Angeline stuck her hand out, like she expected Cricket to shake it. Thing was, Cricket didn't do tricks. Fetch, sit up, beg, roll over, all that garbage. It's demeaning. I trained him a heck of a lot better than all that nonsense. So imagine my shock when he lifted his paw up to her and let her give it a squeeze. I nearly knocked the coffee kettle right over there on the floor, I was so shocked.

"What an exquisite puppy!"

"He's not a puppy," I said. "He's a full-grown adult dog, for your information. And he doesn't do tricks."

"Pardon me," she said. "I didn't mean to offend."

"Don't worry about it," I said. "Milk or sugar in the coffee?"

"However you take it is fine, I'm sure," she said.

"Barebones it is." That means I take it black, no sugar or

milk or anything at all so it's as strong and bitter as possible. I poured the coffee in a little tin mug and handed it to her, along with a plate of salt ham and leftover cornbread.

"I remain firmly in your debt," she said.

Yeah, this girl was definitely weird. I hoped her family was safe and sound, and that they came for her quick, before anybody found out what I'd done. If word got back to Grandpa Widow, I was done for sure.

"Aight, well, me and Cricket got some work to do," I said, "so I'll leave you be. Kindly stay in here and out of sight, if you don't mind. I wasn't exactly supposed to let you into the village after dark, and I don't want folks to worry."

She nodded at me and took a sip of her coffee. She grimaced a little. I tried not to laugh.

I grabbed my fiddle and made for the door.

"Gussy?"

I turned to Angeline, the bandage-headed girl sitting cross-legged on my bed.

"Yeah?" I said.

"Thank you," she said, "for letting me in."

I nodded at her and left.

I didn't know what to do about Angeline. Normally in a situation like this I would have run to Miss Esmerelda's and gotten a posse together to go searching out in the desert for her family. But I couldn't do that, not since I'd broken the rules to let her into the village. If folks found out I'd done that, they would revoke my Protector status and maybe even banish me to the desert for good. I couldn't risk it. But what if her family was hurt, or in trouble? What if they needed help? I flat didn't know what to do. Maybe I could figure a way to sneak her outside when no one was looking and then let her walk in on her own. That way no one would worry, and they'd gather up a posse immediately. Still, it was hard to find a time when the gates were open and there weren't folks coming in and out, milling around, looking for travelers headed our way.

I chanted a Mystery about it, a prayer up to the One Who Listens, and Cricket hollered out his most mournful howl. As always, we were in this together. I hoped soon an answer would come.

Until then, there was work to do.

I did a quick run-through of the village before Midday Salutations, just to see if there was anything amiss. Everything seemed normal, so far as I could tell. Mayor Benningsley was out ordering people around, being a busybody all up in other folks' business, same as usual. I tried to cut around Mr. Jilly's Haberdashery, but the mayor's wife, Lucretia, saw me anyhow.

"And how are things going this fine day?" she said.

Okay, that was weird. Lucretia Benningsley never stopped me just to chat, only to criticize. But maybe it was because I was in charge for the next few days, and that made me worth talking to for once.

"Better than ever."

"All recovered from the storm?"

"Wasn't much to recover from, so far as I can tell," I said. "That storm was all bark and no bite."

Lucretia burst out laughing, a real honest-to-god cackling, and I didn't much know what to do with that. I didn't even think what I'd said was all that funny, or really funny at all. Cricket whined a little bit like he thought it was weird too.

"Yes, yes," said Lucretia, when she'd gathered herself. "You are a delight, aren't you? It's a good thing you're here. We are so grateful for Grandpa Widow and the Rites, indeed. It would be terrible if anything should go amiss while he was gone."

I forced a grin at her.

"It won't." And then a thought occurred to me. "Mrs. Benningsley, can you tell me who that man in the tweed suit was?"

Lucretia's eyes went wide.

"A tweed suit?"

"Yes, ma'am," I said. "He came riding up in that big black

carriage yesterday, before the storm. I saw him go into your house."

"My house?" Lucretia laughed. "Goodness me, I didn't notice any kind of person like that. And I would know, wouldn't I?"

"Maybe you could ask your husband about it," I said, "since I'm the Protector now and I ought to know who is coming and going in the village."

"I certainly will ask him," said Lucretia. She frowned at me. "Must be so hard, a little girl your age, no father or mother to help you, having to carry so much responsibility all on your own. If you need anything, just give a whistle. You know where to find me!"

If there's one thing I hate, it's pity. Go ahead and write that down. If my family was the Benningsleys, I'd be better off an orphan. Far as I cared, Lucretia could take all her pity and shove it.

But as Grandpa Widow always said, "Hate is not worth your time. Not bitterness nor envy either." So I said a Mystery for Lucretia Benningsley and requested the One Who Listens to give her something real to pity so she'd leave me alone.

After Midday Salutations, I came back for some lunch and found Connor Carnivolly sitting on the Rectory floor, trying to burp a toad into his palm. I'd seen Connor try this trick before, but it hadn't worked out so well for the toad. Today Angeline sat there smiling at him, as gleeful an audience for a no-good magic trick show as there ever was.

"I let him in," said Angeline. "I hope that's okay."

"You should have told me you had a stranger in town," he said. "I would have shown up sooner."

For some reason, that annoyed me.

"Just keep this floor free of frog guts," I said.

Connor laughed. "I give you a no-guts guarantee."

I watched as Connor pulled a coin from his ear, gold from his nose, and a rose from his cuff. He also guessed my card right this time.

"It takes a little bit of practice," said Connor. "But I'm getting good."

"It's still not real magic," I said.

"That," said Connor, "is the beauty of it. You've seen what real magic can do to people if they aren't careful. After all, even Lucinda Withern was just a regular old witch healer before she got her head into the wrong books and wound up raising the Seven Forks' Demon. Or that's what they say, anyhow. My magic's just a trick, an illusion. It doesn't pluck the strings of fate, it doesn't alter the path of the moon, nothing like that. It only exists to make people happy."

"But isn't that kind of silly?" I said. "Wouldn't you rather have the power that real magic brings, the kind that could change the world?"

"Maybe my magic has its own kind of power," he said. "I get to make people a little happier, to bring some joy into their lives. That's a noble enough duty for me, I do believe."

"I like that," said Angeline, and I rolled my eyes at her.

I became aware of a strange, somewhat alluring odor drifting through the Rectory.

"Wait a minute," I said. "What's that smell?"

"Connor brought us over some stew," said Angeline.

"Did he now?" I said.

"Yep," said Connor. "And it's delicious. Help yourself, Gussy."

"It's got rabbit in it, but I loved it anyway," said Angeline, and Connor positively beamed. I guess those two were getting along just fine without me. I didn't want to be jealous, but I was nonetheless. Isn't that the way of things? You get all high-minded and virtuous in your thinking, but when it comes down to the actual experiences of life, we always handle things in the same crummy way as everyone else.

"Well, anyway," I said. "My day so far has been just lovely, thanks for asking. Even bumped into Lucretia Benningsley, which was a real delight, let me tell you."

"Lucky you," said Connor.

"Benningsley," said Angeline. "Is that the family that lives up in the big house?"

"Yeah," I said. "How did you know?"

She shrugged. "I snuck outside earlier and took a little look around. Guessing the Benningsleys are rich folks, huh?"

"The richest," said Connor, grinning his gap-toothed grin. "Rumor is they have a secret gemstone that's worth a whole bundle. They dug it up out of the Hidden Mines years and years ago, long before my family even came to the village. It's called the Valley's Heart, and supposedly it's magical."

"It isn't magical," I said. "That's nonsense. The Valley's Heart is just some big glittering jewel, and having it means the Benningsleys get to walk around turning their noses up at everyone. It's enough to drive a body bonkers."

"The Valley's Heart!" chirped Angeline. "What a lovely name. I bet it is magical, at least a little bit. It just has to be, with a name like that."

"That's what I'm always saying," said Connor. "Supposedly it's deep red, like a heart, but it isn't a ruby, no sir. There's never been another gemstone like it, not in these parts or any others. It's the rarest stone on all the earth."

"You've got to stop with this gibberish," I said, but I didn't really mean it. Secretly I loved the way Connor Carnivolly talked things up, how he could make a wild extravagant story out of something so boring as seeing a dog chase around a vulture that just got done eating and was too full to fly. He could stretch a story as long as he wanted, adding all kinds of flourishes that you knew weren't true but made you happy to hear anyway. It was even better when you were involved in the story somehow, like the time Connor and I snuck out to Old Esmerelda's so I could play my fiddle and I made a whole heap of coin in tips.

We would have gotten away with it too, had Grandpa Widow not woken up when I was sneaking back in. He got so mad at me I wasn't allowed to talk to Connor for a whole month. Even afterward, Grandpa Widow didn't let me play around so much anymore. He said I was getting too slack with my duties, and the village needed me to do my job perfectly, every time. He said to be careful, because Connor was just a distraction.

But Connor wasn't just a distraction. He was my friend. I wished Grandpa Widow understood that.

"Where'd you just go?" said Angeline, and I realized I'd drifted off again, thinking about other stuff. It was a real problem.

"She does that sometimes," said Connor, grinning at me. He really did have the best grin of all grins. It made you feel warm and loved and teased and understood all at once.

"So this Valley's Heart?" said Angeline. "I'm intrigued."

"You should be!" said Connor, glad somebody'd taken his bait. "Even the mine where they dug it up is incredible. I mean, it's all boarded up, and you can't get in there, folks say it's hexed, but it's still something to see."

"Hexed?" said Angeline. "How?"

"Well, the story is, the Valley's Heart didn't want to come up out of the earth," he said. "When McGregor Benningsley first found the mine, it was just some crack in the earth, like what had happened in an earthquake or something. He lowered himself down in it, the air all cool and dark and damp and mysterious. As he traveled farther, the crack opened up to a kind of cavern, like a tunnel leading deeper and deeper into the ground. He followed it for hours and hours, until he came to this underground lake."

"A real underground lake?" said Angeline.

"Yep," said Connor. "With no-eyed fishes swimming around, and glowworms and bats the size of bread loaves flying about. And coming up from the earth was one single slender vine, sprouting right out of the ground. And what's more, the vine was glowing."

"Glowing?" I said. This was too much. I never heard anything about a glowing vine in all my life. "Come on, Connor. That's not how it happened."

"Is too," he said. "Mr. Mayella told me himself one time. It was payment for mending his steps. I do odd jobs for him, and he always pays me in stories. It's a good trade."

"I'd rather have coin," I said, but I didn't really mean it. Everybody knows stories are better than money, so long as you still got enough to eat and a roof over your head. Because you can spend money in a second and then it's gone, but a story always grows stronger with the telling of it. The story can change or twist itself or become a whole new story altogether, just the same way the teller can grow and change and become a different person altogether too. They're a mysterious thing, stories, and I'm so happy I'll never run out of them, both to tell and to hear. All my favorite songs are stories, even the ones without any words, and that's a fact.

"Anyways," said Connor, "McGregor Benningsley tugged on the vine, and it jostled the dirt a little bit and gave way. He pulled and pulled and pulled, and the vine kept coming. Only it changed colors every few feet, and it glowed brighter and brighter. Orange and purple and pink and deep blue and a glimmer of green. Finally he pulled until the vine wouldn't move anymore. That's when McGregor Benningsley whipped out his pickax and got to work. Supposedly it took him three days and three nights to dig, without any food and only a small canteen of water. By the end of all that digging, he was half-starved and nearly insane, but he got to the bottom of that vine. It was a red gem, big as a giant's heart, and it glowed brighter than a fire, it hurt his eyes even to gaze on it. He hoisted it out of the hole, and through the crack in the earth, back to the surface, where he strapped it to himself and set off for this very spot—what would one day become the village. He barely survived the journey, and supposedly his horse didn't, poor thing. But that's the story.

That's how the Valley's Heart was conquered, and that's how the village began."

I had to admit, it was a pretty good story, even if Connor had made up most of it, adding all those little details here and there. But you know, in storytelling, the little details are everything. They're the things that help your story come alive in the hearer's own brain; they sprinkle in just enough detail to let the listener paint the rest of the picture in their mind, and then the story belongs to the teller and the hearer too. It's a collaboration like that, between the teller and the hearer, both of their hearts working together to make the story true. That's the best part of stories, to me anyhow.

"I want to see the Valley's Heart," said Angeline.

Connor laughed. "That's never going to happen. The Benningsleys keep it locked up in a safe, deep in a hidden room in their mansion. Nobody's seen it except for Mayor Benningsley himself."

But then again, I wondered if that was true. Surely somebody somewhere had to have seen it, famous as it was.

"Well," said Angeline, "at the very least, I want to see the hole where it was dug up."

"I told you already, it's hexed," said Connor. "Other folks went in, trying to dig up their own Valley's Heart, or something like it. Not a one ever came back."

"That isn't true," I said.

"Oh, isn't it?" said Connor.

"Nope," I said. "One person *did* come back, at least according to Grandpa Widow. But it's true, he's not exactly right in the noggin."

"Who?" said Angeline.

She and Connor looked up at me, waiting so expectantly for the answer. I loved this part of telling a story, having the last final detail that everybody wants to hear. I let the moment linger just a little bit, savoring their attention, the way both of them were so completely focused on me, waiting on what I had to say. I flashed what I hoped was a mischievous smile, doing my best impression of Connor's sly grin.

"Why," I said, "it's Lazlo Dunes, of course."

"No wonder he wanders around town all day," said Connor, "banging on that plate. If he went all the way down in that mine, there's no telling how it warped his brain."

"Pretty brave of him, though," said Angeline, and neither of us could disagree with her on that point.

We sat there a little, quiet while I gobbled up my stew. It was lukewarm, but that was fine with me, considering how hot it was outside. It was nice, having the two of them in the Rectory, Cricket lapping at his water bowl, all of us together. It made me miss Grandpa Widow something fierce, and that thought made my heart plummet. What would he think of this little gathering that could only occur because I broke our most sacred rule? I bet he wouldn't be one bit pleased with me. It'd be a miracle if he didn't toss me out in the street the moment he got back.

"I guess I got to go back to work," I said after a while. "Connor, if you don't mind locking up when you leave, I sure would appreciate it."

"Will do, High Protector Gussy," said Connor. He saluted me, and Angeline burst out laughing.

I sort of wished they wouldn't joke about it like that.

6

THAT EVENING I WAS PRETTY SOLEMN performing the Rites. I stood tall and played "Last Lights Wonder" with all my best intention. The sunset was a deep orange and a glorious pink, a parade of royalty strutting across the sky. I swear to you there is nothing more gorgeous than a desert sunset, clouds like cream puffs, the sky so big you can't imagine the end of it. When I played "Last Lights Wonder," I put my whole soul into it, that new string ringing proud and true out into the desert beyond, while Cricket howled his harmony. It wasn't great, but I hoped it would do.

When me and Cricket walked back to the Rectory, Angeline was sitting on the floor, hunched over a long black raven's feather poking out of a green-and-purple gemstone with a small hole carved in the center of it. Smoke rose from a tiny pile of what I realized was Grandpa Widow's Rites of Reclaiming, secret herbs for calling back something you lost. I stood in the doorway, the door wide open. Angeline didn't seem to notice I was there.

I watched her work, her hands clasped together behind her back, her head bobbing in rhythm, almost like she was swimming. The words were garbled, all yips and squeaks, something like birdsong. This was a crude ritual, a kind of homespun folk work. I'd heard of stuff like this. Grandpa Widow always said it was common magic, far beneath what we did with the Rites. It wasn't anything like my stiff-posture marching and my note-perfect chants, the language of the Mysteries all fancy and highfalutin. No, this was something else altogether.

I slammed the door shut, and Angeline jumped.

"Gosh," she said. "You startled me."

"That was kind of the idea," I said.

"I borrowed some of these gathering herbs. I hope that's all right."

"Those are the sacred herbs for Grandpa Widow's Rites of Reclaiming," I said. I nearly told her how mad he'd be if he found out she'd burned them, but then I remembered she was trying to get her family back. He wouldn't mind her using them for something as important as that.

She shrugged. "We always just called them gathering

herbs where I come from. Though I've never seen a batch of such high quality."

"Yeah, well. Grandpa Widow's a professional."

"Any news of my parents?"

"Nope," I said. "I asked around, and no one's heard a word. If they aren't here by tomorrow morning, I'll send out a posse. It's just hard, you know? Because I wasn't supposed to let you in. Maybe we can sneak you out of here tomorrow morning and tell folks you wandered in from the desert, and they'll send a posse out for them."

Angeline cast a glance at me, her hair falling over her eyes.

"Oh, you don't have to do that," she said.

"Why not? Don't you want to find your parents?"

"Of course I do!" she said. "It's just that, well, you broke a rule in letting me in, and I wouldn't want you or Big Gordo to get in trouble on behalf of me."

"It's not that much trouble," I said. "We just have to find a good moment to sneak you out there. I bet sunrise will be best. You'll have to explain to folks how you survived outside all night, but we'll cook you up a good story."

"Please," she said, "don't make me do that." She fiddled with her fingers, tearing at a cuticle. "It's just that I'm no good at lying, even if it's a lie for a good reason. I always get found out. And besides, you're a Protector. Lying goes against your duties."

So did letting you inside the gates, I thought, but I didn't say it.

"So what do you want me to do?" I said.

"Would it be all right if I just stayed in here and tried to find my parents with my rituals? That's what I was doing when you walked in," she said. "I was searching in my own way, with magic. If you want to hire someone to scour the desert for them, I've got a little bit of gold hidden in my dress, you know, and I can help pay. But please don't gather a whole posse just for me. I wouldn't want you to make such a big deal out of it."

Well, I didn't have a clue how to feel about that. Angeline looked up at me, tears warbling in her eyes, and I knew any moment she would break down weeping and hollering. I was never much good at dealing with crying folks. It makes me uncomfortable. Besides, she had already been through so much, getting separated from her parents and all, not to mention getting conked in the head by hailstones. Maybe I could find somebody to hire on the sly. It'd be easier on me anyhow, not having to concoct some big elaborate story.

"All right," I said. "For now, anyways. But I do think we got a better shot at finding your parents if you'd allow me to put a posse together."

"Thank you, Gussy," she said. "Thank you so much."

Angeline seemed relieved, and again I wondered about her, where she came from, what her family was like. I watched as she pocketed the raven's feather and the little stone.

"What do you call that thing?" I said.

"Oh, this? It belonged to my grandmother. It's called the Peacock's Eye."

"It's pretty," I said.

"It's been in my family a very long time. I hoped it would help draw my parents back to me."

"Well, I'm sure it'll work," I said.

"I hope so."

I took off my robes and just sort of stood there in my tunic, fidgeting a little bit, the smell of Grandpa Widow's herbs lingering in the air. It made me a little nervous, to be honest. I noticed several gaps in Grandpa Widow's bookshelves, and a big stack of books by my bedside. I wondered where else she'd been poking around . . . if she'd seen Grandpa Widow's skull collection. The man is just crazy about skulls—rabbit skulls and dog skulls and cat skulls and beaver skulls and jackrabbit skulls and bobcat skulls and wolf skulls, even a people skull or two. He says if you scratch the top of their heads and hold them close to your ears, those skulls will tell you stories, what it was like to be them, to live their lives, how the moon looked on the nights they all died. It was spooky stuff, what Grandpa Widow did with those skulls, and I didn't much like the thought of Angeline messing around with them. It was strange to know somebody else had been here all day, doing just whatever they wanted.

"Don't worry, I didn't touch the skulls," said Angeline.

"Who said I was worried about that?"

Angeline just blinked at me twice.

I got to work on some dinner, tossing a few scraps first to Cricket.

"Need any help?" Angeline asked me.

"Nah," I said. "I got it."

She picked up the air burial book and got back to flipping pages. There was one illustration in there I loved, of a tall rocky mountain peak, the desert stretching everywhere all around, with a woman in a robe with her hair flayed out black and wild in the wind like a shadow lit on fire. She stood above a body—a man, a dead man, stretched out, his arms crossed at his chest, while above them circled vultures. It was a beautiful illustration, so kind and sad and heartbroke. It seemed sometimes the realest thing in the world to me, that kind of pain and longing. I used to stare at it for hours and hours when I was a little girl. Cricket leaped up beside Angeline and seemed to be reading over her shoulder. He'd never done anything like that with me before. To be honest, it made me a little bit jealous. But then I remembered how Angeline's family was missing, and I figured Cricket was just trying to be extra nice to her on account of all that. I understood. Cricket really was a good dog.

We sat down to our meager meal of cornbread and ham. Grandpa Widow always did the cooking around here, and he was real particular about it, never let me help out or anything like that.

We ate mostly in silence. The food wasn't very good. Maybe I should have fixed some beans or something.

"What was that song you played?" said Angeline.

"Which song?"

"The one at the end of the Rite. The one that goes like this." And she sang the melody off perfectly.

"That's 'Last Lights Wonder,'" I said. "It's how we close out every day."

"It's beautiful," she said. "I don't think I've ever heard anything like that."

"Grandpa Widow wrote it himself, when he first came to the village," I said. "He said that a village besieged by something so awful as the Great Doom needed its own Rite just to get by. He told me it took him months and months of trying and tossing things aside before he finally got fed up and quit. That very night the song came to him in a dream."

"Wow," said Angeline. "I love that."

"Yeah," I said. "Grandpa Widow believes all the best stuff comes to us in dreams, when our brains finally get out of their own way and listen."

"Your Grandpa Widow sounds like a very wise man," said Angeline.

"He sure is. He's the best man I know. I'm real lucky to have him."

"My pop is like that," said Angeline. "He's not real book smart, but he picks things up along the way."

"You get the reading bug from your momma then?" I asked.

Angeline made a face, like she was in pain. "No," she said. "The reading is all my own."

I wanted to ask her more about that, but I didn't want to push it. I don't believe it's good to make people talk about things they don't seem to want to. It can get a body in all kinds of trouble.

Angeline looked toward the window. "I sure hope they come for me soon."

"I have no doubt they will."

"Really?" said Angeline. She turned to me with big tears in her eyes. "Because I'm not so sure."

"I'll light a candle for them tonight," I said, "and I'll chant a special Mystery to the One Who Listens."

"Thank you," she said. "Thank you so very much."

We were quiet then for a moment. The fire crackled, and long far off a wolf howled. I could feel the Great Doom pressing in then, a malingering shadow just outside the gates, and I shivered.

"Maybe you could play that song again for me?" said Angeline. "Your 'Last Lights Wonder'?"

"I'd be glad to."

I picked up my fiddle and began to play, and Cricket howled along, and by the second refrain Angeline had joined in too, her voice high and pretty, like a bird flitting from branch to branch. She sang so well with Cricket and my fiddle, and when the song was over I struck up another, a happy song, a seafaring shanty Grandpa Widow had taught me from the olden days, long before he ever went to the conservatory and learned the Rites, back when he was on the ramble. It was a simple song, and Angeline took up the tune like she'd known it her whole life. Cricket got to barking and hopping around, and before long the three of us began dancing through the Rectory, Angeline singing loud as she could, our song a joyful sound in the cool desert night, all of us safe and protected by the Rites, not a single thought for the Great Doom pacing beyond the gates, ravenous as a wolf.

That night I had a dream.

I was floating in the mist and the clouds, high above the world. I saw the ocean beneath me, the water that stretched deeper and longer than the desert, the frothy tips of it like hills, the cliffs rising steep and jagged from the depths. I saw a lighthouse with its fire burning like a gargantuan single eye, its light cutting through the spray, and I realized I was a bird—a seagull, I'd seen a drawing in a book once—and I was flying, circling and free, while in the far distance I saw the sails billowing like great white ghosts in the wind. And I knew danger had arrived for that lighthouse, for that ship on the horizon, for all near and far in this land.

But it couldn't touch me, no, because I was a bird, a seagull, circling high above, floating on the invisible roads of the clouds, the wind lifting me high, safe and free and unafraid.

7

THE NEXT MORNING, AS I LAY CURLED in my blanket on the floor by the stove, all nice and warm and groggy, sunlight dripping through the window, casting the Rectory floor gold like some sultan's treasure chamber, Cricket nuzzled me awake.

I giggled a little as his tongue lapped the sleep from my face, and for one moment I was filled with such peace and joy I could not explain it to you. I felt home, really home, in that impossibly rare way you can when everything is just right, and the morning feels like a sunlit promise only the rest of your life can fulfill.

Angeline was awake already, drinking leftover cold coffee from yesterday, thumbing through another of Grandpa Widow's books. She had a stack going by the bed. It was like she'd stayed up all night reading or something. The sun lit a glow on her skin, and she seemed to shrink from it a little, like maybe the light would burn her.

Wait, the sun was out? Oh no.

I sprang out of my blankets and scrambled to put on my robes.

"What's the matter?" said Angeline.

"I'm late, that's what's the matter," I said. "Why didn't you wake me up?"

"Oh, you know." She shrugged. "You looked so peaceful sleeping like that, all warm and fluffy like a little cottontailed bunny person. Your body seemed so terribly intent on staying asleep that I didn't want to disturb you."

"Disturb me? I got responsibilities, you know," I said, a crust of cold cornbread stuffed in my mouth, chewing while I tried to find my boots. "I got a whole village depending on me to keep them safe. I can't just be sleeping in whenever I want. I'm usually up before the roosters."

"You do have such lovely roosters in this village," said Angeline. "They sing the sweetest good-morning song."

I bit my lip and tried not to scream at her. She was lucky her parents were lost out in the desert or I really would have let her have it. How in the world had I slept through the roosters? Two days without Grandpa Widow, and I was already failing so miserably at my duties.

I grabbed my fiddle and hustled outside, where Big Gordo

was staring at me all strange.

"Is everything okay in there?" he said.

"Would be better if you'd woken me up," I said. "You ever think of that?"

Big Gordo looked a little hurt. I'd never snapped at him before. It was hard to remember that just because he was so huge and muscle-y it didn't mean he wasn't just about the most sensitive person you ever met in your life.

"I'm sorry," I said. "Just never slept in before. Hope nobody else noticed."

"Actually," said Big Gordo, "now that you mention it . . ."

Strutting down the road came Mayor Benningsley, all huff and bustle.

"Ahh, there she is," he said.

Great.

"Hi there, Mayor Benningsley," I said.

"Getting a bit of a late start today, aren't we?" he said, taking out his gold glimmering pocket watch and giving it a tap. "The gates have been open half an hour, and I have yet to hear the 'Hymn of the Morning.'"

Don't admit that you slept in. He's not your boss, and he has no right to demand anything. You don't owe the man anything, remember that, Gussy.

"Just finishing some chores in the Rectory before getting started today," I said. "If you'll excuse me."

But Mayor Benningsley didn't move. He just stood there

awkwardly, sweating, wringing his hands. His eyes kept darting toward the open gates, the sunlit hazy horizon off in the distance.

"It's imperative that the Rites be performed correctly," he said. "Now more than ever."

Don't tell me how to do my job, I almost shouted at him, but that wouldn't have done me any good. I gripped my fiddle so hard I nearly snapped the neck. I could feel the hair on Cricket standing at end, the quiet rumble of a growl beginning in his throat.

"I'm on it," I said, and I marched right past him through the gates and into the desert to begin my walking widdershins.

Still, I was shaken up a bit. What if Mayor Benningsley told Grandpa Widow I was derelict in my duties? And why was he being so pushy anyhow? Did it have anything to do with that mysterious carriage and the man in the tweed suit? I wish I had asked him about all that, but I was too flustered. Maybe I would get another shot later today. Regardless, I was late enough starting already.

I took a deep breath, cleared my mind, and got to work, trying to make up for lost time.

By noon, I was back at the Rectory, all sweaty and out-of-sorts. I'd had to hustle through "Morningsong Hymn" and missed a few notes, and I'd never walked widdershins so fast. Even Cricket was wore out, tongue lolling all pink and sloppy as he lapped water from his bowl. Something in the air just felt wrong today, you know what I mean? It was like the sky had a crackle to it, like the sun was burning so bright the very air might catch fire and spark. I shocked myself on every piece of metal I touched, little blue lightning bolts leaping from my finger when I so much as reached for the door handle, and my throat was a little sore from all that singing last night.

I had the creeping fearfuls, is what I'm saying. That's what Grandpa Widow called the warning feeling in your guts when something's wrong and you don't know what. He said the creeping fearfuls are usually just in your noggin and you can reason your way out of them if you're smart about it. So I tried to go over my checklist.

Cricket was happy. The morning Rites were done. Big Gordo was mopey and a little nervous, but that was normal. Mayor Benningsley was a jerk, sure, but he wasn't causing me the creeping fearfuls either. What could it be?

"How you feeling?" I asked Angeline.

"Oh, I'm okay," she said. "Had a nice chat with Big Gordo earlier. He's such a friendly person."

"Big Gordo came and talked to you?" I said.

"Oh yes," she said, flipping the page of Ogleman's *Hogthistle Ballads*, a secret Rites book built around nursery rhymes written in code. There's nothing more powerful than a nursery rhyme, especially when the melody's right. It's about the most powerful magic I know of. "He came to see me after you left. Read me one of his poems. He's quite good, you know?"

I had to scrape up my jaw from the floor. I couldn't believe it.

"Big Gordo read you one of his poems?" I said. "He only reads *me* his poems."

"Well then, you know all about it," she said, and munched a bite of my burned cornbread. "You have such a nice life here. All these wonderful books, and people to come read you poems. It's about all anybody could ever ask for."

She was right, of course. But why did it bother me a little to hear her say it?

Maybe because her parents were still lost out there in the desert. Were Angeline's parents the source of my creeping fearfuls? That would make a lot of sense. And if she didn't want a big fuss to be made after her, well, maybe I could get the Rider to go looking for her, the one who had delivered that letter to Grandpa Widow. Of course, if it were me, I'd want the whole village out searching for my parents. But I never knew my parents, and I can't say I've spent a whole lot of my energy trying to find out a thing about them. And this Angeline was a strange bird, no doubt about it. Besides, I bet that Rider would do as good a job as any posse, and she'd be quiet about it. Grandpa Widow had a small stash of emergency coin I could use to pay. He kept it in a toucan skull next to his bedside table.

"So I was thinking," I said. "A Rider came into town a few days ago. She said she was sticking around for a little while. What if I ask her for help?"

Angeline's face went a little flat, her smile vanishing. It must be hard to be reminded that your parents are out there, lost. I'd have to be more careful about bringing it up.

"Oh, I couldn't bother you with that," she said.

"It's no bother," I said. "I'd be glad to help you find them."

"Are you sure it's not too much to ask?"

"Not a bit," I said. "I could hire her . . . as soon as I finish Midday Salutation, of course."

"I'd be much obliged," said Angeline. "You really are so very kind to me."

I thought any second she was going to bust out crying. I was glad I could do something good for her, and I only hoped her parents were okay. Good thing I remembered about that Rider.

It really wasn't a bad plan. I was pretty proud of myself for thinking of it.

8

I REACHED THE BOOK OF NAMES RIGHT
on schedule, blessing it with a protection Mystery (within
these gates, keep these hearts safe, may their minds rest so
nice, in peace and delight, keep the blood well in their veins,
each one as is named) when I decided to go hunting for the
Rider.

Lazlo Dunes clacked around the meeting pole, banging
his pan and hollering. He cast a mean eye at me and I glowered right back at him, hard as I could. I didn't trust that
guy one bit, no sir, and I wasn't about to start now. Miss
Bonnie Blightly Longfeather and Tripoli Sanchez stood by
the meeting pole, gossiping away about the Benningsleys,
which was always where gossip wound up. Even more so
lately, since the Benningsleys had stopped throwing their

lavish parties and inviting people over for tea. You'd be surprised what I hear, making my rounds, performing the Rites. Most folks quit noticing me a long time ago, or else they trust me as some kind of holy person not to be bothered. But I hear everything. Boy, do I. All the rumors about what might be going on in there, despite the mayor's constant smiling and glad-handing. Lucretia Benningsley even canceled her famous book club last year, the one she used to import books into the village for. As much as I don't like that family, I can't fault them this—they gave our village books, and they gave them freely. Even the folks you can't stand still matter to the world, you know? They can still play their part.

When I was sure no one was watching, I hurried myself to Old Esmerelda's. Like Grandpa Widow always said, it was no good for a Protector to be seen in a tavern. Doesn't inspire trust in the villagers. Makes us seem frivolous and flippant, derelict with our duties. How could we keep the village safe if we were out chuckling in the company of the ne'er-do-wells? So I had to be quick, and I had to be sneaky.

"Stay outside," I told Cricket, "and give me a howl if anything goes wrong."

He nodded at me, and I scratched him behind his ears. Then I made my way, clomping across the boardwalk of Old Esmerelda's Inn. The doors swung shut behind me and I walked on past the front desk to the dining room, where a few guests sat around having lunch. But I knew I wouldn't find the Rider in the dining room, no way. The only place for a person like that was behind the back door, covered by a curtain, the kind of place you only went to on purpose—the parlor room of Old Esmerelda's Inn. You couldn't go there if you were just anybody, I knew that, and besides, most people wouldn't even want to. The lighting was dim, and there were only a couple of windows, with great black velvet curtains that hung over them during daylight. A big chandelier held its candles in a crown, and the room was smoky and hot and dusty. You never knew what time of day it was in the parlor room, and the only clock was an old grandfather clock twice my size that hadn't told the right time since before I was born. I supposed the regulars liked it that way. Most folks couldn't stand setting foot in the place. And when they did, they only came for the music.

Lucky for me, the parlor room was nearly empty at noon. The only folks left were the ones who hardly ever went anywhere else in town. Mr. Takahata, the old blacksmith, who had to retire because his hands got too shaky as his hair turned gray. Lucille Downing, the fastest draw in three counties, who's now a pacifist, dedicated to her silence in the far corner of the parlor. It's said she has forty-seven black hearts tattooed on her arms, one for each life she took. Pharaoh K the sharp, with his whispering deck of cards. He might do you a sleight-of-hand trick if it's after midnight—I snuck in and saw him once, one of the few times I ever got bold enough to see Old Esmerelda's by moonlight. That was before I was confirmed as a Protector, of course, when I was just a novice and I could get away with such foolishness.

I always loved these loners and their secrets, little mysteries hunched in their chairs, only speaking when they had to as all the laughing folks frittered around them. They seemed to hold some silent sadness, some key to all the things I didn't know and never would. Theirs was a special kind of power, and they kept their rituals and Rites just as seriously as I did, I knew that. I watched them come and go at Old Esmerelda's all my life, wondered about whatever it was they wondered about.

Best of all was Old Esmerelda's giant grand piano. The thing looked like some sea beast out of a spell book come lurching itself onto land and flopping here to die. It was beautiful, all mahogany and pearly ivories, with a sound so sweet it would make your heart burst. I'd played the upright piano in Doc Myrtle's drawing room, but it was just a plinking middling thing compared to Old Esmerelda's grand piano. I loved to hear the odd notes ring out deep and true through the parlor room. I'd seen Old Esmerelda play it a few times, and she was a genius at the thing, her voice sounding over the keys in a song so sweet and sad and mournful you knew it carried a whole lifetime with it, maybe more. Once she let me sit in on fiddle, and we made music for hours, long into the night. It was one of the greatest times of my whole life, until Grandpa Widow found out. But truly I longed to play that piano myself, to let myself go along with whatever music flowed into my head, to let my fingers do whatever they wanted, the kind of thing I could never do fiddling out the Rites. I took a deep breath and sighed real deep. It was probably best for me not to think about Old Esmerelda's beautiful grand piano.

There were more folks in there too, but I don't have time to go into them now. Sometimes Old Esmerelda's was like church, just as much as the holy day ceremonies me and Grandpa Widow performed at the end of each week. I knew that what happened here was sacred and mattered, even if I knew I would never be a part of it. Places like Old Esmerelda's parlor room just weren't a part of life for a Protector, and there wasn't much I could do about it. It's like Grandpa Widow always said, "Life's about doing what you got to do, not what you want to do." The night when I was nine years old when he caught me sneaking back around daylight from a night of music playing at Old Esmerelda's, I thought he'd skin me alive, and I understood why. Still, it made me sad sometimes, looking in the windows, hearing the laughter and music tumble outside, even in the deep nights when the Great Doom was most on the prowl. There was a warmth to Old Esmerelda's, is all I'm saying; a mystery too. The kind of warmth I couldn't find anywhere else in the village.

Old Esmerelda really wasn't that old. Folks said she'd been calling herself Old Esmerelda since she was six, though her given name was Berenice. She was a big woman with bright silver hair and a golden front tooth and a laugh so high and cackling it was known to crack glass when she really got going. I loved Old Esmerelda. She waved to me in my rounds whenever she saw me, and she would sing along to the "Last Lights Wonder" if she ever happened by the gates just before sunset. She was always offering me to come play her piano anytime I wanted to, but I knew Grandpa Widow wouldn't like that. Still, I appreciated the gesture.

I trusted her too. Everybody trusted Old Esmerelda. There wasn't a chance in the world that she'd ever rat on me for darkening her doorway. Not a lot of folks like that out there, I guarantee you that, and you'd best appreciate it when you find one.

I walked myself to the middle of the room, feeling stuffy and out of place in my robes.

"And what can I do you for, little Protector?" said Old Esmerelda.

"You seen a Rider come through here?" I said.

"In the back," said Old Esmerelda. She pointed to a table in the far corner. "Mysterious one, her. Hasn't said more than two words to me yet."

That's what I like about her, I thought. *That's why I can maybe trust her for a mission like this.*

"Something about her seems familiar, though," said Old Esmerelda. "Makes me think I ran into her before, back in my wandering days." She shrugged. "Could just be my imagination. It's been ages since I last wandered. Problem of starting your own business, you know. It tethers you. Don't get to take off and leave whenever you want."

"You're telling me," I said, and Old Esmerelda smiled.

"Cheer up, Gussy girl," she said. "You got time for wandering yet."

I wasn't quite sure what to do with that. So I nodded at her and walked myself on to where the Rider sat, alone and quiet, sipping her drink. She seemed fresh and bathed and not a bit like the dusty worn-out specter who had scraggled herself out of the desert. She looked dashing in her blue jeans and shirt, her hair untangled and free down her back. She looked like she could up and take off anywhere she wanted, like the whole earth was out there waiting for her and she could claim any speck of ground anywhere as her home. Must be nice.

"Hi," I said.

The Rider just looked at me.

"I come to offer you a job," I said.

I saw her eye flash a little then, like her mind was working fast. I wondered what she was thinking.

"Go on," was all the Rider said.

I looked to my left and to my right. No one seemed to be paying me any attention. The whole parlor room was shadowy and mysterious even at this time in the day, the other patrons silent, lost in their own dreaming. Pharaoh K flipped his cards in a constant clacking, like a critter scuttling in the walls. I heard Marjorie Willoughby, the bull rider, pop her knuckles and sneeze. I felt dangerous somehow, a bearer of secrets. I had put the town in peril, and now I was covering my tracks. I realized suddenly I belonged here in Old Esmerelda's parlor room, with the knaves and ne'er-do-wells, with those who wield their own hearts in a closed fist behind their back.

I took my seat at the table.

"There's a girl wandered up here the other day by the name of Angeline," I said.

"She come up during the storm?" said the Rider.

I nodded.

"And she survived?"

"Yes indeed," I said. "The hail did quite a job on her, but I think she'll be just fine. The problem is, her family's still out there, and they might be in serious trouble. I'm looking for someone brave enough to set out looking for them."

The Rider leaned forward, placing both arms on the table. She was close enough I could smell her breath, all smoky and sweet, the fragrance of the parlor itself.

"Let me get this straight," she said. "Some girl shows up in the morning, telling you a tale of her family passing through this valley—during a storm, mind you—with that grievous specter on the prowl, the Great Doom? If her parents are still alive, it's pure luck, because that's about the dumbest thing I ever heard in my life."

"Maybe so," I said. "But I still owe it to her to look. Will you help or not?"

"I'll help," said the Rider. "But like all things, good help don't come cheap."

I laid a small cloth pouch of coin on the table. The rider raised her eyebrows at me. She picked up the pouch and shook it, the coins jingling in her palm.

"One thing I don't understand," she said. "Where did this girl come from? I mean, I would have heard about some wounded gal wandering up after a night in the desert, wouldn't I? Unless—" She slouched back in her chair. "Oh. So you opened the gates, didn't you? At night too, just like you weren't supposed to." A cruel grin snuck into her face. "Some Protector you are. I bet that old fellow, what was his name, Grandpa Widow? He'd hide your tail for that, wouldn't he? The whole town would revolt. They'd banish you from the village for sure."

It was awful hot in Old Esmerelda's, I suddenly realized. I was sweating something fierce in my robes.

"Yeah, yeah," I said. "You got me." I took a deep breath and let it out slow, trying to meet the Rider's eyes. That was what Grandpa Widow said to do if you were face-to-face with a wildcat. Look it dead in the eyes. Show it you aren't afraid. And that's what I tried to do with the Rider here. "So are you game or what?"

The Rider grinned at me. "I'll take the job. Only I want double what you already gave me. I want two of these little coin pouches clinking in my pockets."

My face went pale. Double? There was no way Grandpa Widow wouldn't notice that much money gone. I'd be caught for sure, even with Angeline's little stash of gold. But then again . . . what about her family out there in the desert, lost and half-starved? Was this one of those moments where there wasn't a right thing to do, just like Grandpa Widow said?

"Fine," I said. "But you leave now, and you don't come back until just before nightfall. And keep all this to yourself."

"Don't you worry," she said. "I don't rat out my employers. And if that girl's family is out there, rest assured I'll find them."

She spat in her palm and stuck her hand across the table. "Good doing business with you."

I spat in my palm, and we shook hands.

The Rider held my hand gripped so tight in her fist it hurt, and she stared deep into my face, a curious squint to her eyes. She let go of my hand and hopped up from the table. She dropped her hat on her head and sauntered to the front door.

"Be seeing you," she said to me, tipping her hat to Old Esmerelda as the door swung shut behind her.

Gussy, I thought, *what kind of mess did you just get yourself into?*

Old Esmerelda stood behind her counter, polishing a glass, a worried look on her face. I stood up from the table. I'd been here far too long, and it was time for me to get back to my rounds. I gave Old Esmerelda a smile as best as I could.

"Come back any time, Gussy!" hollered Old Esmerelda. "My piano will be here waiting on you."

"Thanks," I said, my brain nothing but a big tumbleweed of worry.

9

I WALKED TOWARD THE FRONT LOBBY of the inn, a little bit shaky, when I heard a commotion outside, following by a lone dog's lonesome howl. It was Cricket. I came hustling outside into the dirty dusty streets to find him hopping and panting at me. He barked three times and took off running, and I knew to follow.

We ran all the way to the center of town, the meeting pole, where I'd finished Midday Salutations not an hour before. A crowd had gathered around the pole, all of them gaping and gawking, and I had to force my way through.

It was the Book of Names. It had fallen from the nail somehow, tumbled to the dust. The pages flapped open in the breeze.

I couldn't believe it. Nothing like this had ever happened

before. It was secure on that pole, I knew that, not an hour ago. I had tested it myself.

"What happened?" I asked, my voice coming out barely a squeak.

"It just . . . it just fell," said Mr. Jilly, the tailor, dabbing himself with a handkerchief.

"He's telling the truth," said Bartleby Bonnard. "We were just standing around, minding our own business, and it came tumbling down. Nobody touched it or nothing."

"But how?" I said.

"There wasn't even a wind," whispered Mrs. Cannoli the shopkeeper. "Not even a whisper of a breeze. It just leaped off that nail like a grasshopper."

I looked everywhere for Lazlo Dunes. Where had he disappeared to? It had to be him causing trouble, didn't it? That was when I noticed Lulu Benningsley staring right at me, her eyes gone fierce and glinting like gunmetal in the sunlight.

"This is your fault," she said. "It's your fault the Book of Names fell."

"How?" I stammered. "I wasn't even here."

"That's exactly what I'm talking about," said Lulu. Her face was all red and she had her teeth bared at me like any moment she'd leap up and take my head off, that opal ring flickering fiercely on her finger. I'd never seen Lulu so angry before, not ever in my life. "And in times like this, when my family needs you the most!"

"I'm not here to serve your family," I said. "I'm here to serve the village. And that's exactly what I'm doing."

I grabbed the Book of Names out of the dust and brushed it off. Not a page was missing, not a single name smeared. I hung it safe and sound back on the pole. It wasn't as secure as I'd left it, but it sure wouldn't fall again, not unless someone walked up and yanked it off by hand.

And who in the world would ever do a thing like that?

"I'll come back and fix a second nail to it," I said to the gathered crowd in the lowest, deepest voice I could. "There's nothing here to worry about."

The villagers watched me warily, like they knew I wasn't up to the task, like they knew I was faking it, like they knew I was a phony and a liar.

Truth was, I didn't know why it had fallen. I didn't know what it meant. But I was afraid, standing there in the hot noon sun, the crowd dispersing all around me. And what did Lulu mean about times like this, when her family needed me most? Why was today different from any other day? All it did was make me even more worried.

Cricket woofed and wagged his floofy tail at me, eyes bright in the noontime, his pink tongue wagging happy.

"You're right," I said to him. "Whatever happens, we'll face it together, and I sure am glad of that."

I smiled when he licked my palm.

* * *

I was headed back to the Rectory when a man came running up to me all terrified, like he'd just caught a glimpse of Lucinda Withern herself. It was Petrov Donny the cordwainer, and his wild black mustache hung limp at the edges like a second frown. He was panting and sweaty, all out of breath. I tried to wait a minute for him to catch his breath.

"What is it?" I said.

"It's my cup," he said.

"Your what?"

"My cup!" he said. "It's shaking."

"Shaking?" I said. "But I didn't feel any earthquake."

"Not the ground, and not the house," he said. "My cup. It won't stop shaking." Petrov Donny waved his hand back and forth, in a quivering kind of way.

"All by itself?"

He nodded. "All by itself."

Oh no. I knew what this meant.

I took off running for the Rectory, leaving Petrov Donny panting in the dust outside the gates, Cricket close at my heels.

This is how infection begins. It's the first sign that the Great Doom has breached the gates. According to Grandpa Widow's stories, anyhow. I've never seen it before in real life.

When the Great Doom enters the village, it latches itself

first on one single object. In the case of Maybelle the botanist, twenty years ago, it was a magnifying glass. This was the last time the Great Doom successfully snuck into the village. Maybelle came home one day after scouring the desert for a specific type of flowering shrub, only to find her magnifying glass had gone dark. I mean that when she tried to look through it, all she saw was darkness, like someone had spilled coffee on the lens. It shuddered and swished when she picked the magnifying glass up, but the liquid stayed contained, like the glass itself had melted and blackened. The glass shook and quivered in her palm like it was alive.

From an urge she could not fight nor later describe, Maybelle was drawn to the magnifying glass, as if it commanded her to pick it up. It felt furry and soft, a living thing; she could feel a heartbeat in its handle. She peeked through it and saw things the likes of which she refused to speak about ever again, even to Grandpa Widow.

But her screams had been enough to get the neighbors running.

Grandpa Widow got lucky that time. He was able to contain the infection and expel the Great Doom from the village using the Cleansing Rite, the kind of thing he's grilled me on since I was two. Later he was able to discover how the Great Doom got to the magnifying glass in the first place. Turned out it had snuck in due to a clerical error on his part. As Maybelle was only a visitor to the village, staying at her cousin Armand the tinker's shop for a short time, Grandpa Widow had neglected to write her into the Book of Names. But just the week before, Maybelle had decided in her heart that she belonged in the village and she would make it her home, only Grandpa Widow didn't know about it. That alone was enough to let the Great Doom in. It was enough to put the whole village in danger.

That's what I mean when I say the Rites have to be performed perfectly, with not a single error or deviation. And that's why I'd messed up so seriously by opening the gates at night, why I had to be perfect from here on out, assuming I hadn't doomed us already.

I flung the Rectory door open. Angeline was sitting on the floor, messing around with the raven's feather and the Peacock's Eye. She jerked her head up toward me, startled, and knocked over her feather. The look on her face was strange, guilty even, like I'd just caught her doing something she ought not to. Then I saw the big pile of Grandpa Widow's quiet herbs smoking on the ground, which Angeline knew good and well she had no business burning.

Well, I'd deal with that later. I hustled through the room, snatching up Grenaldine's *Sacred Rites in Practice*, a small bundle of cardinal feathers, a tiny bottle of holy oil, and a bag of cleansing herbs. Just as I headed for the door, I grabbed my favorite book of travel ballads, for luck.

"What's wrong?" said Angeline.

"No time to talk," I said.

And I ran out the front door toward Petrov Donny the cordwainer's house.

I wasn't sure what I would do when I got there. I mean, was I really ready to face the Great Doom all on my own? Maybe it was a false alarm. Maybe some of the village boys were playing a trick on him, the kind of thing Chappie Benningsley used to pull all the time when he was running around with his gaggle of minions, breaking into houses and rearranging all the furniture, cutting holes in Mr. Jilly's finest garments, tearing entire end chapters from the traveling library's books. They were always causing a ruckus, and it wouldn't be too hard for them to rig a table to shake a cup. I could only hope, gripping my fiddle and my supplies tight, and chant a Mystery to the One Who Listens.

Why oh why wasn't Grandpa Widow here?

Petrov Donny's shop was shut and locked, so I walked around to the side door that led to the kitchen. I had to bang on it for a whole minute before his wife, Marylou, would let me in. She was a smallish woman in her forties with a slight hunch to her back. I always liked Marylou. She was kind and snuck me treats every solstice, cookies cut into strange little shapes like constellations. Marylou stood there wringing her hands, a worried look in her eyes.

"Where's Petrov?" she said.

"I left him outside the gates," I said. "I ran the whole way here."

"Good girl," she said, a little sparkle of hope in her eyes. I had to be honest, that made me feel better. At least Marylou didn't think I was out of my depths.

"Well, come on in," she said.

Marylou slammed the door shut behind us and locked it. The house was small, only the storefront, the workshop, a bedroom, and a kitchen. I stopped a moment in Petrov's workshop, where he made his shoes. I always loved walking through that room, the smell of leather and the strange sharp instruments dangling from the walls, the disconnected shoe parts everywhere, soles hanging like footprints all over the walls. I loved the hammers and the tiny nails and the precision that went into all of it, shoes in racks on the walls patiently waiting for someone to need them. I can think of worse things than being a cordwainer, worse jobs than making sure everybody's feet don't hurt.

The workshop seemed unnaturally dark, and not just because the windows were shuttered. Marylou carried a candle that hardly gave off any light at all. It was as if the darkness lay thicker in that house, like it was a living creature lapping up the light like milk from a bowl. I felt it swirl and tingle all around me, surrounding us, drawing closer. From the corner of my eye I thought I saw something move, a shadow flinching in the candlelight. Cricket let out a low growl.

"This way," said Marylou, and she led me to the kitchen.

The cup was a simple dented tin thing sitting by itself on the kitchen table. It was right side up and rattling, the only sound in the house. It clattered against the table in a constant shivering, like it was cold. I reached my hand out to touch it, and the cup went quiet.

A knock sounded at the door. Marylou went to see who it was.

I stood there in the dark and silent kitchen, watching that cup in its stillness. What was happening here?

A feeling came over me. I felt it like a wet hand on the back of my neck, prickling my skin.

Me and Cricket weren't alone in this room, not by a long shot.

No, something else was here too. The creeping thing, the menacing darkness, the destruction I had worked so hard to keep outside our gates.

The Great Doom had come into the village.

It was my fault, and now I had to fix it.

Petrov Donny came bustling into the kitchen, damp and sweaty, wore out.

"It's still now," he said, pointing to the cup.

"Yeah," I said, "but it won't be for long. I need to get started."

I sprinkled cleansing herbs in a circle around the kitchen table, and I anointed each corner of the room with oil. I walked three times around the place in the darkness, chanting a protection Mystery over all who entered that house and all who would leave, so that nothing of the Great Doom could latch on to them, nor could it follow them anywhere they went. I burned the tiniest pile of the herbs and smeared dust in a triangle on Petrov Donny's and Marylou's foreheads, for protection. I did it to Cricket as well. He was trembling under my hand, scared, I could tell, which was a first for us. I gave his back skin a couple of good tugs to make him feel better.

Now it was time to begin.

I flipped open *Sacred Rites in Practice* and turned to my feather-marked page. It was a musty old book and dust covered, and I tried not to sneeze. That would really kill the mood. Nothing like a squeaky little sneeze spilling from my mouth when I'm about to go to war with a dark and malevolent force.

I began to read in the deepest, most serious voice I could muster.

"We beseech thee, the One Who Listens, to hear the words of your servants gathered here against the infernal forces of darkness . . ."

The cup clanked on the wooden table once and then was still.

". . . against the infernal forces of darkness who work against us. We ask thee for favor in our endeavor, that by thou mercy we might prevail. If we have trespassed against any creature, we ask forgiveness. . . ."

The cup began to shake, violently this time. It clacked up and down on the table like it was asking to be refilled.

You know not what power you trifle with, little girl, whispered a voice.

I whipped my head around the room but could see nothing. Even Cricket was focused on the cup.

"Did you guys hear that?" I said.

"Hear what?" said Petrov.

"Nothing." I shook my head and continued. "We command the Great Doom to leave this place, or else be swallowed in light! Begone or be consumed by the flame of the candle, by the flame of our hearts!"

I used Marylou's candle to light my own. The tiny flame wasn't much good against the fierceness of the Great Doom, but that little glow did my heart some good. I picked up my fiddle and began to play "Hyssop and Brine," a mournful little repetition, just a few notes, that circles around itself, changing only slightly, like the way a dog curls up all comfortable before a fire. It's a cozy tune, one that grows in gentleness the longer and louder it repeats. I began to hum along softly, feeling my way into the hymn, giving it more and more of my heart, just like a Protector is supposed to. Because that's one thing you need to defeat something like the Great Doom. You got to do this kind of thing with your whole heart and your best intention or it won't work at all. You might as well be dropping your lantern down a well for all the good it will do.

The cup clanged harder and harder against the table, denting itself into the wood. I was scared it would knock the sacred candle over and spoil the Rite. I should have set the candle on a stool or something. Rookie mistake. Cricket paced the floor around me, whimpering, his mottled fur standing up like a cat's all over his back. The racket was so great I had to shout the rest of the words in order to be heard.

"Flee, darkness!" I shouted. "Be banished back from whence you came! Be swallowed in light!"

The cup lifted off the table and flung itself at my face.

It conked me hard, right on the noggin, knocking me on my back.

Cricket howled. All the candles in the room lit themselves and the shutters burst open, flooding the cordwainer's house with light.

I lay there on my back, my head throbbing.

"Oh dear, are you okay?" said Marylou, leaning over me.

"I think so," I said.

"Did it work?" said Petrov Donny.

I tried to sit myself up. Cricket walked over and licked my hand.

"Of course it worked," I said. "The Rites never fail."

"The Rites never fail," they both said, in unison.

Petrov Donny helped me to my feet. Marylou took a gander at my head.

"It doesn't look too bad, dear," she said, "though you might have a bruise."

Despite the pain, I felt pretty okay. The Rite had worked. I hadn't messed it up. I got up and was making my way to the door when Marylou took my arm and stopped me.

"Gussy?" she said.

"Yes?"

"Why did this happen?"

I wished I had a good answer for her. But I couldn't tell her the truth, that it was all my fault. So I came up with the most general, almost meaningless thing I could possibly say.

"The Great Doom is a wily force," I said. "It comes and it goes with a purpose we do not understand."

"But why our house? Why my Petrov's cup?"

"That I can't answer you," I said, which at least was true. "But rest assured, you didn't do a thing wrong. Please don't worry about that."

"Okay," she said, but she didn't much seem to believe me.

"Can you do me a favor and keep this quiet? I don't want

a panic breaking out in the village."

"We won't tell a soul," said Marylou. "You have my word."

"Much obliged," I said.

"Thanks," said Marylou. "We'd be lost without you."

"Just doing my duty."

I acted all confident, but I was deeply shaken. I had to find a way to fix this before it was too late.

10

THAT NIGHT, AFTER LAST LIGHTS, I PER-
formed an extra Protection Rite over the village, just in case.
To be honest, I was thankful the infection hadn't spread,
that things weren't any worse, but it was still a disaster. I had
to make sure an infection would never ever happen again. I
came home worn-out and exhausted, with Cricket panting
at my heels. I was crabby and frustrated and I didn't feel
much like talking.

Angeline seemed to sense my mood, and she didn't say
much.

"I talked to the Rider," I said. "She said she'd go looking
for your family. Might take a few days."

"Thank you, Gussy," she said. "As before, I remain firmly
in your debt."

Angeline was sipping some weird tea she'd brewed, probably with leaves pilfered from Grandpa Widow's stash. Something gross from the stink of it, the kind of thing you have to haggle for with ominous warty folks in sackcloth, hawking newt eyes or something. I hate when those peddlers stop by the village. Grandpa Widow always brings them in here and fattens them up like they're royalty. The whole time they just keep glancing at me with their weird roll-y eyes asking me all kinds of questions about where I come from. I always tell him they could be secret witches or roving warlocks or even poltergeists in human disguise, but Grandpa Widow just laughs me off.

"Did you spend all day in here?" I said.

"Nope," said Angeline. "Not today. That sweet boy Connor Carnivolly came by, looking for you."

"Did he now?" I said. I kept my eyes staring down at the floor.

"Uh-huh," she said. "He did some card tricks for me. They weren't very good, bless his heart, but he has a lot of showmanship. If he gets better, he could really be a great magician, you know?"

"Is that so?" I said.

"Then Connor snuck me out to the village and showed me some of the sights. I wore a shawl and kept myself quiet. We saw a brown cat and a three-legged dog named Homer. He was just bouncing around, nearly the friendliest pup you ever saw, except for Cricket of course. Connor bought me an apricot tart from the baker too."

"Wow," I said. "Sounds like you and Connor had the best day ever."

"I wouldn't go that far," she said. "But he's a very sweet boy. I'm glad you have such good friends in the village. You're lucky to be here."

I gritted my teeth and kicked at the floor.

"So nice of you to say."

Yeah, so I was pretty jealous. I wanted to do things like play with Homer the dog and eat apricot tarts. I couldn't remember the last time I'd had a tart, much less a pleasant afternoon during which to eat it. The very thought of Angeline having all this fun while I was out working my tail off made me glum right down to my bones.

I sat on the bed in a huff, not saying a word to anybody. I wouldn't open my mouth again, not for the whole night. All I wanted was peace and quiet and a good happy dreamless sleep.

That's when Angeline began humming a little song from her corner, where she'd propped up a few pillows and her books, sipping that sludgy tea of hers.

I put my hands over my ears and tried to ignore it, but I just couldn't. There was something about the tune, a melody I thought I knew from somewhere long ago, the way certain words out of a stranger's mouth will hang familiar in your mind for days and days and you can't ever figure out why. She just kept humming and humming that little tune over and over again, her eyes burrowed deep into her book— Saint Bartlelingua's *Book of Musical Skeletons*, a technical volume about turning human bones into instruments, like femur flutes and rib-cage xylophones and all kinds of arm-bone clangers, the sort of practice that ought to be banned, I tell you that right now—and I just couldn't take it anymore.

"Do you mind?" I hollered at her.

"Not at all," she said, and went back to whistling.

I jumped off the bed and walked over to her, then snatched that book out of her hands and slammed it shut hard as I could, for emphasis.

Angeline just looked up at me from the floor, her eyes wide. The teacup trembled a little in her hand.

"You know, just because something is strange to you, that doesn't mean that it's wrong," she said.

"What in the world are you talking about?" I said.

"Bone flutes," she said. "It's a beautiful practice, really. People make music from the dead. They honor the ones who've passed by transforming them into vessels for music. They blow their breath through loved ones' bones in songs of praise. What could possibly be wrong with that?"

I just glared at her for a moment, and she stared right back. Thing was, Angeline had a point, and I knew it. I was wrong, dang it, but I wasn't about to admit it.

"What was that stupid song anyway?" I said.

"What song?" she said.

"The one you've been humming nonstop for the last hour," I said. "It's been driving me nuts."

"Oh, you know," she said, shrugging. "Just something I made up."

"How could you have possibly made it up?" I said. "I know that song. I've heard it before, a million times at least."

"Hmmm," said Angeline. "Interesting."

"It's not interesting, it's annoying," I said. "I can't even remember where I even heard it before."

"Well, perhaps if you sang it yourself, you might remember," she said.

Again, this was a good idea. Again, it made me really mad.

"I don't sing," I grumbled. "My voice sounds like an old hag gargling gravel. I sound like a coyote sneezing."

"I do believe you're mistaken about that," she said. "But if you find your own voice so disagreeable, perhaps you might play the melody on your fiddle?"

"Yeah, well, I guess I could."

"I should like that very much," said Angeline.

Cricket perked his ears in attention. I snatched up my fiddle and picked out the notes. Like I said, the tune was simple enough, repetitive, and besides, it was like I'd known it already my whole life, like it was already inside me, long hidden in my blood or something. Angeline began to sing a harmony over the line, to change it a little, tweaking the repetitions. I could follow her, I realized. It was like I knew what she was going to do before she did it, like somehow the music flowing through us was communicating itself, like it didn't have anything to do with us at all.

"That's it," said Angeline, smiling, her eyes shut. "That's exactly right."

When it came time to change parts, it was so simple, it was like my fingers knew exactly what to play, like the song itself had just been floating around in the air forever, waiting on us to put it into music.

I'd never done anything like this before. I'd never written a song, or helped write something. I'd never created something I could take part in before, something that could be mine.

"Ours," said Angeline.

"Yeah," I said. "Ours."

"Want to play it again?"

"Very much so."

We began again, this time both of us playing together, diving right into the song. Angeline kept changing things, adjusting the melody here and there, adding different parts. She was improvising, I realized, building on it, adding to what I was doing. I tried to follow her lead, and I began to add little things too, Angeline picking up on them, stretching some notes out and speeding others along. We were working together, making something new, both of us locked in and synchronized, like we could read each other's minds.

And then something funny happened. I still don't really know how to explain it. It was like the world went dark, like the ceiling disappeared and the night sky opened and the stars came down to meet us, like they were just fruit on these big nighttime trees dangling close enough to pluck, like I could bite into them and all that glow would come streaming down like juice, like I could fill her belly with all the stars' light. I mean it. I could taste the burning glow of the stars on my tongue, I could feel the fiery sweetness of that music dripping down my throat.

Just like that, the song ended. Angeline sat there staring at me, a quiet little look in her eyes. I didn't know what to say. I'd never experienced something like that before. The air still crackled with our music. I suddenly felt like I could do anything, make anything, be anything at all I ever wanted. The world seemed huge and possible to me, full of options, of places I could go, of people I could become. It made me wonder if my dreams were actually memories, and if I had been born elsewhere, into a world of ocean and cliffs and lighthouses, ships sailing on the horizon. Or were my dreams some glimpse into a possible future, a me I might become one day, a world I could enter all on my own?

But no, I was a Protector, had been trained that way from my birth. There were no other possibilities for me. I had duties, I had responsibilities. The village was my home, and it needed my protection. Especially now, with the Great Doom having just breeched the gates, all because of my mistake.

"What's the matter?" said Angeline.

I shook my head. "I'm just tired, is all. Let's chant a Mystery for your family, how about that?"

Angeline looked sad all of a sudden.

"Yes," she said. "I'd like that very much."

Together we lit a Candle of Request for Angeline's family, that they might be safe out in the desert at night, and one for the Rider too. While I chanted, Angeline watched the candles flicker, the flames reflecting in her eyes. Something else was there too, some hidden little feeling, a sadness maybe.

Or a warning.

That night I dreamed like never before.

I had dreams you wouldn't believe.

I dreamed I was a seagull sailing high above the waters as a storm blew on the horizon.

I dreamed I was a four-mast ship flung about by storm winds, lifted airborne like a ghost ship, slung about by the wind, until my heart was dashed on the rocks.

I dreamed I was a lighthouse burning, casting my glow out upon the waters, trying to pierce the darkness with the only song I knew, the fire burning in my chest.

I dreamed I was a family trapped in the cargo hold. I

dreamed I was the ocean water flooding in, rising higher, higher, to their knees, to their hearts, to their throats. I dreamed I was the last bubbles of air escaping from their mouths.

I dreamed I was their tired hearts giving out, their blood slowing. I dreamed I was Death come to meet them, to gather themselves in my arms and shepherd them to the Quiet Lands.

I dreamed I was an ocean full of fishes and darkness, that I had depths in me where blind creatures thrashed and hunted, where impossible lights glowed, where silky slithering things floated near invisible, clutching their secrets.

I dreamed I was a little girl, barely more than a baby, pulled from the wreckage, wrapped in blankets, staring at the moon while strange-tongued women spoke softly around me.

11

I BURST FROM MY SLEEP AS IF IT WAS DEEP water and I was a drowning person. I gasped and sputtered, coughing, my lungs burning, my arms tired from thrashing. Cricket leaped on top of me and licked my face until I calmed down. Angeline was already awake and watching me from her book and teacup.

"See anything interesting?"

What was all that I had dreamed? And what could it mean?

"Maybe," I said.

I rubbed my eyes and spat. My head ached a little bit from where Petrov's cup had whacked me. The sun wasn't quite up yet, and Angeline was reading by candle, so at least I wasn't late today.

"You know that I'm very good at interpreting dreams," said Angeline, "if only you will tell them to me."

Grandpa Widow didn't care much for reading dreams. He said in most cases it was "two-bit hoodlumism from no-account charlatans." He said interpreting dreams was a blurry art at best, and you were better off trying to decipher the meanings in slug trails.

"Don't you ever be trusting somebody who talks on and on about dreams," he would say. "They're just little fragments of things, scraps blown in from the wind. Any meaning you make from them is your own, straight from your noggin. Invented, is what I'm saying."

"Let me guess," said Angeline. "Your Grandpa Widow doesn't approve of oneiromancy?"

"Angeline," I said, "I never heard that word in my life."

"It's the interpretation of dreams," she said. "It's an art. A science even. All good ritual workers can do it."

"Is that so?" I said, flinging my robes over my head. "Well, Grandpa Widow works the Rites better than anyone this side of the river, and he said it was bunk."

Angeline fixed me a glare the likes of which I'd never seen before. For the first time I caught a hardness in her eyes, a flinty power hidden deep, like something capable of burning an entire village down.

"Has it ever occurred to you," she said, "that your Grandpa Widow might not be quite the sterling source of wisdom and knowledge that you think he is?"

I could not believe it. I'd never heard such a crazy notion in all my life. I stomped myself over to Angeline and stuck a finger right at her face.

"Grandpa Widow is a great man," I said. "He's head Protector of this village, and you and I both owe him our lives. I won't have his name profaned in his own Rectory. And if you don't like that, you can scamper off for all I care."

Angeline cast her eyes down, her red hair drooping over her face.

"I . . . I apologize," she said. "I didn't mean any offense."

"I don't give a skunk what you meant," I said. "And if you'll excuse me, I got work to do. Come on, Cricket."

I snatched up my fiddle and the two of us headed for the gates, leaving Angeline sulking alone, her head hung low, silent in the corner.

I walked my widdershins and chanted the Mysteries, my voice a cracking scratchy thing. Boy, did I hate hearing my voice. Well, at least my fiddle sounded fine, and Cricket was in top form as always. I kept thinking about my dreams, the taste of the salt in the air and the boom of the storm, wondering what it all had to do with me. Were those memories? Did I come from a faraway land, rescued in a shipwreck? How did I wind up in the desert?

I was thinking these thoughts so hard I walked an extra

turn around the village, messing up the whole Rite. I had to back up and walk one clockwise, just to reverse it, and say the Mysteries backward, which is a lot harder than it sounds. I'd already let the Great Doom in once (I had a plum-sized bruise on my noggin to prove it), and I wasn't about to let it get a foothold again. Why couldn't I focus? What in the world was going on with me?

It was all too much: the Benningsleys and Lazlo Dunes and the fallen Book of Names and the infection, and now all these strange dreams, worries about my past. Not to mention how weird everyone in this whole village was acting. How could I focus on protecting us from the Great Doom when I didn't even know what was going on with the people in my very own village? And to top it all off, I had Angeline filling my head full of all kinds of thoughts and notions and homemade magic. And to bad-mouth Grandpa Widow in the Rectory? I'd had about as much of her as I could take. Even if she was the most fun person to play music with I'd ever met in my whole life.

But fun wasn't the point of music, was it? Maybe for the folks over at Old Esmerelda's, but not for me. Music was for the Rites, music was for the protection of the village. Maybe sometimes it could while away the long nights under siege from the Great Doom, but it wasn't frivolous, it always had a purpose. For me, music was my job, just one mechanism in the long clockwork of my day. Who cared if it was beautiful or fun or if it came from my heart? I needed it to *work*.

I was being a jerk, I knew that. I just wished the Rider would get on back from wherever she was, with news of Angeline's family already, and that everything was okay with her.

But I could not for the life of me stop thinking about my dreams. I couldn't get the smell of the waters out of my head, the wet spray and the lighthouse fire burning, the enormous freedom of sailing above it all, capable of going anywhere I could ever want, riding the invisible streams of the air, same as a fish does in water. It opened up these strange desires in me, things I'd never thought about wanting before. What worlds lay out there beyond the desert? How many possibilities could ever exist for me? Had I really come from somewhere else? Was my birthplace maybe where I belonged, really and truly? Did I still have any family there?

It wasn't until my second round walking that I realized something was wrong with the cardinal feathers hanging from the four corners of the village. I always made sure to give them enough twine so that they dangled in little fiery clumps, flames of red burning for protection and life, dancing in the wind. And yet the first two bundles were missing feathers, down to only two apiece. The third only had one feather left, a bright red exclamation mark against the brown

of the village walls. The fourth bundle was missing altogether.

It was so strange. Never before had so many feathers
gone missing like this. I mean, sure, during a particularly bad
windstorm we'd lose one or two here and there, but never so
many and all at once. Besides, they were all in place at Last
Lights, not thirteen hours earlier, and there wasn't much of
an overnight wind, at least not the feather-snatching kind.
On the fourth bundle, it appeared as if the twine had been
bitten in half, chewed off by some kind of wild animal. But
what sort of creature wants cardinal feathers so bad? Certainly not a coyote, much less a wolf or something vicious
like that. So what could have done it?

I'd have to make a stop at Mr. Mayella's cardinal hatchery
as soon as possible so this village could be good and protected again. As a matter of fact, that would be the very first
thing I did after the morning Rites. While I was at it, I could
ask him about what he was doing the night of the storm, not
that I was likely to get a straight answer from him anyhow.

But on my way back inside the village gates after rasping
out the "Hymn of the Morning," I stopped myself at Big
Gordo's hut. I knew I should hustle off to the hatchery, but I
had a question bugging me that I figured only Gordo could
answer. I gave his door three good raps.

"Hi there, Gussy," said Big Gordo.

He had a notebook in his hand, full of scribbles, his big

loopy handwriting unreadable to anybody but himself.

"Howdy, Gordo," I said. "Whatcha working on?"

"Oh, you know," he said. "Just writing a poem."

I can't describe the feeling I had right then. It was like a bug buzzing around in my belly, a quick spark that flittered up my body and into my brain, bright and crackling. I had a curious feeling around Big Gordo's poem.

"What's this one about?" I asked, the words all sticky in my mouth.

"A seagull," he said. "It's funny. I had a dream."

I felt dizzy, like I was about to fall over.

"A dream, you say?"

"Yep," he said, scratching his big bald head with his pencil. "I had a dream I was a seagull soaring above open water, a big lighthouse in the distance. It was the strangest dream I ever had."

"Yeah?" I said, my voice croaking a little. "What was so strange about it?"

Big Gordo shrugged. "It didn't feel like my dream, is all."

"What does that mean?"

"I'm not rightly sure," he said. "Who can tell with dreams? It just seemed like somebody else was dreaming this dream, and I had stumbled into it. Like I was just along for the ride."

This wasn't any small deal, no way. When you dream so hard it bleeds over into someone else's sleep, well . . . that's serious business. Grandpa Widow didn't put much stock in dreams, but he most definitely would have raised an eyebrow at something like this. It was an omen, sure as anything.

Ask it, said a little voice in my head. *You know the question.*

"Gordo," I said. "Where did I come from?"

His eyebrows raised high in little squiggles on his massive forehead.

"I mean, where did Grandpa Widow get me?" I said. "Was I born here in the village? Did I come from someplace else?"

"Well, Gus, I'm not real sure what you want me to say. Didn't Grandpa Widow tell you all of this already?"

"No, he didn't," I said. "He always just told me that I'd come to him as a blessing from the One Who Listens, given as a Protector, born to serve the village."

"Then that's the answer I would stick with," said Big Gordo. "If that's what Grandpa Widow told you, then he must have had a good reason for it."

A week ago, that might have been a good enough answer for me. Even two days ago, that would have sufficed. But not now, not anymore.

"Gordo, please," I said. "Is there anything at all you can tell me?"

"I'm sorry," said Big Gordo, "but I don't know much more than you do. One day you weren't here, and then you were. Just a tiny little thing, couldn't hardly talk. You should have seen the look on Grandpa Widow's face, though. I'd never

seen him smile like that before. You really changed everything for him, you know?"

"I did?"

"Of course you did. He was a much different character
before you showed up. He changed a lot with you. He got . . .
much kinder, I would say. He smiled more."

"He still doesn't smile much," I said.

"Well, you should have seen him before."

I had to laugh a little at that.

"If you're really curious, there's probably a record of you
somewhere at the courthouse. The Book of Names isn't the
only place where new arrivals are logged, after all."

The courthouse. I'd forgotten all about it. There was
a whole set of laws and proceedings that had nothing to
do with the Rites. I often forget they even existed, I got so
wrapped up in my duties. Maybe the courthouse would
have a record of my entry into the village. Maybe Grandpa
Widow had even formally adopted me. Who knew? I'd
never thought to ask before.

"Thanks, Big Gordo," I said.

"No problem, Gussy. But do be careful, okay? Sometimes
what's unknown is best left that way."

"Maybe so," I said.

I didn't really think that, though. I mean, it was my life,
wasn't it? I deserved to know everything about it I could.

I knew I needed to replace those cardinal feathers, that it was really important for the safety of the village, but I could always do that after Midday Salutations, and besides, how could I perform the Rites properly with so much other stuff on my mind? I couldn't possibly give them my full intention, not when I couldn't stop thinking about where I came from.

So instead of heading to Mr. Mayella's cardinal hatchery, I hurried myself all the way to the far end of the village, where the old courthouse sat. It was a squat, strange little building, one of the first constructed around here. It was built out of clay bricks, straight from the earth of this place, and it looked like a weird, malformed giant bird that sat down one day and turned itself into stone. When I was a kid, I called it the Birdhouse, and in my mind it would wake up one day and crack the clay off its feathers and rise up to sail away through the sky, seeking its destiny elsewhere.

Since most actual legal trials (few and far between as they may be) were held in the town circle, right by the meeting pole, the courthouse was really just a grand storeroom for records and documents, whatever was deemed worth guarding by the village folks. It was run by this old woman, Madame Golescu, who over the years had come to sort of resemble the building itself. She squatted at her desk like a big old mother hen roosting, guarding all those court documents like they were her eggs. The room was decorated with little knick-knacks, bird bones painted in wild colors, masks made from the shoulder blades of coyotes, bird feathers everywhere. For a woman who spent her whole life guarding village records, Madame Golescu seemed like an awful grand mystery to me. There were rumors that she'd traveled the world, that she was a witch, that she had a dozen children in different countries, that whatever was out there, she'd seen it all. And yet she'd just sit there behind that desk, a sly smile on her face, and offer you shortbread cookies.

I always kind of liked the courthouse, come to think of it. It had been ages and ages since I'd dropped in for a visit, a year maybe. I was glad I'd come there today.

I opened the door to a clattering of chimes hanging from the ceiling, gold coins in foreign currency clanging together, little bells tinkling like glad raindrops, echoing through the room. It was a whole chorus of sounds there to greet me, like I'd just walked right into a cacophony of winged things all singing out to the morning. It felt good, is what I'm saying. It's the kind of welcome that makes you always want to come back. So many people hated Madame Golescu's doorbells, but I sure wasn't one of them.

Madame Golescu wore a big purple dress and long dangly earrings painted like eyeballs, her gray hair piled high up on her head like a cactus. She sat behind her desk, blocking the bolted door to the records room, same as always.

"Well, if it isn't ol' Gussy girl," said Madame Golescu. "What brings you to my little government chateau today?"

"I was looking for a record," I said.

"A most suitable place to search for such a thing," she said, smiling. "Any record in particular?"

"I'm looking for . . . well . . . I'm looking for my own record," I said. "For some kind of documentation of how I came to the village."

A curious look came over Madame Golescu's face, just a quiver of a grin and a sparkle to her eye, something I wasn't quite sure how to interpret. Then that placid smile was back on her face, like nothing had happened at all.

"I recall that day quite well," said Madame Golescu. "You were a wee tiny thing in your little dress, staring out at the world with the widest, roundest eyes I ever saw. A strange child, you were, and full of secrets. Grandpa Widow was so happy to have you."

"Do you know where I came from?" I said. "How I got here, I mean."

"No, dearie, I'll rightly say I don't. But the records never lie, and Mayor Benningsley made sure a full account was made of your arrival."

"You never read the report yourself?" I said.

"I try never to mind other people's business," she said. "Unless of course I don't like them. I've read Lucretia Benningsley's file at least a dozen times, and don't you go repeating that. But folks I like, I tend to let alone. They'll tell me what I need to know when I need to know it. I'm not a busybody."

"I gotcha," I said, even though I wasn't quite sure I did. "Would you mind if I take a look myself?"

"Of course not, darling. The public records are for the public, after all." She stood up and pulled a giant jangling key ring from her desk drawer. It took her just a moment to find the right key, and soon the great wooden door was swinging itself wide open for me. "Wait just a moment now. I'm sure I'll find exactly what you're looking for."

Madame Golescu disappeared into the back room for a moment.

I stood there, surrounded by all these trinkets from other places, umbrellas and statues and champagne flutes and dark vases with skinny warriors painted all over them, a million souvenirs from a million different lives lived, all by this odd quiet woman in the records office, the woman no one knew really, the one who kept to herself. I wondered what it would be like, to live a wild life like that, with no responsibilities but to myself, no village to look out for. Only me and what I wanted, all the time, no one else to worry about at all.

It seemed nice, if I was going to be honest. It seemed like a dream.

Madame Golescu came shuffling back a few minutes later, her grin vanished, replaced by a rather perturbed frown. I'd never seen a look like that on her face, not in all the years I'd known her.

"Gussy dear," she said. "It appears that your file is missing."

"Missing?" I said.

"Yes," she said. "I can see the spot where it should be—you're the only Pearl in the village, after all—but it just isn't there."

"Has it been misplaced?"

Madame Golescu huffed a bit, hands on her hips, puffing herself up like a too-ripe grape.

"Not by me, of that I can assure you. I can't even recall ever plucking your file from the library after I first put it there, and I'm the only one with a key. It appears as if someone pilfered it."

"As in . . . someone stole it? My very own record?"

"Not to put too fine a point on it," she said, "but yes."

"So who could have done it?"

"I can assure you, darling, that I haven't the slightest idea."

I didn't like that, not one bit.

"Truth be told, I haven't been this stupefied by something since the one day I met Lucinda Withern."

"You met Lucinda Withern?" I said. "And lived to tell about it?"

Madame Golescu frowned.

"Aye," she said. "I did indeed, in a tavern far from here. We were sitting around, ten of us, waiting out a storm, and in walked the most fearsome witch I'd ever seen in my life. The next thing I knew, it was two weeks later, and I'd been wandering the desert with no shoes for days. Couldn't remember a thing that happened. Those two weeks were stolen from me, and I never got them back. I found out later the tavern was destroyed, ten sets of bones left over. I was the only survivor." She coughed and shook her head, tugging on a little squirrel-skull necklace. "Funny I would think of that story at a time like this."

I couldn't believe it. Madame Golescu had met Lucinda Withern and hadn't wound up a roadside skeleton! She really was a mystery. I wished there was time to hear all her stories.

"Yeah, well, thanks anyway," I said. "And let me know if my file turns up."

"That I'll do, dearie, and don't you doubt it."

I was nearly to the door when Madame Golescu called out to me.

"Gussy?"

"Yes?"

"Do be careful out there."

I nodded at her and left, making my way into the dusty village streets. What in the world had happened to my record? Had Grandpa Widow taken them for some reason? Why would anyone want to keep my past a secret, even from me?

The sun burned high above me, and I realized it was already time for Midday Salutations. I'd just have to get those cardinals feathers from Mr. Mayella later. Worry started inching its way up my shoulders. Was I already messing up again, so soon after an infection? Grandpa Widow was going to be so ashamed of me. . . .

No, it would be fine, I told myself. It had to be. Just so long as I got the feathers up by nightfall.

I set off for the village gates, fiddle in hand, my mind full of questions, the intention of my heart gone in a million different directions, wind scattered and wild as the dust blown from my fingers at Midday Salutations.

It sure was hot out there today, the noontime sun roasting me in my robes. I tell you what, part of the troubles of being a Protector was how toasty the uniform could get. I shook the worries out of my head and picked up the dust and let it fall, chanting the Mysteries, scanning the horizon the whole time for the Rider. But the desert was a dusty blanket, still and silent, as if it was waiting on anything to come and disturb it. Even the clouds seemed to be lingering, not blowing much of anywhere.

I always wondered if there wasn't something inside clouds more than rain, if clouds were just the clothes angels wore when they were bored and peering down at us. If maybe clouds themselves were alive, like the spirits of dreaming people off wandering the world. It seemed like a good life, to be a cloud, to get whisked along by the wind far above everything else, only to drop your gentle rain on whoever needs it most. I figured you could get a lot of good done, being a cloud, and see the world to boot.

That's what I was thinking, not minding one bit of my own intention, walking the four hundred and sixty-seven steps to the meeting pole, where I was supposed to bless the Book of Names. Yep, my mind was drifting wander-y and cloudlike when I hit on step number four hundred and sixty-six, only to realize I was about five feet from the Book of Names. I stopped dead still. I mean, I couldn't take an extra step. That would invalidate the whole Rite, and I'd have to reverse my steps, chant backward, and start the whole thing over. Besides being a colossal waste of my time, I'd look pretty foolish, all these people walking around, going about their business, waving at me, trusting me to keep them safe, and I couldn't even perform the same ritual I'd done every day since I could remember right. It would just give them one more reason to think I wasn't good enough to be their Protector, that Grandpa Widow was absolutely nuts to leave me in charge.

I didn't know what to do. I was going to have to take a

mighty big leap to make it all the way to the Book of Names, and I couldn't risk making myself look like a fool. Bartleby Bonnard was already staring at me kind of funny, and Martina the locksmith gave me an uncertain wave. How could I make them think I wasn't stuck?

I looked down at Cricket, and he looked at me. *Thanks for understanding, buddy,* I thought, and scratched his head.

I guess I'd have to improvise.

I pulled my robe over my head and lifted my arms up wide, like I was invoking the sun itself, like I was imploring the One Who Listens to lean its ear a little closer my way, because I had something important to speak to it.

I began chanting a Mystery—an ancient chant to conjure salamanders, I don't know why, it was the first thing that popped into my mind—in High Speak, which is the language of the Old Protectors. I like High Speak quite a bit, all those fancy words and weird endings. It just sounds showy and impressive, even if nobody ever can understand quite what you're saying. I sure was glad Grandpa Widow wasn't there to see this. He'd be furious at me for pulling a stunt like this. But regular folks don't know any better. A few of them stopped to notice, nodding their heads approvingly, like "Look at our little Gussy, doing something extra to protect the village," before getting bored and moving along. Finally even Bartleby Bonnard shrugged and got to walking.

This was it, the big moment. Maybe I could tell them it was a symbolic "leap of faith" or something. Yeah, I could do that.

Unless I fell flat on my butt. Then I wasn't sure what in the heck I would tell them.

I took a quick glance to my right and to my left, to see if anybody was paying attention to me—especially if any of those Benningsleys were watching—and then I crouched low as I could and took the biggest leap I'd ever leaped in my life.

I landed about two feet from the Book of Names. Close enough. I could finish the Rite from here, anyways.

Not so bad, I said to myself. *Not so bad at all.*

Then I saw a face in the topmost floor of the Benningsley mansion, a pale ghost-looking figure peeking out from behind a curtain. Now who could that be, and why on earth were they in the attic?

The eyes met mine for just a second, and I realized it was none other than Chappie Benningsley staring down at me. Something about his look showed me he knew what I was up to, that I was faking that whole scene down here. It was a knowing look, and a sad one too. He closed the curtain and vanished from my sight. With my luck, he'd probably tell his dad all about what I'd done, and that would get back to Grandpa Widow for sure. It gave me a terrible shameful feeling, deep in my heart, like I was some kind of fraud, like I wasn't even close to worthy as a Protector.

I gritted my teeth and held my head high and played "Hymn to the Noonday Sun." I did my best, but it sure didn't feel like enough. Now I had to hustle off to grab me some cardinal feathers before anything worse happened.

Mr. Mayella's cardinal hatchery was the fanciest place in all the village, except for maybe the Benningsley mansion. It was no dogs allowed, so Cricket had to wait outside as I opened the door and walked myself in. The front room was a crisp, lavish, dust-free place, a near miracle considering we lived in the desert. A rug from somewhere far off lay thick and wild colored on the floor, depicting all sorts of strange patterns and designs and swirls all over it, little hex symbols from all over the world, magic I didn't know a thing about. A magnifying glass hung from the wall, a series of tiny pinkie nail-sized portraits of fancy-haired women mounted in a glass case next to it. Why anybody would paint a portrait so small as that made no sense to me, but I did enjoy looking through that magnifying glass at them, seeing all the little details the tiny-minded artist had hidden there—little white stars in a blond woman's green eyes, an itty-bitty tiger tramping through the dark tresses of another woman's hair, impossibly small icicles sparkling at the fringes of the third woman's smile. They seemed mysterious to me, these women, from worlds away, and I always wondered where they came from, how Mr. Mayella came to get their portraits, or even who had painted the portraits in the first place.

Mr. Mayella just called them his sisters.

"Sisters?" I said once. "They don't look a thing alike. Not like each other, and not like you either."

"You will find," he said, his odd grin spreading across his skull, "that there is more to family than bloodlines, child."

I hated that. I hated when he called me child.

I should probably tell you that I didn't like Mr. Mayella much. Or maybe that's not it at all. More like it was impossible to like Mr. Mayella. He just wasn't a likable kind of person, and so far as I could tell, he didn't much want to be. In fact, he was one of the few people in this village with the power to intimidate me.

Maybe I ought to tell you a little bit about him and let you decide for yourself, how about that?

Mr. Mayella was a bone-thin man six and a half feet tall who wore nothing but perfectly tailored black suits he had delivered from places far, far away, made of the strangest, shiniest material. Not even Mr. Jilly knew where his suits came from. They had a shimmer to them when they caught the light, and if he should step outside in the daylight (which he almost never did, not even to buy supplies—I mostly only saw him outside the hatchery at dusk light, when he would scuttle through the village like a cold breeze blowing down the boardwalk, that great big ghastly smile stretched across his face, waving stiffly at everyone while they stared back frightened, like it was all some big game to him) the suit would ripple with colors bright enough to make you squint. He smiled all the time, like I said, this horrible cheek-splitting smile that showed you each and every one of his teeth, so bright white they gleamed. He had thin silver-and-white hair combed close to his skull, and he wore this wide-brimmed hat, even indoors. His voice was this deep booming thing, and he made every statement like a pronouncement, like a judge banging down his gavel.

No one knew where Grandpa Widow had found him. All we knew was that, shortly after Grandpa Widow showed up in the village, Mr. Mayella came too. Don't get me wrong, the man was indispensable—we needed those cardinal feathers for the Rites, and there were no two ways about that. It's hard to keep birds like that happy in a place like the desert, and Mr. Mayella was a genius at birds, that was clear enough. His cardinal feathers were of the deepest, richest red hue, clearly from healthy birds, and they definitely seemed to have a power of their own. I'd seen a few other feathers from travelers here and there, and I couldn't find a lick of power to them. But I could spot a feather from one of Mr. Mayella's cardinals half a mile away, and that was a fact.

However, it still did not endear me to the man. Not even his lobby of oddments did either. When I was a little kid,

I'd gaze at them for hours and hours while Grandpa Widow and Mr. Mayella vanished behind the back door that led to the hatchery itself, where all the birds hid and lived. The door was carved with birds and strange writings in the old esoteric languages of the first Protectors, even older than High Speak. It was ritual writing, I knew it, and of a kind that I'd need a dictionary and about seven hours to decipher. Which I would have done already as a kid, except the symbols on the door were always changing. Don't ask me how, as I know wood isn't in the habit of recarving itself, and yet it was true. Every time I set foot in this room, the door was somehow different. No one was allowed behind the door except for Grandpa Widow. Not that I knew of, at least. Mr. Mayella had a way of overwhelming you when he talked, of being all mysterious and more than a little intimidating. I hoped I'd have the courage to confront him about the storm night.

A bell sat on the desk of Mr. Mayella's desk.

I walked up and rang it. I couldn't hear a thing, but outside Cricket got to howling, same as always. I guess it was pitched to a frequency only dogs could hear.

Well, dogs and Mr. Mayella, of course. The door to the hatchery opened and out he strode, dusting a small scrum of brown wood filings from his shoulder.

"Ah, little Miss Gustavina, is it?"

"Gussy is fine," I said.

"Indeed it is," he said. "Have a seat."

He lowered himself into his chair, an event he somehow made seem dramatic.

"Yes, Gustavina?" he said. He held up his hands, his bony white fingers waving in a mock apology. He touched one long pointer finger to his heart. "Excuse me. *Gussy.*"

"I come for some cardinal feathers."

"Of course you do! Why else should you be here? Certainly not to visit dear old me." He sighed. "You never come to see me anymore, Gussy. My sisters have missed you terribly."

"I'm sure they have."

His smile seemed to grow bigger then, so wide and wild I could see his molars.

"Is there something troubling you?" he said. "Some matter about which you've come to seek my advice?"

How did he know? But I wasn't going to give him the satisfaction.

"I just come for feathers," I said, "and then I got to scram. Lots to do today."

Mr. Mayella widened his eyes a little, staring so deeply into mine that my eyelids burned. He held that gaze for just a moment too long. Then he clapped his hands together so hard I jumped.

"Feathers, indeed!" he said. "And how many do we need today?"

"Eleven," I said.

Mr. Mayella raised one thin white eyebrow. It hung there on the pale of his face like the seagull flying in my dreams.

"Eleven," he said. "My, my." He squinted his eyes at me. "This wouldn't have anything to do with that small matter at Petrov's house, would it?"

My hands went all clammy.

"I wouldn't know a thing about that," I said, "and you shouldn't either."

"You're right," he said. "I shouldn't."

He sprang from his chair, jolting upright like an exclamation mark behind his desk.

"Eleven feathers for Gustavina. I shall return shortly."

Mr. Mayella opened the great wooden door to the hatchery, all scrawled over with sigils. He only opened it a crack, just enough to slip his slender body through the doorway. As if offering me a present, Mr. Mayella stuck his head out the door and grinned at me, opening the door a little wider.

And then I caught a glimpse. For just a moment, I saw everything. In gold glittering doorless cages sat the cardinals, regal and plump, the females a mix of gray and gold and brown and just a hint of red, like campfire smoke crossing the sunset, the males bright and red as the deepest velvet, little flames of them in all their splendor. Feathers floated around the room, catching the sunlight from the window, glimmering fire-like in their slow falling.

The door creaked itself shut, and the splendor vanished. I stood there in the quiet lobby, the strange artifacts of Mr. Mayella's life surrounding me, my heart thudding from the joy and wonder of what I'd just seen. It was like that every time for me, like staring into a treasure room in a palace, like getting a tiny glimpse into the inside of the sun.

A few minutes later the door opened—this time just a crack—and Mr. Mayella slipped through. He held in his hands a bouquet of feathers, bright red and burning. I could feel the power of them, all the wonder stored deep in their quills, ancient magic old as the earth, passed down from bird to bird. My hands shook with it.

"Thank you, Mr. Mayella," I said, and bowed to him.

"No, Gustavina," he said. "Thank you."

And there was a sad look in his face, a sorrow to his eyes. That smile twitched a little around the edges, drooping somewhat.

If I didn't know better, I'd say Mr. Mayella was worried about me. I'd say he knew something serious that maybe I didn't.

"Mr. Mayella," I said, "what were you doing that night of the storm?"

His eyebrows rose.

"Pardon me?"

"I saw you from my window, just as the storm hit, wandering toward the gates. What were you doing? Why were you out there?"

"I think," said Mr. Mayella, "that you are much mistaken. You didn't see me out there. I was in here, in this very hatchery, taking care of my birds."

"But Mr. Mayella, I saw you. I saw you with your hat pulled low, walking your way through the storm."

"No, you did not!" he shouted, slamming his fist on the desk.

The violence of the gesture shocked me. As frightened as I'd always been of Mr. Mayella, he'd never once raised his voice at me, or at anyone. I didn't even know the man could yell.

Silence settled into the hatchery, a moment of fierce quiet while Mr. Mayella composed himself. He straightened his tie and adjusted his hat and sat with his perfect posture, hands folded on the desk, facing me.

"Mr. Mayella," I said.

"I think you should leave," he said, his voice gone quiet, whisper soft.

"But listen. I was only trying to figure out what's happening in the village. I mean, things are getting really strange. . . ."

"Get out of my office," he said. "Now."

Maybe I should have stayed. Maybe I should have pushed

him to tell me his secrets, called on my authority as Protector, sworn an oath on Grandpa Widow's honor, anything to find out the truth. Maybe things would have turned out differently if only I had.

But I didn't. I was shaken by the way Mr. Mayella had screamed at me, at the cold silence I now faced sitting across from me. In fact, I hate being yelled at, and I was awful close to crying. Like I'd ever give a jerk like Mr. Mayella that satisfaction.

So I did the only thing I could do. I gathered my dignity and stood up and walked to the front door.

"Be seeing you," I told him.

I hoped it sounded like a threat.

Outside Cricket lay in the dirt, looking all tired and hungry.

"Come on, boy," I said. "Let's get us some grub."

But as we started back for the Rectory, I saw Lazlo Dunes sitting in the shade of Donald Dithery's Shop of Dentistry and the Tonsorial Arts. He chuckled to himself and spat in the dirt.

"What's your problem?" I said.

"I got words for you, little Gussy," he said.

"Oh yeah? Well, go ahead and spit them out. I got places to be, work to do, Rites to perform, all that stuff you hate."

"Is that what I do?" he said. "Hate things? No, no, Gussy, you misunderstand me. I love this village, and I love the people in it. But they've gone astray. I'm here to lead them back to the righteous path."

He rose to his feet and came clanging my way.

"No one's gone astray here," I said. "We're just trying to live a good life and be safe. I perform the Rites for you too, you know."

Lazlo Dunes was nearly to me, his haggard face, his old tattered clothes. As he got closer, Cricket began to growl, and Lazlo stopped where he stood.

"That you do, Gussy," he said, "and I suppose you think I should thank you for that. But I don't thank you. No, I am not grateful, not one bit. The only thing you're protecting us from is the truth."

"What truth?" I said. "That the Great Doom wants to destroy us? We all know that."

Lazlo Dune's eyes sparkled a bright blue, a look of rapture coming over his face.

"You're just one of them. Just a pawn of that old fraud Grandpa Widow and the Benningsleys."

"I'm nobody's pawn," I said.

Lazlo Dunes shook his head at me and laughed.

"You think you will escape?" he said. "None of you are safe. We built this bed long ago, and we shall have no choice but to lie in it."

I just stared at him stupidly, my mouth hung open.

"The Great Doom is coming," he said, "and there's

nothing you can do to stop it. In fact, it's already here. It's in this place, right now, as we speak, among you."

And he shuffled off, his pan dangling at his side, not saying another word.

I wondered if maybe it wasn't me opening the gates that caused the infection. Maybe it was something else entirely.

Maybe it was Lazlo Dunes.

12

ME AND CRICKET WERE NEARLY TO THE
Rectory when Big Gordo came running up to me all frantic
looking, waving his arms.

"Hey, Gus!" he hollered. "I think you need to see this."

I groaned.

"What is it now?"

But he just beckoned me onward, through the village
gates, to where the chicken foot was supposed to be safe
and buried.

Because it wasn't safe and buried.

No, there was a big hole in the ground, all dug straight
up, dirt and clay tossed aside, no chicken foot to be seen.

"Who did this?" I said. "Was it a bobcat? A wild desert
dog?"

"I must confess, Gussy, I just don't know," he said.

"What do you mean, you don't know?" I said. "Sometime in the last three hours, something came out here and dug up the chicken foot right under your nose, and you're telling me you didn't see who did it?"

Big Gordo scratched his bald head all sheepish, and sighed.

"I was writing," he said. "A poem about volcanoes. And then I got stuck on this one line—you don't know a word that rhymes with salamandrine, do you?—and then it was gone, all dug up, no one around."

"You and your poetry," I said, and Big Gordo winced, which made me feel bad a little bit. But gosh, maybe he should feel bad. He was the one who had gotten careless and derelict about his duties. "Well, did anybody else see what did it?"

"I don't think so," he said. "I didn't see anybody standing around. I would have asked, but I thought the fewer people that know about this, the better."

That actually was pretty good thinking. Still, it would only be a matter of time before folks noticed a hole dug up right outside the gates.

"Aight, aight," I said, and slumped my head a little. "I'll take care of it."

"You okay, Gussy?" said Big Gordo, his big blue eyes looking all concerned for me. And for a moment I felt like leaning my head against his shoulder and bawling my eyes out, telling him how wrong everything was going, how scared I was, how much I missed Grandpa Widow. But I couldn't do that. I had duties to perform, Rites to complete. I didn't have time to cry. I bit my lip, made two fists, stomped my left foot, and tried to get myself all mad and stern, just like Grandpa Widow did when he saw someone make a mistake.

"Well, I'd be a heck of a lot better if you'd do your job," I said in my lowest, meanest voice. "So if you'll excuse me, I'm going to grab some grub and a glass of water, and then I'll rehang these cardinal feathers, and *then* I'll set about looking after the sacred chicken foot you let get stolen."

It was a hateful tirade, I'll tell you that right now, and I'm not proud of it. But I won't whitewash the truth of the matter either. I was angry, and I took it out on sweet old Big Gordo. Sometimes you just have to be ashamed of yourself, don't you?

I huffed myself away toward the Rectory, spitting furious. I was sick of this day already. I couldn't figure how it could possibly get any worse.

I opened the door to the Rectory to find the place midnight dark, with Angeline sitting cross-legged, facing the back wall, nothing but candlelight flickering. On the wall she'd drawn a gate with some kind of chalk, little stars around the outside of it. I could hear her humming a strange melody, her long red hair flopped all the way down over her face, covering her head and neck like a hood. Her hands were outstretched, beckoning to the wall, as if calling something to come this way, to walk itself straight through.

A gust of wind blew the door shut behind me.

Angeline jolted out of her trance, whirling toward me, the candle flame reflecting little fires in her eyes, the veins bulging in her neck, and she bared her teeth at me in a growl, her fingers curled at me like claws. She looked furious, ghastly, like any moment she would leap at me and tear me apart.

I staggered back against the door. Cricket let out a whimper. I held the bouquet of cardinal feathers up to my face, as if to protect me.

Then, just as quickly, Angeline's claws turned back into fingers, her snarl calming into a smile, the flames in her eyes tampered down to their usual soft gray.

"Hello, friends," she said. "I'm sorry. I didn't hear you come in."

A banging sounded on the Rectory door, Big Gordo shouting outside.

"Gus! Come quick!"

I didn't know what to do. I didn't know what was happening. I looked back at Angeline staring sweetly up at me from the corner, and then I yanked the door open and there he stood with Mr. Jilly, the tailor. He was all frantic and crying.

"My clothes!" he said. "Oh, my poor beautiful creations!"

"What happened?" I said.

"Why, they tried to kill me! To strangle the very life out of me!"

"Who tried to kill you?"

"I already told you—my clothes!" he said. "They came alive, Gussy. And they tried to murder me! Me, who made them! And I have loved them so!"

He burst into tears and flung his arms around Big Gordo's neck, heaving and sobbing.

I knew what this meant. It was the Great Doom. It was still in the village.

"Wait here one second," I said.

I stepped back inside and shut the door behind me. I had to move quick. I grabbed the cardinal feathers and my fiddle and Grandpa Widow's book on Cleansing Rites.

"Is everything all right?" said Angeline, her voice sparkly and light as moonsilver. I looked at her sitting there, surrounded by candles, that dark strange doorway seeming to glimmer behind her, and my whole body gave a shiver. I gave her a fierce look.

"I'll deal with you when I get back," I said.

I backed outside and pulled the door shut. Then me and Cricket took off running toward Mr. Jilly's.

13

MR. JILLY'S TAILORING AND HABERDASH-
ery was shut tight against the bright afternoon, as if it was
trying to keep the sunlight out. I clutched my fiddle and my
bag close. I took three deep breaths and let them out slow. I
chanted three Mysteries and bunched my fists a few times.
It was time for us to move. I opened the front door a foot,
and me and Cricket slipped inside.

The shop was candlelit and brighter than daylight, all the
lanterns glowing, the still-flickering flames of the candles
in every corner. It was hot, I tell you, much hotter than out-
doors, and the room carried the faint whiff of burning, of
kerosene and flint and tinderboxes. A stove glowered in the
corner, the coals bright as hellfire.

Clothes were strewn everywhere. Evening gowns and

dresses with gingham and floral patterns, top hats and tux-
edos and three-piece suits, they all lay about on the ground
or slumped over the staircase railings, as if they had been
full of people just moments ago and everyone had up and
vanished. They lay about like carcasses, like a windstorm
had scattered them every which way.

All was silent, and nothing moved.

I didn't trust it.

Cricket lay low and growled.

I opened my Rites book and read a short passage about
brightness, about the light banishing the darkness, about
how the darkness feared the light. It seemed stupid, considering how bright this room was. I mean, how scared could
the Great Doom be of the light when it had just lit every candle in the room? It was ridiculous, I realized, all those big
and pretty words that meant exactly squat in this situation. I
slammed the book shut.

A breeze wafted through the room, scattering a blouse
from the table in a whoosh. It wafted across the floor with
the sound of a snicker, little muffled laughs all around the
room. I didn't like this, I didn't like it at all.

*Don't panic now, Gus. You're the Protector, after all. You're
the one in charge here.*

I stood myself up straight and snapped my boots together,
my head held high, at perfect attention. Then I lifted my fiddle to my neck and began to play. It was a mournful hymn,

slow and quiet, "The Desolate Bones of Saint Mary Keene."
I liked that song. It was the closest a hymn ever got to a murder ballad. I sang it too, but just to myself, so quiet no one else could hear, not even Cricket. I don't know why I picked that one to play. It was just the first thing that popped into my mind.

When I got to the second verse, the one about Saint Mary Keene trying to seduce Lonely Handsome Royal so as to save his life from the murderess Princess Beaconbright, one of the dresses, a beautiful long-sleeved jade-green one, an elegant woman's dress, lifted right up off the shop floor. I couldn't believe it.

The long sleeve pinched up the hem of the gown and began to twirl, slow waltzing circles across the immaculate hardwood. Say what you will about Mr. Jilly, he was no slouch when it came to cleanliness. I'd never seen a dinner plate shine so bright as his showroom floor did. The dress spun and danced, swishing the floor in time with the beat I played. When I got to the refrain ("All praise Saint Mary Keene, holy tart of Beebottle Abbey!"), another dress lifted itself from the ground, a floral housedress with a big waistline, and joined the jade-green dress, and together they danced themselves across the floor. It was beautiful, I tell you, the elegance of those dresses, filled by nothing but wind, no sound but the slightest rustle of fabric against floor.

Cricket whimpered at my side, tugging on my robe sleeve, as if to ask me to stop.

But that was when something funny happened.

See, I realized I didn't want to stop playing. I didn't want to see those dresses cease their dancing. I loved having them dance for me. It was like an honor, you know, to finally have an audience, for something to enjoy my music so much. I played the next four verses, and when I hit that final refrain, I had tears in my own eyes. As the last notes of my fiddle rang out, the dresses released each other and slumped lifeless to the floor.

I walked over to the jade-green one and toed it with my boot. It was completely empty, not even any air inside. I stooped down and picked it up.

It was a beautiful dress, it truly was, one fit for nothing less than a ball at the Benningsley mansion. I wondered if I would ever wear such fine clothes and go dancing at a ball. Not necessarily this sort of dress—I'm not sure gowns are much my style—but something that made me feel fancy, anything but my Protector's robes. I wondered if that would ever be a part of my life, if I could ever feel elegant and free, twirling around a dance floor like those two pretty dresses just had.

I felt something in me, what Grandpa Widow would maybe have referred to as a *call*. It's when you get a feeling you don't understand that tells you to do something you think doesn't make any sense. Grandpa Widow always told me to fight the calls. He said they were irrational, and they were often in conflict with the duties and responsibilities of a Protector.

"We have codes and rules for a reason," he always said. "Follow the rituals and follow the Rites, and perform them to perfection, no matter what. Do not listen to the tiny voice urging you to the right and to the left. The path is clear before you. It is the path laid out by the Rites. Anything else is danger."

But it wasn't so simple as all that. This call wasn't some curiosity telling me to poke my head into somebody else's larder or something. It wasn't even words, or a notion. It was a song. A melody I could hear, five measly notes, a looping sound so strong in my noggin it might have been Cricket howling it right in my ear.

So I did something maybe I shouldn't have. I stood up straight and pulled my fiddle to my neck and I played that song, just the same as the call told me to. It was a jaunty little tune, and I could tell it wanted to be played fast, so I picked up the pace, hurrying the melody along a little bit.

The gingham dress lifted itself sleepily off the floor, stretching as if coming out of a long nap. It swayed a little bit to the song, sashaying in its own little corner. Then the jade dress up and did a twirl, spinning out like a flower in full blossom. A tuxedo with a floating top hat took a bow and whisked its way onto the floor, arm in arm with a long-trained wedding dress, moving so elegantly to the music I was making.

Soon the entire room was full of suits and dresses and gowns and bodiless hats of all kinds dancing wild, a ballroom of invisible dancers flinging themselves in unison, the wildest party I ever saw in my life. Nothing like this happened even in the parlor room of Old Esmerelda's, of that you can be certain. It was uncivilized, dresses twirling, four- and five-piece suits hopping over each other, swinging themselves from the banister. I played faster and faster, the garments spinning themselves in bright little whirlpools, twisters of candy-colored fabrics, a whole universe of colors. I felt like I was creating a world here, a song that breathed the entire cosmos into life. All those fancy clothes dancing to the tune I played, all of these worlds being created and living and dying to the tune of my fiddle. I felt lightning zapped, the power of the universe flowing through my fingers, what it must have felt like for the One Who Listens to fashion the world out of its own breath.

The pace rose to a gallop, my blood pounding in my veins, my fingers blistered and burning, my heart thumping so hard in my chest I could see it through my robes. And yet still the call came faster, the song increasing in speed like floodwaters down a gulley. I stomped my boots on the hardwood quicker and louder, until in my head it sounded like a whole battalion of wild horses barreling across the desert, the clomp of hooves thunderous in my ears, and I could hear laughter all of a sudden, jokes and conversation, men's voices laughing loud and ribald and women cackling at each other, the clang of empty cups slammed on hardwood tables, the shattering of a dropped glass, a partygoer's hysterical whooping.

I spun and twirled and fiddled harder and faster, I danced myself, boots clomping, scuffing up Mr. Jilly's immaculate floor, the song of my calling ripping through the afternoon, the shop alive and wild with music and joy and dancing. I couldn't help it, I played faster and faster. It was as if I was being controlled by something else, like my soul had been lit on fire and all I could do was play. I danced around the room, my own robes swishing, the dresses dancing with me, porkpie and pillbox hats flinging from the shelves, tossing themselves about in celebration. I couldn't stop laughing, I was so happy, all my invisible friends in a great big fancy ball, just for me. It was so beautiful, all the whirling colors, like the whole night sky had come down to Mr. Jilly's Tailoring and Haberdashery just to dance with me, just to sweep me up into their twirling and let me be one of them for a time. It was maybe the happiest I'd ever been in my life.

It was only Cricket's howling that snapped me out of it.

Suddenly I realized what I was doing, how I was dancing

around like an idiot, in thrall to the Great Doom's calling. I stopped my dancing, and I stopped my playing too. All at once the clothes dropped lifeless to the floor, same as they were when I'd found them.

I was panting, all hot and sweaty and out of breath. I'd been hoodwinked, I had, lured in by that siren call. If it weren't for Cricket, I probably would have played that tune faster and faster until my fingers bled and my heart gave out altogether. It would have been the death of me, as certain as I do stand here now. Once again, Cricket had saved my life.

I bent down and let him lick my face. When we got back home, I'd find him a good tough bone to chew on.

These clothes weren't all elegant and pretty, they were hexed, filled up with cursed air and puppeted about by the Great Doom. They might as well have been poison. Mr. Jilly ought to have them burned.

I was a Protector, and I had a duty to do. I would cleanse this whole place of every trace of darkness, of the foul infection caused by the Great Doom, and nothing was going to stand in my way.

The clothes were settled down, a whole floor of bright scattered flower petals. I wasn't messing around anymore, no sir. I'd lost my focus for just a bit, but I wasn't going to let that happen a second time.

I cleared my throat and chanted a Mystery. I would have walked around the room, blessing every corner, but I was a little afraid of what those garments might up and do. Instead, I stuck a cardinal feather straight upright in a notch in the floor. I spread the cleansing herbs in a great big circle around myself, and I made ready to begin the Rite.

I had barely got into the "We beseech ye" part when a little girl's pink holy day dress began slinking its way snakelike across the floor. It curled up next to my ritual circle and rose, swishing against the floor in a hissing sound. I ignored it and kept reading.

"We ask thee for favor in our endeavor, that by thou mercy we might prevail. If we have trespassed against any creature, we ask forgiveness. We plead to be shown the error of our ways, so that mercy and justice might prevail."

A black funeral frock lifted itself from the floor and flew at me. I flinched, my hands in front of my face, but it stopped dead when it hit my ritual circle, same as if it had been a brick wall. The frock flopped straight to the ground. A fedora half-heartedly whizzed at me and clattered away.

That was good to know. My ritual circle worked.

One by one the lights went off in Mr. Jilly's Tailoring and Haberdashery. The candles snuffed themselves out, and the lanterns blinked and sputtered, and suddenly I found myself in the dark. I could just barely see the print of the book through the daylight glow from the shut windows. It wasn't much, but it was enough.

I kept reading.

"May the deeds of our ancestors not be held against us, and let knowledge and understanding guide us toward paths of righteousness forevermore."

A pair of velvet trousers flung itself at me from off a fitting dummy, flitting away when it tried to cross the barrier. They weren't going to stop me from finishing this Rite, not no way, not no how. I took a deep breath and let it out slow. I only had another page to go.

That was when I saw a big mink coat dangling itself like a jumper from the staircase railing. It lifted a furred sleeve all dramatic-like to where its head might be, and then it flung itself from the balcony, arms angel wide, in a freefall, spreading itself open like a cape, right at the foot of my ritual circle.

The whoosh it made swept a tiny bit of the cleansing herbs aside.

My circle was broken.

I stooped to fix it.

Quick as a whipcrack, a long-sleeved dress swooped up from where it had lain hidden on the floor, noosing itself around my neck. It was a nasty gray thing, and it was no wonder I hadn't noticed it slinking along the floor. I grabbed at the fabric, but it pulled itself tight, choking me. I watched in terror as the dress rose higher, lifting me off the floor. My legs kicked, and I tore at the sleeve, but its grip was too tight, and I was strangling. My vision got all splotchy, and I couldn't breathe anymore.

Cricket took a mighty leap at the dress, catching it by the hem in his teeth. The dress tottered in the air a little bit, dipping me down to where my feet could touch the floor. I gave the dress a yank, and together we pulled it from the air. Cricket tore the dress hard, ripping the sleeve wrapped around my neck just enough for me to slip out of its grasp. Cricket fought the dress alone now, tearing it to pieces until it lay still on the floor. I was alive and breathing, barely. My throat ached. The dress had almost crushed my windpipe.

I scrambled for my Rites book and read, quickly as I could, the rest of the ritual. Fancy garments flung themselves at me, trying to smother me, but still I read. Cricket ripped them off me as best as he could, but they piled higher and higher on top of me, crushing me, until finally I got the last bit of the Rite out.

"In the name of all that is light, I banish the darkness from this place forever!"

And the clothes burst off me in a whoosh, dropping here and there around the tailor's shop.

About then Mr. Jilly came running in, all out of breath. He saw the gray dress that had tried to kill me lying in scraps on the floor, and he clapped his hands to his cheeks.

"My beautiful creation!" he hollered, and began to weep.

I don't know. I probably could have said something mean to him about how his "beautiful creation" had nearly murdered me, but what would the point of that be? He'd made that dress with all his heart, ugly as it was, and he was sad it got ripped up. I understood that.

It's hard loving things.

I struggled myself back to my feet.

"Your shop is clear," I croaked.

Mr. Jilly looked at me, his eyes all red from crying.

"Thank you," he said.

I just nodded. Then I gathered my things, and me and Cricket left.

14

BY THE TIME WE GOT OUT OF MR. JILLY'S,
I was flat wore out and exhausted. My neck hurt and my
throat was scratched and I needed a nap. But I'm a Protector, and Protectors don't get to nap. It was getting late in the
afternoon already. I had to hurry if I was going to hang all
those cardinal feathers and replace that stolen chicken foot
in time. And then there was the whole matter of Angeline
and her doorway spell. I didn't even know what to think
about that, and to be honest, it scared me.

The feathers were easy enough, just twining them together
and chanting a Mystery and breathing on them and we're
all good. But you'd be amazed at how hard it is to find a
chicken foot some days, especially if the creature had to die
of natural causes. I mean, most chickens don't get to live

long enough to expire peacefully in their coops, and that's just the truth of the matter.

I checked Petrov's coop. I checked Old Esmerelda's. I stuck my head in Bartleby Bonnard's shop, to see if any of his chickens had recently kicked the bucket. No luck. By sunset, I'd run myself ragged all over the village, looking for any old chicken that might be on death's door. Nothing doing.

All the chickens around here were in good health, thank you very much.

That meant I had to take some drastic measures. That meant I had to use eggs.

I do not like using eggs for ritual work, especially not this particular Rite. I simply don't. For one, they are life at the beginning, not at the end, and that's a different sort of power altogether. A raucous power, less reliable, less inclined to be stable. The ritual power of an egg is about dealing with the possible, with things not yet realized, and possibilities can get you into all kinds of trouble.

I sprinkled salt in a circle around the earth, walking backward clockwise three times. I bent to my knees and kissed each spotty egg individually and blew on them, chanting a Mystery as quiet as the breeze. I buried the eggs in the dust, patting them over carefully, trying not to break a single one. I thanked the chicken for giving me these eggs, the product of such careful work, and the eggs themselves, for keeping us safe. It is a fearful and wonderful thing, sacrifice. You never should take it for granted. I said a prayer to the One Who Listens that these eggs would keep the village safe, that the power they brought would be kind and gentle and strong, that no harm would come to anyone listed in our Book of Names.

You know, the usual.

Then I set about replacing the cardinal feathers. When I made it to the far northern point of the wall, I saw a little dug-up spot at the base of one of the posts, like a dog or coyote had been trying to tunnel underneath. I got down on my knees and shoveled some of the dirt out with my hands, just to see how deep the hole went. I didn't have to go very far. Because at the base of the wall, a tiny symbol was carved into the wood, no bigger than my palm, a spirally-looking thing, all hooks and feathered lines, like a strange star shimmering in the night. I knew what this was, and it terrified me.

A Sigil of Discord.

It was a spell against the wall, a disruption of the Rites. Old dark magic, evil to the core. It was expertly cut, detailed down to the tiniest curl at the end of each pointed line, and it was worn a little, like it had been there a few days. This was how the Great Doom was sneaking into the village—it had to be. The Rites couldn't work properly with a hex like that scribbled onto the wall.

I didn't understand. Why would anyone sabotage the

wall like this? Who would want to? Lazlo Dunes? But how could someone like Lazlo know such magic? Where would he even have learned it? Mr. Mayella was a more likely candidate. I had seen him wandering around the night of the storm, hadn't I?

I bent down and took the tiny knife I carried to cut the twine for the cardinal feathers, and I scrawled a big protective circle over the sigil, scratching through its heart with an X and a spiral, to nullify its effects. I chanted a Mystery over it and spoke it backward three times, to reverse the effects of the sigil back onto the carver. Just think of it, putting the whole village in danger like that. Whoever had done it deserved the spell to rebound on them threefold.

I checked the rest of the wall as carefully as I could, but I didn't see any more Sigils of Discord or spells carved into anything else.

As I headed back to the Rectory, there was one particular thought I couldn't quite shake. There were only a couple of folks in the village who would know how to carve the Sigil of Discord. Mr. Mayella, for one, and though he was acting awful squirrelly, I couldn't figure why he would want to let the Great Doom in. After all, keeping it out was his whole livelihood, with the hatchery and all. That left one other person: Angeline. Hadn't I caught her reading Grandpa Widow's forbidden books on esoteric Rites? And what was she doing with that doorway chalked on the wall? Had she been summoning the Great Doom into Mr. Jilly's shop? Was she the one who had been causing all these problems from the very beginning?

But that didn't make any sense either. I mean, why would Angeline want to disrupt the Rites like that? Hadn't she come here to escape the Great Doom? Was anyone who they were pretending to be? My mind was a tangled-up ball of confusion, and I didn't have a clue what to do.

I picked up my fiddle and began "Last Lights Wonder," playing it soft and sad and slow, the burns on my neck throbbing, my back and arms aching in pain. It wasn't a perfect rendition, but it was heartsick and strong, and I knew I meant it with all my heart, with my fullest intention. I did my best. It was all I could do.

Afterward, me and Cricket walked all exhausted and wore-out back to the Rectory. Just on a whim, I decided to peek into the window first.

Angeline sat on the floor, the chalk doorway erased, little smudges where the stars were on the wall. Grandpa Widow wouldn't like that. She was curled up just reading away, surrounded by her candles and books. She looked so peaceful, so innocent like that, the focused inscrutable look on her face, the soft splash of red on her cheeks. She seemed utterly harmless, a scared girl stuck in a strange place, missing her family, wiling away the time with books.

I didn't know what to do. I was confused and alone, lost

in this world of things I didn't understand. Where oh where was Grandpa Widow when I needed him most?

I walked to the front door and stepped inside. I took a deep breath and bolted the door. The girl didn't look up from her book, just flipped the pages rapidly. I couldn't believe how quickly she could read, especially with books as strange and old as the ones she pored through nightly.

"Angeline . . . ," I said.

"You know," she said, "these Rites you perform every day are all very particular."

"Angeline, I really need to talk to you about something."

"It just makes me wonder about the nature of the magic you do every day," she said. "Have you ever considered the grander implications of those cardinal feathers, for instance? Or the substance and source of those Mysteries you're always chanting? They have a defensive spirit. They're about keeping things out."

That made me a bit angry, to be honest with you. I didn't like being lectured about my own duties, about how I spent every day of my life on this earth.

"First off," I said, "it's not plain old magic. It's our Rites. Second, the Rites aren't about keeping 'things' out. There's just one thing—the Great Doom, and I've been battling it all day."

"But that's just it," she said. "There's so many other kinds of magic. Magic of discovery, of hope and joy and learning.

This is all defensive magic. It's deceitful, in a way. This is magic to hide something."

I didn't quite know what to make of that. It was taking everything in me not to wring Angeline's neck.

"You wouldn't know anything about Sigils of Discord, would you?" I said.

"Of course I know about Sigils of Discord," she said. "There's three books on them here, and how to subvert them too. Why? Did you find one somewhere?"

"Yes," I said. "In fact, I did."

Angeline jumped to her feet.

"You didn't touch it, did you?"

"I did. Just to see if it was fresh or not. Freshly carved, I mean." Angeline's mouth hung open, as if in shock. "I . . . I scratched an X over it. I said the Mystery backward to reverse it."

Angeline took my hand in hers, the same one I'd carved over the sigil with. She whispered something into my palm and then spat.

"Gross," I said, and tried to yank my hand away, but Angeline held my wrist tight. Angeline kept whispering over my hand, guiding her finger in a long slow circle over my palm. My palm began to brighten and flicker, like parchment paper that catches fire. It began to tingle, a crackling feeling, but it didn't hurt any.

"What are you doing?" I said.

"Watch."

In lines of orange fire there appeared a symbol on my hand, all curves and arrows, a star in the middle of it.

"Just as I thought," said Angeline.

I knew exactly what that was. It was a hex, burned into my skin. I had picked it up from touching that sigil. I felt like the stupidest person who ever walked the earth right about then.

"It's okay," said Angeline, "it's an easy fix."

She walked over to Grandpa Widow's herb cabinet and dug around for a while, my hand crackling with light. It wasn't exactly an unpleasant feeling, only strange, like when you've accidentally fallen asleep on your arm. I waved my hand back and forth in the gloom of the Rectory, watching the light trace the dark air.

"Pretty, isn't it?" said Angeline as she returned, her hands full of herbs. "But it won't be tomorrow, when you wake up and all the skin is melted off your hand."

Angeline sprinkled herbs in a tiny stone mortar of Grandpa Widow's and ground them with a pestle, whispering all the while. When the herbs were properly crushed into powder, Angeline picked up a pinch of them and sprinkled it onto my hand.

"Almost finished," she said. She walked over to the kitchen table and grabbed a knife.

"What are you about to do with that?" I said, alarmed.

"Nothing to you," she said. Quick as a blink, she poked her thumb with the knife blade and squeezed a single drop of blood onto my palm. She closed my hand into a fist and brought it to her face, whispering to it.

"Okay," she said. "Count to five and open your hand."

I did as she asked. The fire was gone, and so was the hex. All that was left was a handful of ashes.

"Now walk backward to the fire and dump them in there," she said, "and we'll be done here."

Again, I did as Angeline asked, stumbling a little over a pile of books she'd left on the floor. I was careful not to spill any of the ashes before tossing them into the fire.

"Whew," she said. "That was a close one."

"Thanks," I said. "I don't know what else to say."

"You don't have to say anything," said Angeline, smiling real big at me. "I'm just glad you're safe."

"Yeah," I said. "Me too."

I felt like a phony and a liar, standing there like that. I couldn't believe that I'd thought this girl who had just literally saved my skin was the one letting the Great Doom inside the village. I was thoroughly ashamed of myself.

"Angeline," I said, not even able to look her in the eyes, "what were you doing with that doorway spell?"

She blinked at me. "Doorway spell? Oh, you mean the thing with the chalk."

"Yeah, yeah," I said, "the thing with the chalk."

"That wasn't a doorway, it was a window. An awfully big window, I know, but a window nonetheless."

"A window to what?"

"A magic window," she said. "I wanted to see who was causing the darkness in the village. I hoped they would pass by the window I'd made, and I would see them for who they really were."

"You know those things work both ways, right? When you're looking out, something else could be looking in." I was downright furious. What could possibly be more irresponsible than trying a spell like that in a time like this?

Angeline's head drooped. "I know, it was dangerous. But I was trying to help you. I was trying to figure out how the Great Doom was getting inside."

"I don't need your help," I said. "I'm Protector of this village. I might not be doing a very good job of it right now, but so long as it's still my job, I'm going to do it. And if I need your help, I'll ask you for it, thank you very much."

I stormed off to the stove in a huff. To calm down, I set about making dinner, just whatever scraps I could throw together last minute. I was weary and angry and exhausted. My neck still throbbed from my near-strangling, and all I wanted to do was collapse on the bed and not wake up for a week. Cricket was already snoozing in a little curl on the floor, my truest friend. He'd saved my life today, and that was a fact. What had I ever done for him? Plus I was starting to feel real bad for how I'd snapped at Angeline. She was just trying to help, wasn't she? I'd be a liar if I said I wasn't rightly ashamed of myself.

As we sat over dinner (cornbread that I burned, salted ham, a few runny eggs), Angeline was quiet, not catching my eye, like she had a question in her mind she was scared to ask. I hate when people do that. If you want to know something, get bold and say so. That's why the One Who Listens gave us mouths. Finally I got fed up and just asked her myself.

"What is it, Angeline?"

She picked at her food, which was admittedly pretty bad. "Oh, nothing."

"Hush. It is something, and I want to know what."

Angeline sighed and looked up at me. She clicked her tongue three times like she was trying to get up the courage to say the thing.

"Well, it's about your dreams."

"My dreams? What do my dreams have to do with anything?"

"It's just that . . . the Peacock's Eye here is a powerful tool," she said. "A scrying tool. I think I can use it to see your dreams, if you want me to. And if I can see your dreams, I think I might be able to find the place you're dreaming of."

"Does that mean you could find out where I came from?"

"Maybe so."

I probably should have thought a little bit more before I said what I said next, but I sure didn't. Maybe I was just too wore out, or maybe I'm just dense in the head, I don't know.

"But if the Peacock's Eye is so powerful," I said, "why haven't you been able to find your parents with it?"

The smile fell off Angeline's face.

"Well, it isn't foolproof. No magic ever is. My point was that I could try." She slumped facedown on the table. "You're right. It's a stupid idea. I don't know why I even mentioned it."

How thoughtless I was, bringing up something like that.

"No, it's not stupid," I said. "And I believe in you, that you could do something like that. I just . . . well . . . how about we focus on one set of missing parents at a time, all right?"

"Okay," she said. "Yeah, that makes sense."

"Is there anything I can do to help you?" I said.

"You've already done more than enough."

Angeline got up from the table and went back to her books, her face hidden under all that red.

To say I felt like a jerk is to so thoroughly understate the sentiment that it's useless. I felt like the scum at the bottom of a hog trough. I felt like something a fly wouldn't even want to land on. Why couldn't I ever just keep my mouth shut?

As I cleaned up the table, Angeline did her same ritual using the Peacock's Eye and that black feather. It was amazing the way Angeline worked, not so much reciting old Rites as making up her own, changing them, doing little variations on rituals I knew so well. Even the Peacock's Eye was a stone of unwieldy power; I could feel it from across the room. How did she know all this stuff? Because it was clear she'd learned it from somebody, and it sure as heck wasn't someone like Grandpa Widow or his books. As homespun as her magic was, there was definitely technique to it, some kind of order.

After dinner I lay myself down on the bed and fell asleep, Angeline's soft voice whispering away in the corner, performing some ritual I'd never heard of, something I'd probably never even understand.

That night I had a dream.

I was a bird again, a seagull swooping high over the wreckage of a ship, lightning gouging the sky, rain pelting me. Why didn't I seek warmth and protection? Why didn't I head for my safe perch among the rocks? Because I wanted to see. I wanted to see the suffering sailors, the men and women and children flung into the icy water. I wanted to see them kick and thrash and swim, swim with all their might, that giant boat rising up high in the water, sinking oddly, teetering on the edge of two worlds, its white-sailed mast like the last finger of a drowning man reaching out from the water.

Then nothing.

The sea was lurching and wild, water and foam hurled high, and I sailed away, far above it all, as a woman set a child safely on the rocks, just before the current wrapped itself around her ankle like an evil hand and the water yanked her backward, out into the ocean, into the depths of the sea, the new underwater world from which she would never escape, from which she'd never return, no one would ever see her again.

Leaving that poor baby crying alone on the rocks.

15

WHEN I WOKE UP THAT MORNING, I
knew something was wrong. You could just feel it in the air,
a crackling feeling, a kind of dangerous sparkle to everything
around you. Even Cricket awoke whimpering. Angeline lay
sleeping on the floor, the feather and Peacock's Eye still out
in the open, gleaming at me like strange treasure, a riddle I
couldn't solve. I reached for my breakfast fork, and it shocked
me so hard I dropped the thing clattering on the floor. I was
worried a moment, but Angeline hardly stirred. Lord knows
how late she had stayed up scrying for her parents, trying to
find them lost somewhere out in the darkness.

If Angeline hadn't carved the sigil, someone else had, and
I needed to find out who. I gritted my teeth and took three
breaths and steeled my mind. I had a job to do, and I was

going to do it. With that, me and Cricket set off to start the Rites.

Just as I finished walking widdershins, the sun a bright fire on the horizon, I saw the Rider galloping this way, crossing the desert on her horse.

I grabbed my fiddle and began "Morningsong Hymn," playing it longer and slower than usual, like I was drawing the Rider toward me with the song. By the time I finished, the Rider rode up on Darla all panting and huffing, laid over the poor horse like she'd just crawled half-drowned out of a river. Big Gordo drew the gates shut behind her.

"I'll grab you some water," said Big Gordo, and hustled off.

"Gussy," said the Rider, her voice a scratchy croak.

"Just you rest a minute," I said. "There'll be time for talking later."

"You don't understand," she said. "It's that girl you were asking me about. That family."

My eyes perked up at that. They might be safe, finally. They might be alive.

"Yeah? What did you find?"

"There was no family in the desert," she said. "Nobody heard any word of travelers coming through that storm night, not in any camp around these parts. I rode every last stretch of this desert, Gussy. There wasn't any carriage broken down, there wasn't any flood wreckage either. No bones, no debris, nothing."

"What are you telling me?" I said.

She looked down at me, her face all sun blistered and dusty.

"I'm telling you that girl's lying to you," she said. "I don't know where she came from, or how she got here. But she wasn't a part of any wagon crossing, and that I can guarantee you."

Big Gordo came back with a jar of water for the Rider, and he took Darla by the reins and led her to the stables.

I didn't know what to say. If Angeline was lying, how had she gotten here? Why had she come at all?

I didn't have much time to think about it, though. Because right then, up came Connor Carnivolly running toward me all frantic and terrified.

"It's my daddy," he said, all huffing and out of breath.

"What's the matter?" I said.

"The Great Doom's got him."

My eyes went wide.

"Got him how?"

"It's inside of him," said Connor Carnivolly. "My daddy's infected."

Connor burst into tears. I probably should have thrown my arms around him and hugged him close. I should have comforted my friend. But all I could do was stand there, slack-jawed, scared out of my wits. The Great Doom had infected somebody, my only real friend's father, and it was all my fault. I should have stopped this a long time ago. I already would have if I was half the Protector that Grandpa Widow was.

"Connor?" I said.

He looked up at me, face all swollen from crying, not one bit of his old wit hiding there in his smile. He looked broken and terrified, a kid in trouble. And I was the only one who could fix it.

"I'll be right back."

I ran into the Rectory and gathered my things, stuffing every cardinal feather and potion and powder I could into my knapsack. I grabbed a purple-black candle and a spare set of fiddle strings and a jackrabbit's ankle bone, for luck.

"What's wrong?" said Angeline.

"Nothing I can explain right now," I said. I took a deep breath and cast her the meanest eye I could. "And don't you dare set foot outside the Rectory, do you hear me?"

Angeline wilted a little in my gaze, shrinking all scared like. It made me feel bad to do that to her, but I wasn't about to risk her getting loose.

But never mind that right now. I had a father to cure, a village to save. I kissed my turtle-shell necklace and rang the silent bell twice, where only the One Who Listens could hear it. Never before had I called on such powers as this to aid me. Never before had I faced an evil quite like this.

I ran outside and found Connor where I'd left him.

"Take me to your father," I said.

He nodded.

Me and Connor and Cricket took off running toward the Carnivolly house, the fate of the entire village in our hands.

16

RUNNING ALL THAT WAY TO THE CAR-
nivolly house, I went over the Cleansing Rite for infected
folks in my mind, trying to remember every detail exactly.
I'd never done one of these before in real life, of course, but
the ritual itself was a doozy. I'm telling you, it isn't easy to
cure a person from infection. You have to pin them down
and light a candle at their head and perform the Cleansing
Rite, which is a pretty hard thing to do when someone is
filled to the brim with the Great Doom. I wasn't sure how
me and Cricket were going to do it, but I knew we had to
succeed, that there wasn't any other option.

I took a deep breath and let it out slow, trying to regain
my focus and intention. Then I pushed that door open and
walked inside.

I loved the Carnivolly house, I always have, ever since I first got to go inside it. Grandpa Widow didn't let me do things like that much. ("It's not good for folks to get too familiar with you," he said. "It's best to be a bit aloof.") But I always treasured any chance I got. The Carnivolly house was a kind of a dream, a home full of strangeness, but not like Mr. Mayella's lobby. This was more of a homemade strangeness, not a gathering of things from afar. Mr. Carnivolly's wooden marionettes hung from their pegs on the walls, while Mrs. Carnivolly's corn-husk dolls gazed up at me with black button eyes. Mr. Carnivolly collected bones too, and what's more, she painted them—coyote skulls colored bright and pretty with flowers, deer vertebrae with faces illustrated on them, the hip bones of cows turned into wild-faced masks. Antelope skulls with the horns painted purple, tears streaming down from their eye sockets.

All of those had caused me so much delight the few times I'd been allowed to come over, and yet in the darkness they seemed so threatening, the bones all a promise of the end to come, the fate of everyone and everything, no matter how pretty you colored them up. Mrs. Carnivolly always said she was honoring the dead, decorating their bones like that. I wondered if the dead critters truly liked it, or if some speck of their souls remained, seeking revenge.

I heard a snickering sound in the darkness, a high-pitched giggle.

"Who's there?" I said, waving the candle around.

But I couldn't see anyone. It was all darkness and silence, the gloom so thick it seemed to swallow the candlelight.

I heard a crackling sound, like a giant beetle scuttling across the floor. The walls groaned, the darkness brushed against me like fur. I could feel someone watching me, eyes on me in the darkness, and I shivered in the heat.

Cricket growled by my side. I knew Mr. Carnivolly must be close. But where?

A drop of something splashed me on the top of my head. I thought it was rainwater, like the roof had a leak in it. But it wasn't raining, was it? What in the world could be dripping on me from above?

When I looked up, I saw him. Mr. Carnivolly, on all fours, crawling across the ceiling, a long string of slobber dangling from his lips.

I screamed and dropped the candle. All became darkness.

I heard the clatter of fingernails scraping the ceiling above me. How was he doing that? It must have been the Great Doom inside of him, giving him powers like that. I tried to follow the scuttling, which sounded like a giant spider clacking across the ceiling. I tripped over something—a kitchen chair, I guessed—and went tumbling, my fiddle banging on the hard floor. I heard laughter in the darkness above me. I backed myself against the wall and strained my eyes, looking everywhere for Mr. Carnivolly, seeing nothing at all. He was close to me, I knew that. I could hear his breathing.

Well, I couldn't fight him in the dark. This was going to require desperate measures.

I grabbed my candle and cupped the wick and whispered a little Mystery that Grandpa Widow had taught me. "Light from above, light from below, light from my heart, light this flame aglow." It was low magic, he'd said, and not worthy of folks like us, only to be used in a pinch. And yet it worked— the candle crackled into light. Thank goodness.

I held the flame up to the room.

I saw Mr. Carnivolly's face barely a foot away from mine, his eyes burning a flame-bright blue, his smile stretched to the breaking point, a ghastly grin, all his teeth exposed. He was hanging from the wall, horizontal, his fingernails and toenails dug into the wood like claws.

Mr. Carnivolly growled at me.

I screamed and stumbled away, waving the candle at him as if it were a knife. He bounded away from me on all fours, landing sideways on the wall. He scampered up to the ceiling, hissing at me like a cat. I waved a cardinal feather in the air and held it above the candle until it crackled and caught.

"By the light of this feather," I hollered, "Mr. Carnivolly, you come down here now."

Mr. Carnivolly leered at me, his eyes shimmering.

"*No,*" he snarled, his voice rough and ragged, like a thousand miles of desert.

"I'm not giving you an option here," I said, waving the flaming feather for emphasis.

"I only want what is mine," he said. *"It's all I've ever wanted."*

"Then you let Mr. Carnivolly go!"

"No!" he roared, leaping from the wall, landing no more than a few feet from me. It scared me so bad I tumbled backward.

He staggered toward me, fingers outstretched like claws, and I knew I didn't stand a chance. Cricket growled, ready to protect me. Mr. Carnivolly yanked a cow-bone mask from the wall and flung it at him, hitting my dog right in the face.

"Cricket!" I hollered, and he lay whimpering, dazed.

Mr. Carnivolly lunged at me. I had a tiny bit of burning feather left and I shoved it into Mr. Carnivolly's face. He screamed and scrambled backward, cowering in the corner on all fours.

I whipped out a piece of chalk and sketched a ritual circle around myself, but not quite finishing it, leaving about a foot of it wide open, chanting under my breath all the while. I motioned for Cricket to come join me inside, and he did. He was hurt, but not too badly. We were going to make it. We could do this.

I opened the *Book of Common Rites*, and I began the invocation, calling on the One Who Listens for aid.

"Hear ye, One Who Listens," I said. "Hearken your ears

to our prayers. We are lost and alone on this world, and we wander. Send your light to guide us, send your stars and moon to show the way. Send your sun to burn the land clean and your rain to fill it up again. We thank thee for the light. Always for the light."

So far so good. Next I had to chant a Mystery, and I began with my best intentions.

But a strange sound came from the room then, as if it was whistling up from beneath the house. It was a kind of whirlwind noise, like a twister was coming, like the big wind was swooping itself through the living room. My candle flickered, and its glow seemed to shrink and diminish, and the edges of the room vanished into gloom. I heard singing, voices like a choir of children. I saw the corn-husk dolls staring at me with their black eyes, and I knew it must be them, their voices high and warbly. The marionettes began clapping their little wooden hands together, swaying on their strings. Wind whistled through the mouths of the deer and antelope skulls; cabinet doors banged themselves open and shut. Doors slammed themselves with cracks like gunfire, and books leaped from their shelves and went scuttling across the floor like spiders. The walls complained, whispering back all the secrets they'd ever overheard. I saw a white shape shudder past, translucent as moonlight, the ghosts of this old land buried deep beneath the clay. Louder sang the corn-husk dolls, their black eyes staring back at me, a chorus of children's voices whirling through the tongue-less bones of the animal skulls, the wooden clacking of the marionettes.

This was not good. This was very, very not good.

I continued the Rite, placing the candle at the head of the circle, clearing my mind of all but my best intentions. As I spoke, the whirlwind sound got louder, the dolls' singing bouncing around the room, ringing so loud I could hardly hear myself. I shut my eyes and clamped my hands over my ears and shouted my invitation. "Come, darkness," I hollered, "come face the burning candle of pure light!"

Only then did I open my eyes. Mr. Carnivolly was there, just outside the circle, growling at me like a wolf.

"Go, Cricket!" I said.

Cricket sprang from the ritual circle and clamped his teeth around Mr. Carnivolly's pants cuff, dragging him into the circle. I jumped backward and finished the last foot of chalk line just as Cricket leaped outside. Mr. Carnivolly was trapped in the ritual circle now, and he wasn't going anywhere. I shook a bone rattle at him and chanted a Mystery, one that should have calmed him, that should have made him still and silent as a sleeping baby. But he just snapped his teeth at me and paced inside the circle like a caged animal. At least the circle held. That was something. What was I supposed to do now?

Well, if nothing else seems to work, there's always music.

I picked up my fiddle and began to play a dirge called "The Seamaiden's Lament." It's about a woman sailor who is the captain of her own ship, and she sails from island to island, country to country, trying to find anything that can be truly hers and hers alone. But every sunset belongs to the sea, and the moonlight and starlight glimmer off the scales of the fish that leap from the water. Every flower she finds shares its petals with the sunlight and its roots with the soil, and even the clouds pour their rain down on all the undeserving earth. She finds that nothing can be hers alone. In despair, she thinks of a song, a perfect melody of power and darkness and light, and she holds it in her mouth like a coin. A song of her very own, one she'll never play for anyone, that she'll never share with the world. And she carries that song to her grave. I don't know why that's the one I picked to play, but something in me wanted to hear that one, something in me felt that it was right.

A blue light seemed to shimmer in the room. Mr. Carnivolly staggered away, hands over his ears, the light flickering in his eyes. He stumbled backward and fell to the floor.

I moved the candle by his head and waved the half-burnt cardinal feather over him while he thrashed and moaned, his eyes still glimmering blue. I chanted the Mystery again, with Cricket howling along over me. Mr. Carnivolly hollered out, and a great big plume of black smoke billowed from his mouth. He lay limp on the floor, gasping for air.

But the Great Doom wasn't done yet. It swooped through the room, a black buzzing cloud of anger and disgust. I chanted louder, the whirlwind sound so loud it hurt my ears.

"Be gone already!" I hollered.

The black cloud swooped down into Cricket's mouth. My dog lifted up off the ground, his legs kicking and spasming, thrashing back and forth in the air. He was higher than my head, all the way to the ceiling.

Then he fell.

His body slammed into the ground, and he lay there whimpering in pain. His mouth filled up with white foam, and his tongue hung out like a great black slug.

I didn't know what to do. There aren't any Rites for cleansing animals, not from something like this. Or if there were, I didn't know any. Where was Grandpa Widow? What was I supposed to do? Mr. Carnivolly just lay there useless on the ground. There was nobody to help me.

Cricket was barely breathing. I put my head on his chest, and his heartbeat was just a little murmur. I didn't know why he was reacting this way to infection. Maybe dogs are different. Maybe they are just so purehearted they reject the control of the Great Doom, like they'd rather die than be taken over by such a powerful evil. I didn't know, but if something wasn't done fast, Cricket was going to die.

"Please!" I shouted. "Somebody help me! Somebody save my dog!"

A voice cut through the darkness, one I'd come to know very well. It was singing, a high and lovely thing, a sound that pierced the darkness like starlight.

The voice was Angeline's, and she stepped into the candlelight, her eyes shining in the glimmer.

"What are you doing here?" I said.

"I came to help."

Angeline went back to singing, and she came closer to where Cricket lay. She kneeled before him and held out her hands, like she was some high priestess blessing him, a Mystery woman of the most sacred Order of Protectors, ones I'd only read about.

The song seemed to calm Cricket. He stopped jerking, and the foam settled in his mouth. I watched his chest rise and fall in shallow little breaths, and I was afraid he was dying.

"Don't be scared," said Angeline. "Just take up your fiddle. Play what I'm singing, just do it with your fiddle and your best intention."

"How do you know what to do?"

"I'll explain later," she said. "Just follow my lead."

I didn't understand that at all, but I didn't have any other choice. I began to play along with her while Cricket lay limp on the floor, and something strange happened. It was like my mind flooded with starlight, like in my heart I could hear the moon itself singing its light down in a blessing upon me, like the One Who Listens wasn't just some giant invisible ear in the sky, but a being and a mind and a heart, and in that music it lowered its hand to me and laid it on my shoulder.

I wasn't alone anymore, is what I'm saying; I wasn't hopeless or afraid. Angeline's song gave me courage, and the sound itself was magic. When her voice and my fiddle sang together, twining around that melody, I felt a joy and a power I'd never experienced before. My heart cracked open, and I understood for the first time that what gives the Rites power was the same thing that lay hidden in my own heart, that kept my blood pumping and my mind alive. It was the love of Grandpa Widow and Cricket, my affection for the villagers, the lonesome coyote howl in the desert. I can't explain it, not really, but in that moment I was a part of everything, and everything was a part of me, all throughout time, all throughout the world.

One day others will sing this song, I thought. *One day this will be a Rite known the world over.*

The darkness rose up out of Cricket's mouth like a flock of black bees and crashed through the window, swooping out into the night.

The gloom lifted. The candle flame cast light across the whole room. Mr. Carnivolly sat up, rubbing his head, and Cricket leaped up and licked my face all over. Connor and Mrs. Carnivolly came running into the room, and they pounced on Mr. Carnivolly, burying him in hugs. They were such a happy family, all together like that. Everything had turned out okay.

But then I saw Angeline, standing there with the strangest smile on her face, like she was happy, but hurting too, and I remembered that she was a liar, that she had lied to me about where she had come from. How did she know how to cure Cricket? What else was she not telling me? I wondered how seeing Connor with his family made Angeline feel. I wondered if she had a family at all.

Angeline saw me staring at her and the smile fell right off her face, like she knew exactly what I was thinking. She started backing away from me, but I grabbed her by the wrist.

"How did you do that?" I said. "Who are you?"

Angeline let her hair fall over her face, so I couldn't see her eyes anymore, I couldn't tell what she was thinking. But I held on tight to her and pulled her toward me.

"I know you lied about your family," I said. "I know they aren't lost out there in the desert. Who are you? Why did you come here? How do you know so much about magic?"

Right then Mayor Benningsley burst into the Carnivolly house, thudding his way across the floor like he owned the place. My word, the rich and how they treat every patch of ground they walk on like it was their own personal property! It's enough to drive a body crazy, it surely is.

"Gussy, I need to have a word with you," he said.

"Not now," I said. "I'm busy. As you can obviously tell."

"Yes, *now*," he said, and clamped his hand on my shoulder so hard it hurt. Angeline jerked away from me and went running from the room.

"Wait!" I hollered, but it was too late. I watched her disappear out the front door.

Cricket crouched by me, growling soft and low, but I signaled to him to keep quiet.

"Who was that girl?" said Mayor Benningsley.

"That's what I was trying to figure out," I said. *Before you came busting up in here like some kind of deranged mule and interrupted me.* That's what I wanted to say, but I held my tongue.

Mayor Benningsley frowned at me.

"Well, that's not the kind of thing that inspires confidence," he said. "You're supposed to be our Protector, and not only have there been three infections in the village so far, strangers are running around uninhibited in spaces the Great Doom has touched. This simply cannot stand, Gussy."

"Listen here," I said. "I'm the one risking my neck trying to protect everybody. I'm doing the best I can."

"Pardon me, but I don't recall you being the one infected by the Great Doom," said Mayor Benningsley, wagging his finger in my face. "Mr. Carnivolly here could have died."

"You hush up," said Connor, walking over to us. "Gussy here saved my daddy's life."

"Have you considered, you impudent little brat," said Mayor Benningsley, "that your father's life wouldn't have been in danger at all if Gussy had actually done her job in the first place?"

"That's not true," said Connor, clearly taken aback at being scolded by the so-called mayor. "She is doing her job."

"Thank you, Connor," I said, "but I don't need you sticking up for me. I can manage quite fine myself." I turned back to Mayor Benningsley. "And I don't answer to you either. So back up and let me out of here, so I can finish the Rites and do my job."

I yanked my shoulder free of Mayor Benningsley's hand, and I marched myself right out of the Carnivolly house, Cricket by my side.

I was not, however, prepared for what was waiting on me outside.

A crowd of villagers, all of them people I knew and had devoted my life to helping, were gathered around the Carnivolly doorway. I didn't know how they'd heard about the infection, but somehow word had traveled fast. All those scared and angry faces, screaming at me. I knew I had let them down. It was the worst feeling I ever felt in my life.

I raised my hands to calm everybody, same as Grandpa Widow would, and then I tried to figure out what to say.

The villagers looked at me and I looked right back at them. I was sweating something fierce under my robes. I cleared my throat and spoke.

"The situation is under control," I said, which wasn't even really true. This particular situation was under control, sure, but I still didn't know how the Great Doom had gotten inside the village, or why it kept happening. But there was no way I could tell the villagers that.

In the front row, there was Mr. Alvarez the cooper and Ms. Orlean the chemist and Mr. Showalter the schoolmaster and Leonidas Tucker who didn't seem to do much of anything at all. All the way back were folks I'd spent my whole life trying to take care of, staring at me with nothing but anger in their eyes.

"How could you let this happen?" hollered Mr. Gargantua the cowboy.

"What kind of danger have you put us in?" said Samantha Mulberry, the fanciest lady in town.

"I didn't put any of you in any danger, and that's a fact," I said. "I'm getting to the bottom of this, I promise you that."

I sounded ridiculous, I knew that. It was just a jumble of words that didn't mean much, that couldn't offer any real comfort to these folks. It broke my heart to talk to them like that, to lie to them like they were idiots. But I had to do my best. I had to try.

"What about that little girl that came running out ahead

of you?" said Sylvana Plainclothes, the meanest geezer I ever met. "Did she do this?"

"Was it her, Gussy?" shouted someone else, so many voices I could hardly keep up. "Did she let the Great Doom in?"

"Everybody needs to quiet down a minute!" I said. "Don't you worry about that girl. She is an innocent who got lost in the storm. Don't you go bothering her."

I was lying to them, though, just as Angeline had lied to me. What did I owe these people anyway? It was so hard to be a good Protector. I'd never known, never understood for a moment, all the trouble Grandpa Widow had to deal with. Performing the Rites was a piece of cake compared to dealing with a bunch of angry villagers, and that was the truth.

"She's lying!" boomed a voice. It was Mayor Benningsley, snuck up behind me. "She's lying and she knows it. That young girl you were asking about, come running through here a second ago? She didn't come in the morning after the storm, no sir. That girl came in the middle of the storm."

A gasp rose up from the crowd.

"It's a fact," said Mayor Benningsley. "A certain Rider told me herself not one hour ago. Gussy here opened the gates in the middle of the night, during the worst storm in a decade. She broke the cardinal rule of the whole village, betraying her most sacred duties as Protector."

"Is it true?" said Connor Carnivolly, who was standing by the doorframe, watching us.

"Yeah," I said. "Yeah, it's true."

The crowd erupted then, everybody hollering and screaming at me, calling me a fraud, calling me worthless, telling me I was reckless with the village and bad at my job. Telling me how this never would have happened if Grandpa Widow were here. For a moment I thought they were going to scoop me up and toss me out into the desert this very second, banish me into the wilderness for good to account for my sins. I supposed I deserved it.

"Listen," I said, "that isn't how the Great Doom got in."

"Oh yeah?" said Mayor Benningsley. "Then how did it get in?"

I thought about Mr. Mayella and Lulu Benningsley and Lazlo Dunes and the Sigil of Discord on the wall and all the other strange things I'd seen the last few days.

"I . . . I'm not rightly sure," I said.

"Hah!" hollered the one voice I most did not want to hear right now, that of Lazlo Dunes himself. "This child does not have a clue about which she speaks, and that's the truth of the matter."

Right then I thought about blaming this whole thing on him—the infection, the Great Doom, all of it. I could do that, I realized. I could pin the whole thing on Lazlo Dunes, and the villagers would believe it. It sure would make my life a lot easier, get all these folks off my back. But no, that wasn't right. A Protector protects everybody, and that included

Lazlo Dunes. I couldn't blame it on him without proof, and so far all the evidence I had was merely circumstantial.

"You can't protect this village," said Lazlo, clanging toward me with his rattling plate. "No one can. It sowed the seeds of its own destruction long ago, before you ever set foot inside these walls. And there's nothing you can do to stop it."

"We'll see about that," I said.

"Oh yes, we will," he said, laughing, cackling his head off. "The reckoning is at hand! You can't stop it! It's already begun!"

The villagers erupted in hollers and screams again, accusations flung at me like rotten old fruit. I hopped up and down and waved my arms until they got quiet again.

"Listen," I said, "regardless of whether or not you all think this mess is my fault, one fact remains. If you want this village safe, then you need to disperse right now, and let me go about finishing the Rites. Those are the only things that can protect this village, and already we're losing daylight. It's too late for Midday Salutations, and if I'm going to do a thorough job of Last Lights, I best get back to work. So if you'll excuse me."

Mr. Demetrius the chessmaster stood in my way, as if to stop me. I looked up at him square in the eyes, aware of Cricket by my side.

"You got something you want to say to me, Mr. Demetrius?" I said, and I turned my fiercest scowl on him.

I met his eyes, and they were full of meanness. But you know what? My eyes were meaner, and that's just a fact. When it comes to staring contests, I can outmean anybody in the whole Darkling Valley, you better believe it.

Mr. Demetrius's face softened. "No, Gussy."

"Then step out of my way," I said.

I walked myself through that crowd, my head held high, my hands shaking so bad I nearly dropped my rucksack.

I went straight back to the Rectory and had myself a good cry. Sometimes you just can't help it. All the fear and worry come pouring out of your eyeballs and you just lay on the floor and moan a while. There's nothing wrong with crying, and that's just a fact. Plus, I had a warm dog to cuddle with and make me feel better.

I gave myself all of fifteen minutes. Then I wiped the tears from my cheeks, picked myself up, and got right back to work.

Whether they liked it or not, the village did depend on me. Even if this was it, my last days ever being their Protector, the fact was I was all they had.

I spent the rest of the day finishing the Rites and searching for Angeline. I fortified the cardinal feathers, rehung the Book of Names, and finally tracked down a safely dead chicken whose foot I could bury, but I couldn't find Angeline anywhere. Not even Cricket could sniff her out. It was strange, you know? I was so thankful to her for saving Cricket's life, but I was also angry at her for lying to me about her family. Mostly I was worried. Where had she gone? Hopefully not the desert. I didn't want to imagine her back out there all on her own. Besides, I hadn't meant to scare her away like I did, asking her about her family. I should have hugged her and told her how grateful I was. I should have handled every single bit of this day differently.

By the end of Last Lights, I was so low down and disappointed with myself I could have just curled up in a ball and slept the rest of my life away. I could have just found a cave somewhere and crawled up inside. Nobody bother me, villagers, I'm just going to hide away forever.

I decided to make one more sweep through the village just as the sun went down to see if I could find Angeline.

It was strange to wander the village at dusk, the final glimmers of light casting everything in haze and shadow, knowing everybody hated me now. I felt eyes watching me from the windows all suspicious like, eyeballs stuck in the faces of people I once called my friends. Disappointment trailed me like a shadow. It weighed on my shoulders like some lumpy invisible devil. I couldn't believe the way I had failed them, how quickly they turned on me.

Didn't they see I was doing my best? That I was out here every day busting my back trying to keep them safe? Didn't it matter to them that I'd been nearly strangled by infected clothes, or barked at by a grown man climbing on a wall? I was liable to have nightmares about Mr. Carnivolly for the rest of my life. And what kind of thanks did I get? Nothing but angry glares and a lack of faith. It made me downright indignant. I passed Alonzo Atticus's periodical reading room and he slammed the door in my face. It wasn't like I wanted to hop inside and scan the books at this hour, but it would have been nice to sit a spell. Mr. Atticus usually even offered me a glass of milk, which I tended to turn down, but the offer was always nice. Good lord, I bet even my only pal Connor Carnivolly hated me too, now that he thought it was my fault his daddy got infected. It was a miserable night setting in over the village, and that was the truth of it.

Cricket came running back up to me, and for a second I figured he'd caught a whiff of Angeline. But my dog just shook his head forlorn at me, and I knew the search was useless. If Cricket's nose failed us, then I didn't know how my eyeballs could do any better. Angeline had probably performed a hiding ritual or something like that so we couldn't find her. Not a bad idea. Maybe I ought to do something like that, leave all these villagers in a lurch, see how they liked it. Yeah, they'd wish I was back if they had to deal with an infection on their own, you better believe that. They'd come running up to the Rectory, pounding on the door, begging me to come and save them, oh, please, Gussy, we're so sorry, won't you come back and help us? Wouldn't that be a sight to see? I grinned in my hood, my first real smile of the day.

I was just about to turn myself around and head home when I saw Mayor Benningsley skulking down an alley. He had his coat on despite the heat, and his collar turned up over his face and a wide-brimmed hat pulled low, as if he were in disguise. What in the world was he up to?

I decided to follow him and find out.

Mayor Benningsley walked his own swift way through the village, cutting between shops and houses, any narrow place where the shadows were thick. I figured he really must be up to something no good to be hiding himself like that. He usually walked so pompous and upright through the center of every street and boardwalk like he owned the place, like every road in the village was built just for him. It made me feel good, just a little bit, to see him walking all spooked and suspicious, like he was some kind of criminal, like he had a secret to hide. I followed him past Mr. Chen's place and behind the Abednegos' cottage, behind the Wilders' chicken coop and past the Clanking Bones Cemetery, where people used to get buried in the olden times, all the way to Old Esmerelda's, where he stopped dead still, like he could tell something was off, like he knew he was being watched.

I crouched myself behind a wheelless wagon somebody'd left out in the street and huddled into a ball, hoping the darkness and shadows were enough to keep me hidden. I kept my eyes on him through a hole in the wood. I watched as Mayor Benningsley looked to his left and to his right before ducking inside the front door. I tiptoed myself down the side of the building and peeked in through the window. There he stood with the tiny man in the tweed suit, the one who I saw at the Benningsley mansion stepping out of that black carriage with his metal box. They headed toward the parlor room, talking close, with Mayor Benningsley bent down low enough to speak into the tiny man's ear. I headed to the front door. If I couldn't follow them into the parlor room without being seen, at the very least I might bump into that Rider who'd betrayed me to Mayor Benningsley. I had a word or two for her, no doubt about it.

"Where do you think you're going?" said a girl's voice.

It was Lulu Benningsley. Of all people, on this wretched endless day, why did it have to be her?

"You're always snooping around my daddy," she said. "What is it you think you're going to find? Or are you just jealous that I have a daddy, and a rich one at that? Isn't that all you want, really? To be me? To have a family like mine?"

I rolled my eyes at her, not that she could see it in the dark.

"If you were half as smart as you are arrogant, you might be worth the time I'm wasting talking to you," I said. Lulu looked a bit hurt at that, and for just a second I felt bad. I guess I'd never considered that a girl as mean as Lulu had any feelings at all. "For your information, I want to know who that man in the tweed suit is. You know, the one your daddy's always talking to? I got a duty to protect this village, and I need to know who all is coming and going."

"That a fact?" she said, all her haughtiness come back in full force. "Well, you're doing an awful poor job of it, I'd say."

"Yeah, you and everybody else."

Lulu just shrugged. I was about to tell her off when I noticed that Lulu wasn't acting like her usual sneering, domineering self. Her shoulders slumped a little, and her face in the moonlight was all red and tear streaked. That magic opal ring of hers shimmered a melancholy blue.

"You okay?" I said.

"Why wouldn't I be?" she said, a little bit of the old snark come back. I knew sadness when I saw it, and Lulu's heart was all busted up. I didn't know what to say. We stood there a little awkwardly, a few gray clouds like rabbits hopping across the moon.

"You looking for that girl?" said Lulu. "The one you let in against the rules?"

"Why?" I said. "You seen her anywhere?"

"If I had, I'd bust her skull," said Lulu. "Putting us all in danger. Especially in a time like this."

"You and your daddy both said that same thing to me, 'in a time like this.' What's so special about this time?"

Lulu shook her head. "For somebody who's supposed to be in charge, you sure don't seem to know a lot about what goes on around here."

The moon scooted out from behind a cloud and cast its light over the both of us. Two girls outside in the dark of the empty village, the moonlight so bright our shadows were tall and long as giants. It suddenly felt like me and Lulu were the only two folks on earth.

"Why don't you tell me?" I said.

"Because," said Lulu, her eyes bright with tears, "I can't. I can't say a word."

And she turned to leave.

"Lulu," I said. "Wait!"

Lulu stopped a minute, starlight shimmering all over her.

"If I see that girl," said Lulu, her back still to me, "I'll be sure and send her your way."

And she ran off into the darkness, back toward her mansion. She seemed to me the loneliest, saddest girl on earth.

I took one look back in the window of Old Esmerelda's, but I didn't see Mayor Benningsley or the Rider or the man in the tweed suit anywhere, and it wouldn't do for me to go busting up into the parlor room just to eavesdrop. I didn't have a clue what to do.

I walked around a few more alleys, back to hunting Angeline, but I didn't have much heart left in it. This day had totally worn me out. All I wanted was a plate of hot cornbread and about a zillion hours of sleep. Right as I was about to call it a night, I saw weird Mr. Mayella come bustling up all frantic. He wasn't wearing his hat, and his normally perfect hair was wild and sticking up all over his head. His eyes were bloodshot and he had stubble on his chin. I'd never seen the man look so disheveled, and it scared me a little bit. He ran up and grabbed me by the shoulders, his long fingers clutching me a bit too tight.

"Gustavina," he said, his voice all high and scratchy, "where is the Rider?"

I shook myself free of him and gave him a stare to wilt daisies. Nobody lays hands on me like that, not if they know what's good for them.

"You mean the one who sold me out?" I said. "How should I know?"

"If you know anything about her whereabouts, it is imperative that you tell me now."

"Haven't seen hide nor hair of her," I said, "not since earlier today. Turns out she talked to Mayor Benningsley, gabbing all my secrets. I could wring her neck."

His eyes got big and those eyebrows seemed to spring right off his forehead. "The Rider met with Mayor Benningsley? When?"

"Yeah," I said, a little confused. "According to him, anyhow. Why? What's the matter?"

"I have to go. Stay inside tonight, Gustavina. Lock your doors tight."

And he hustled off into the darkness, his pointy shoes clacking on the boardwalk. What was that all about? Had the whole village lost its mind?

A few minutes later, I met Cricket back at the meeting pole. There was no sign of Angeline. I looked toward the wall, and the desert blackness beyond. The stars were millions of silver coins cast into the sky. I hoped Angeline was safe out there. I hoped all that shimmer and sparkle rained down in blessings on her, even if she was a liar. I didn't know what to do, all these questions hopping around like grasshoppers in my skull.

Right then the sky lit up, a big red burning thing streaking across the dark. Grandpa Widow called those meteors, and he said they swooped in from far-off planets, stars so distant we didn't even have names for them yet. Never before had I seen one so big. It cut a red arc through the sky, a split in the great blackness up for all the light to leak out. It was an omen, it was, a sign. A good omen or a bad one, that I didn't know.

What would tonight bring, and would I be ready for it?

"Come on, Cricket," I said, and the two of us made our way back to the Rectory.

I had one more dream, the last before it all went wrong.

I was a baby, a wet, squawling, terrified little bundle of rags perched on a rock, screaming my head off. I was cold, I knew that, and I could feel terror too, grasping my tiny fingers at the air, as if I could snatch the wind and spray everywhere and take hold, be carried off to safety like all those pretty birds up there, swooping in their white arcs. But I was just a baby, I couldn't save myself, I couldn't crawl, I couldn't do much of anything at all.

It all felt so new to me, everything—the booming of the thunder, the wild shrieks of wind, the hot sizzling purple streaks of lightning in the sky. I saw a massive funnel rise up out of the water, a gray thing like a giant swiveling and dancing across the surface of the sea. I heard the cracking of a ship broken in half, its mast shattering in the waves. I heard the screams of folks swimming for safety, the terror in their voices, the gasps as they dragged themselves onto land. I was in the middle of a maelstrom, more sound and light than ever I'd seen before.

And suddenly it was like I could see through the clouds,

into the black depths of the sky, the sea inverted, the moon and stars and sky all impossibly immense, an ocean of emptiness dotted by stars that bloomed like white-hot flowers in the abyss. It was beautiful, this world, all of it, and I was seeing it for the first time, breathing the sea-sharp air, peppered by the spray. And though I was hungry and cold and shivering and feverish, that great rush of the universe swarming my senses was grand and powerful. I realized I was in the world now, and it was a place of wonder and joy and awe.

Me, as a little baby abandoned in a shipwreck on the rocks, despite all that, I tilted my head back and laughed.

I was in the world, and it was beautiful.

17

I AWOKE TO CRICKET BARKING AND yowling at some kind of clamor going on outside. I threw my robes on and hustled into the night. The moon was out and bright, casting a blue glow to the world, a shimmering softness covering everything, and the stars were the silver mouths of angels up in the sky. I heard voices in the distance, the sound of people marching through the streets, gathering for some purpose. Cricket howled out a big question to the moon and beyond, all the way to the One Who Listens, a mournful prayer.

That's when I noticed something that shuddered me down to my bones.

The village gates were open in the middle of the night,

the long empty desert spread out blue and sparkling as the ocean in my dreams.

How was this even possible?

I ran toward the gates and saw Big Gordo sprawled out facedown in the dust. He looked dead, crumpled in a heap, like someone had just tossed him there. I ran to where he lay and bent down to him and shook him as hard as I could.

"Come on, Big Gordo," I said. "You got to wake up."

He groaned a little and I was so happy I fell right over. I was scared he'd be a goner. I was scared somebody had killed Big Gordo while I slept inside the Rectory all useless. Big Gordo sat up and held his head, like it hurt him. He looked around confused-like, as if he were in the middle of some strange dream, adrift on a clutter of wreckage in the midnight sea.

"What happened?" I said.

"It was the Rider," he said. "She put some kind of hex on me."

"The Rider?" I said. "Why would she do that?"

"I don't know," he said. "It was like she had magic, like she was a witch. She . . . oh, Gussy, she opened the gates."

He stood up as if to go close them, and stumbled back to the dust.

"You just rest up," I said. "I'll get those gates closed."

So the Rider was a witch, and an awful powerful one at

that. I really had failed the village if I couldn't even tell a messenger from a witch. But still, she had fooled Grandpa Widow too. I just didn't understand how any of this could have happened.

Connor Carnivolly came running toward us, his eyes wide and terrified.

"Gussy!" he hollered. "Something's wrong with the village. There's some kind of magic here, a spell cast over the place. Can't you feel it? Can't you feel the grim crawling all over your skin?"

This was more than I knew what to do with. I started breathing too hard and my vision got spotty. I had to get ahold of myself. "One step at a time, Gussy," I heard Grandpa Widow's voice echoing in my head. "Fix what you can, in order of importance. Stay calm, and show that you're in control."

"Connor, can you help me get these gates shut?"

"I'll do my best," he said.

"I can help," said Big Gordo. He rose unsteadily to his feet, and for a second I thought he might topple right back over. But Big Gordo shook his head and stood up tall. "I got this, Gussy. It's my job."

The three of us made our way to the gates and together began drawing them closed. We had them nearly shut when I heard the sound of a great wind, that horrible rushing noise like a twister come blowing through the village. The gates burst open, knocking me and Connor and Gordo back as a whoosh of wind roared through. They splintered and shattered, cracking open. The moon was darkened in the sky, and one by one the stars went out. A shadow fell over the village, the air grown cold. Cricket reared back and howled, the gloom swallowing his voice, making it no more than a squeak from a puppy.

I could feel the terror creep in, the darkness clutching my heart.

It had finally come, in full force. All of our protections, all my work on the Rites, was now for naught.

The Great Doom had breached the gates, and there was nothing we could do to stop it. All my training—my whole life's work—had come to nothing. I'd failed them, each and every last villager. I'd failed Grandpa Widow. I'd even failed myself.

I heard a cry rise up from the village square.

I ran toward it, Connor and Big Gordo fast on my heels. The darkness was so thick it was like a fog. I could barely see my hand in front of my face.

Lazlo Dunes and his cronies were cowering around the meeting pole, torches in their hands.

"Gustavina!" shouted Lazlo Dunes. "I told you it was coming, did I not? I warned you, and now it's too late."

The villagers were coming out of their houses then, sleepy eyed, to a world slathered in gloom.

"What is it?" said Polly Odongo the toymaker. "What has happened?"

"The darkness has come," said Lazlo Dunes. "And we are not prepared."

That was when I saw her.

The Rider stood in front of the Benningsley mansion, her arms outstretched, hollering curses at all the protections Grandpa Widow had built over the place. Her hair shot up wild around her like lightning bolts, and shadows danced off her fingers. She roared in a voice as low and deep as the earth, shuddering the ground beneath me, chanting in some strange language that I'd never heard. The walls of the Benningsley mansion creaked and groaned, crying out into the storming darkness.

Without looking back, she called to me.

"Does the little Protector come to see my triumph?" The Rider let out a cackle that shivered my heart. "It's too late, you know. The Rites are broken. The gates have shattered, and the Great Doom roams the village freely. You failed, Gussy."

"I'm not done yet," I said.

A flicker of blue lightning traced the scars on the Rider's face.

"You don't even know what you have here, do you? The nature of that treasure locked in the rich fool's house? You never even wondered. You just did your duties, Grandpa

Widow's mindless little minion. For this alone you don't deserve what power is hidden in this village. No, the spoils must belong only to the worthy. And no one is worthier than I, little Protector. Not in the entire Darkling Valley and beyond."

Power crackled from her skin like electricity, and I was afraid.

"Who are you?" I said.

The Rider grinned at me, her eyes fierce in the lightning's glow.

"You mean you don't know? Why, I am the thing you have always feared most," she said. "I am chaos unleashed, born of a falling star and a cold desert stream, a wolf's howl and the flutter of a bat's wing. I am a sorceress so mighty not even your Grandpa Widow could stop me. My name is Lucinda Withern, and I will grind your village and its people into dust!"

I made a holy sign over my heart and spat three times in the dust. Lucinda Withern, a name that had terrified me ever since I was a little kid. How could someone like her have snuck into our village undetected? How had Grandpa Widow not known the moment she handed him the letter? How could I not have sensed the power rippling out from her as I sat across from her at Old Esmerelda's? Some kind of Protector I was. Our destroyer waltzed right in through the front gates, and I didn't hardly notice. I guess it was true then, and Grandpa Widow had been wrong. I wasn't worthy to guard this village and its people. I had already failed them all.

"And now," she said, "little Protector, you will see me in all my glory, as I was born to be."

But then a strange thing happened. The laughter seemed to die on Lucinda Withern's lips, and her body did a kind of involuntary shudder.

"No," she said. "Not yet. This cannot happen. Not when I'm so close."

Lucinda Withern's arms went stiff, her eyes burning a bright blue. A kind of billowing darkness rose from the ground and swaddled her up, and she rose into the sky, swallowed by the clouds lit alive and pink and brain-like by lightning.

The ground beneath the village shook, knocking me to the dust. Shutters clacked open and windows exploded, doors swinging themselves shut. All the village dogs began to howl, and the chickens squawked in their coops. Darkness swirled around us—it seemed alive, a creature made of shadow and smoke. Yellow eyes stared at me from alleyways like watchful angels, or maybe demons, who could tell now? The sky shuddered, lightning falling down in streaks.

I turned to Lazlo Dunes.

"Did you do this?" I said. "Are you working with the Rider?"

"I have not seen or known that woman until this very day," said Lazlo Dunes, his eyebrows raised. "I knew our destruction would come, but I did not know what form it would take."

A bolt of lightning fell from the sky, striking the meeting pole. Sparks shot from the wood, splintering it. The Book of Names burst into flames, the pages catching and rising like birds in flight. The ground shook again, and Lazlo Dunes fell to his knees. Buildings cracked and groaned, and the roof fell in on Mercy Montague's shack. People began to scream, to panic in the streets.

"Get back inside!" I shouted. "Lock your doors! Light a Candle of Protection in every window!"

"You're still trying to save this place, aren't you?" said Lazlo Dunes.

"Of course I am," I said. "It's my job."

"Gussy," said Connor Carnivolly. "Look."

Outside the gates of the village, off in the desert, there loomed a twister bigger than any I'd ever seen before, lit alive by fire. It didn't move, it wasn't barreling down at us, determined to rip the village to pieces. It twirled in place like a ballerina dancer, a whirling burning gyre so bright in that pitch-black I had to squint to look at it.

"What is it?" said Connor.

"I . . . I don't rightly know," I said.

"It's so angry," said Big Gordo. "Can't you feel it? Doesn't it make your very hair stand on end?"

Lazlo Dunes gazed up at the twister, his eyes glistening in the firelight. The look on his face wasn't terror—it was awe, joy even. He really did want the village destroyed. I realized he wasn't kidding. This was the best day of Lazlo Dunes's whole life.

"Gussy," said Connor Carnivolly, "I'm scared."

"Me too."

For the first time, I had to be completely honest with somebody about it. I was in way over my head now, it was just a fact.

"So what do we do?" said Big Gordo.

"You two go back home," I said. "I'll figure something out."

"But I can help!" said Connor.

"Your responsibility is to your family," I said. "I know they're worried sick about you."

"Gussy . . ."

"I said go home!" I shouted, the fire of the meeting pole hot on my face. "Go home now, and I will send for you when I need your help. I promise you that."

"Okay," he said, turning away from me, and I could tell I'd hurt his feelings. Big Gordo too. He cast me a worried look and loped along after Connor. But there was nothing I could do about hurt feelings now. The only thing that mattered was keeping everyone safe. I had to get to the Rectory and figure out some kind of plan. Cricket let loose a long howl, and Lazlo Dunes hobbled toward the burning meeting pole, calling out to all the people in the streets.

"The Reckoning is upon us," he hollered, "just as I said it would be! And you laughed at me! Gather round, children, and repent! Repent before it's too late!"

I watched folks gather round him like he was some kind of prophet, as the Great Doom fell upon the village, cloaking it in darkness.

And all the while that twister burned in the desert in a crackling column of fire, our final destruction lingering just outside the gates, as if waiting for some diabolical purpose that I did not know or understand.

18

I KEPT THE RECTORY SHUTTERS CLOSED and the door double locked and the room candlelit and quiet. No fire would burn in my hearth, no fiddle music would play to dispel the darkness. The Great Doom covered everything, a darkness deeper than darkness, a shadow no light could penetrate. It was a feeling too, a gloom, a despair so complete it was hard to raise yourself out of a chair, much less pore through ancient Rites book after ancient Rites book, trying to find any ritual strong enough to put a dent in it. Even Cricket lay tongue out and whimpering, curled in his little bed on the floor. I flipped page after page, tossed leather-bound volumes and unwound scrolls in a pile on the floor, finding nothing that would help, nothing that could puncture a dark so complete.

Where oh where was Grandpa . . .

No, I wasn't going to ask for Grandpa Widow anymore. It was useless, and he was gone. This was all up to me now. I'd let the villagers down three times now, and it wasn't going to happen again. The answer had to be somewhere in Grandpa Widow's library, in some book I hadn't read yet, some obscure ritual to vanish the Great Doom forever. It just had to be here somewhere, if only I could find it.

A loud boom shivered the walls, sending dust and splintered wood cascading down from the ceiling. The Great Doom sure was doing its best to barge its way inside the Rectory. Good thing that wasn't happening, not with all the Rites of Protection that Grandpa Widow had set up in here. It'd have to be one sly hex to slip its way past these doors, ritually guarded as they were, with cardinal feathers and sigils and chicken feet and salt lines and Holy Dioramas in little glass jars buried under the floor. The Holy Dioramas were my favorite things to make when I was a little kid, and sometimes I used to sell them in the market when I'd made too many. They're little scenes from the lives of saints, with figures made out of clay I baked myself in the fire. I have a tiny shelf of them in Grandpa Widow's workshop. He's so proud of them, even though I guess they aren't very good. You have Seer Horatio and Paladin Ludovico and my very favorite Protector of all, Saint Petunia the Bold, squaring off against the devils and demons of their day, performing their miracles and rituals, staving off the wickedness so the rest of us could live in peace. I wished I had the power of any one of those old-timers with me. I bet they would know what to do.

Oh, hush, Gussy. If a saint or a holy seer was here, they wouldn't have let any of this mess happen in the first place. I looked at the chaos I was making of Grandpa Widow's library, volume after volume chucked in a pile on the floor, my head throbbing with the effort it took just to keep searching, to not give in to the misery and despair scratching at the door like a hungry kitten, begging to be let inside. This was hopeless, and I knew it. The village was too far gone for me to save it, even with all the rituals and Rites and knowledge I had bouncing around in my brain. None of it was any use against a force as strong and powerful as the Great Doom.

I clutched a cardinal feather in my fist and said a silent prayer to the One Who Listens. Maybe at least my intentions could pierce the heavy dark clouds of the Great Doom and make it up to the heavenlies. It was my last hope.

You know what I prayed? Just one word.

Please.

It was the only thing I had left.

A knock sounded at the door. I was suspicious, lest it be the Great Doom somehow in human form, trying to sneak its way in and take over the Rectory for good.

The knock came again, harder, faster.

"Who's there?" I hollered.

"It's me," said a tiny voice. "It's Angeline."

For a moment I hesitated, I'm ashamed to say it. What if this girl, this stranger in town, the very same one who had lied to me about her missing family, who knew so much more about magic than anyone I'd ever met next to Grandpa Widow, had something to do with all the chaos happening outside?

Well, if that was the case, then so be it. Angeline was still my friend, and she had saved Cricket's life. You don't leave somebody like that out at the mercy of the Great Doom. I opened the door and yanked her inside. I was about to slam the door, but she stopped me.

"Wait!" she said. "I'm not alone."

That's when Connor Carnivolly walked into the Rectory. I stared him down.

"I thought I told you to go home," I said.

"Gussy," he said. "I know you're trying to take care of me, and I appreciate that. It's your job, and your job is important, sure. But if you think I'm going home right now, you've lost it."

"You don't understand," I said.

"No, you're the one who doesn't understand," he said. "My dad got infected by this thing, and now it's taken over the whole village. Gussy, you're the bravest person I ever met in my life, but you can't do this alone. You're going to need some help, whether you like it or not."

"This isn't up for discussion, Connor."

"You're right, it isn't." He smiled at me, that prestidigitator's glimmer in his eyes. "I'm coming with you, and I'm going to help. There's no two ways about it."

Well, it didn't look like I was going to win this fight, no matter how much I didn't like it. I looked down at Cricket, and he tilted his head at me, like "What are you waiting for?"

"Fine," I said.

I slammed the door shut and bolted it behind them. I turned my attention to Angeline. She stood there before me, tattered and beat down. Her dress was torn and her cheek was bruised, her lip all swollen up like somebody had socked her good. I wanted to know where she'd been last night, if she was okay. Mostly I was so glad to see her I could have thrown my arms around her and hugged her, which is something I almost never do. But all of my feelings would have to wait, because right now, before anything else, I needed answers.

"You got a lot of explaining to do," I said. "So talk."

"I'm so, so sorry," she said.

"That may well be true," I said, "but that doesn't help me much at the moment, so we can skip all this apology nonsense. What I want are facts. Why did you run away? Why did you lie about your parents? Who are you really?"

"That's what I was trying to apologize for," said Angeline. "Lying to you about my parents, I mean. I know it was a wretched thing to do. But I didn't think I had much choice in the matter. Truth is, I ran away from home over a week ago. My parents are no-account charlatans, nothing but con artists who travel the desert, ripping people off. At first my mom's sister, Aunt Bawdie, was with us. She was the magic one of the family, the one who was touched with something greater. She saw my potential and taught me ritual work ever since I was little. But Aunt Bawdie was old, and when I was four years old she grew sick and died. My parents don't have a lick of magic between them, so after Aunt Bawdie passed, they use me for their schemes. People are so scared nowadays they'll believe anything, fall for any little swindle that comes their way, just so long as they think it might help them fight back the darkness. Do you understand how awful that is? My magic is the most precious thing I have, and I got pretty sick of using it for nothing but evil. I always thought my gift was destined for more, for something greater, but my parents wouldn't have it."

At least you know who your parents are, I wanted to say, but I figured it was best if I kept my mouth shut. I mean, how happy would it make me to find out I was the kid of a couple of swindlers? Maybe it was better not knowing some-times. Maybe the best thing was to focus on what you had right here, right now, not something in the long far-off and gone.

"So how'd you end up here in the village?" I said.

"Well, I heard about you, Gussy," said Angeline. "Specifi-cally, I heard there was a Protector who was training a young orphan girl to follow in his footsteps. Now, that's something pretty rare around these parts, someone who will just take in a stranger and teach them the Rites. It takes a special kind of person to do something like that. Because the truth is, Gussy, all I ever wanted in all my life was to use my magic to help people, and I figured the best way to do that was to become a Protector, same as you. That way I might be able to do some good in the world. I was headed to your village when I got caught up in that storm. It was a miracle I sur-vived at all. I wouldn't have, if you hadn't broken the rules and opened the gates for me."

I sat down, my brain reeling. Angeline had come all this way just to become a Protector, all because she heard of Grandpa Widow and me? I couldn't believe it.

"But why did you lie about it?" I said. "What's with that whole story about your family?"

"I didn't think you would let me stay if I didn't have some kind of sad story to tell," she said. "I guess that's something I learned out on the road, swindling folks. The truth isn't much good out there, especially when the truth is something so pathetic as what all my parents are up to. Besides, I was intimidated by you. Your ritual work is so formal and meticulous, and mine is so haphazard and homemade. I didn't think you'd want me here. I thought you'd never let me stay if you knew I wanted to be a Protector too."

Me, intimidating? That was just about the most ridiculous thing I had ever heard in my life. But maybe it was true. Maybe I was pretty tough to get along with, seeing as how seriously I take my duties. Maybe that did scare Angeline a little bit. Maybe I was a little bit harder to get to know than I ever thought. I wondered again what I looked like to the other kids in the village, if maybe they didn't dislike me so much as they were intimidated by me too. That would make sense, wouldn't it? After all, their lives were more or less in my hands. I could see why that would scare a kid who didn't know any better.

"She has a point, Gussy," said Connor. "You cut a formidable figure. It's the robes, the Rites, the way you walk with your back all straight, like you're on some mission." He grinned. "It's part of what I like about you."

"Anyways," said Angeline, "thank you for letting me into the village and saving me from the storm, for giving me your home to stay in. It's the kindest thing anybody ever did for me in my life."

"You really have Cricket to thank for saving you, you know

that, right?" I said. "He's the one who finally convinced me to break the rules."

"Of course, I'm thanking Cricket too," she said. "I'm thanking both of you, because you're a team. And Connor too. I think you guys are the only people who've been nice to me since my aunt died."

"I'm glad you're here, Angeline," I said. "And so long as I have anything to say about it, you can stay with me as long as you want."

For a second I thought Angeline was going to cry right then and there. But then she jumped forward and threw her arms around me and hugged me so tight I could hardly breathe.

"Okay, okay," I said after a minute. "Now let's get down to business. Any idea of how we can beat the Great Doom?"

"Nope," said Angeline. "But I did find out some things about the Rider while I was out there. I followed her into that inn—what do you call it, Old Esmerelda's, even though Esmerelda doesn't seem to be that old. I snuck in there just fine, told Esmerelda I was looking for my pa. Anyways, when the Rider got up from her table I went over and found a long brown hair of hers and snatched it up in my fingers. I took it out back to an alley and did a reading of the hair using the Peacock's Eye. Guess what? She's a witch, a great and mighty one. It's Lucinda Withern herself!"

I dropped my head into my hands and groaned.

"Trust me," I said, "I'm well aware."

"Oh. Well, it's still incredible, isn't it?" said Angeline. "I was a little bit honored to be holding one of her hairs."

"I'm going to pretend you didn't say that," I said.

"What would a witch so powerful want with our little old village?" said Connor.

But I already knew the answer to that.

"She wants the Valley's Heart," I said.

Angeline nodded. "It's the Valley's Heart, no question. She's been scrawling these Sigils of Discord all over the place. They're even under the tables at Old Esmerelda's. She must have had this all planned out."

I had to admit, it was a pretty good plan. Even the letter to Grandpa Widow must have been part of it, calling him away to a far-off town so he couldn't stop her. The only person standing in her way would be me, and I'm sure Lucinda Withern figured there was no way tiny young me could stop her. It was humiliating for me to realize how right she was. I'd blown it, just the same as if I were following her orders on purpose. I was pretty much no good as a Protector. If we ever did get out of this mess, Grandpa Widow would banish me to the desert for good, I knew that. And you know what? I would deserve it.

"Hey," said Angeline, laying a hand on my shoulder. "It

isn't over yet. Not by a long shot. Not with a library like your Grandpa Widow's right here, all sorts of esoteric Rites to sort through."

"But what if it's not enough?" said Connor. "What if we can't beat the Great Doom? I mean, you saw what it did to someone as powerful as Lucinda Withern. It just sucked her right up into the sky like she was nothing."

"All we can do is what we can do," said Angeline. "If it doesn't work, then at least we went out trying, right?"

"I've got to be honest with you," said Connor. "That doesn't make me feel very good."

Angeline blushed. "That wasn't much of a speech, was it? Gosh, I'm awful at speeches. Pa used to make me speak my spells out loud when we were scamming folks. He told me to project my voice, said if you can get folks with their eyes and their ears then they'll be too busy to notice you're picking their pockets. But I just wasn't ever good at saying the right thing."

"It's okay," I said. "I was never one for big talk. I'm more about doing. So let's get to work already."

I gazed at the giant wall of books in the Rectory, shelves and shelves of volumes in languages I could barely translate. This was going to take ages. Right then a big whooshing noise passed the Rectory. It was like a great winged bird soared over us, a dragon-sized wind of cooling darkness, and it shivered the roof. I felt it down to my bones, the dread and despair, the whole village in the clutches of the darkness Lucinda Withern had unleashed, now far beyond her control.

How were we ever going to get out of this?

We only had one option: back to work.

19

A COUPLE OF HOURS LATER, WE STILL weren't any closer to figuring out what to do. Angeline had found some rituals that might work in an especially ancient and crumbly book called *Verities of the Soothsayer's Daydream*, but I wasn't sure if we were powerful enough to make them work. Not to mention the difficulties in translation and measurements and all that. Connor held up a book so old I wasn't even sure Grandpa Widow could make sense of it.

"Ugh," he said. "These books are so hard to read. Some of them aren't even in the right language."

"Well, they're in the language of the person who wrote them," said Angeline, "so it technically is the right language. We just only know the wrong ones."

"Yeah, yeah," said Connor. "A lot of good that does us."

"There has to be an answer somewhere," I said. "We just aren't seeing it yet."

"The thing I don't get," said Connor, "is why the Great Doom came into this town in the first place. I mean, what's it doing here? What does it even want?"

"It doesn't want anything," I said. "It's an evil force that haunts the desert and takes things over, same as how a twister doesn't exactly want to destroy houses and villages. That's just what it does."

"I'm not so sure you're right about that," said Angeline.

"Well, it's what Grandpa Widow always told me," I said, "and he would know."

"Your Grandpa Widow is certainly a brilliant and capable man," said Angeline, "but maybe he was wrong about this particular thing."

That made me about as mad as I knew how to be. I wasn't about to let Grandpa Widow get insulted in his own Rectory.

"Are you trying to tell me Grandpa Widow didn't know how to do his job?" I said.

"Come on, Gussy," said Connor. "Let's hear her out for a minute."

"Fine," I said. "Go ahead."

"I really didn't mean to offend you," said Angeline, "but let's think about it for a second. What if the Great Doom isn't just some totally wicked evil thing here to cause destruction? What if it actually has a purpose, an intention?"

"You saying the Great Doom has a mind?" I said. "The next thing you're going to tell me is that it has feelings too."

"Sure," she said. "Why not? If something's got a mind, then it has wants and desires too."

I'd never thought of it that way. My word, how sometimes the only question you don't think to ask is the only one that really matters.

"You know," said Connor, "that actually makes a lot of sense."

"Thanks, Connor," said Angeline, smiling all big. "It's like I keep telling you guys. All these Rites are about keeping something out. So we know the Great Doom wants inside the village. We just don't know why. We don't know what it wants with the village."

"How do we find out?" I said. "You want me to walk outside and ask it myself?"

"No," said Angeline. "I say we ask the one person who has actually communicated with it, or who at least has claimed to."

"And who might that be?" I said.

"Lazlo Dunes."

"You're kidding me," I said. "That guy hates me and Grandpa Widow both. He has no respect for the Rites."

"Which might be why he could help us," said Angeline. "You know, he might actually know something we don't."

I hated to admit it, but Angeline had a point. And as much as I didn't want to have to go back out there, especially not to talk to somebody like Lazlo Dunes, we weren't getting anywhere sitting inside like this, cowering, while the whole village was in danger.

"Fine," I said. "Let's get to it."

We set out into the darkness of the village. It was as if everything had changed in a moment, the whole village gone eerie, transformed into a shadow of itself. It's hard to explain what it was like now that the Great Doom had fully taken over the place. I guess it was sort of like a dream, the kind where you are walking around in some place you know very well, but there's something strange about it, something off, like the whole place just doesn't feel right. That's what it was like walking into the village that night—like wandering into a bad dream. The Great Doom covered the sky like a black curtain drawn over the world. It was in the air we breathed, thick as fog, with the burning smell of sulfur on the wind. Doors and windows swung open and banged shut, all on their own. Infected folks ran through town, screaming in gibberish languages. I saw old Mister Luther McNamara leaping from rooftop to rooftop, cackling his head off. Strange-colored eyes peered at us from the shadows, and I wasn't sure if they were infected people or animals or somehow the Great Doom itself.

And all the while that flaming gyre burned outside the gates, like a final punishment biding its time.

This was the world we walked into that night, me and Angeline and Connor and Cricket, our tiny troop against the darkness. I'd performed a Protection Rite over all of us, anointing our heads with sacred oil and the tears of a bat, speaking a Mystery for each and every one of us. We carried saints' bones and cardinal feathers and the dried tails of lizards in our pockets and around our necks for protection. So far as we stayed close, I knew the magic of us together could keep us safe.

We walked in single file, holding hands, in case the dark grew too great and we couldn't see in front of our faces. I held Connor Carnivolly's hand, which was a first for me, but I wasn't about to lose a single one of us to the Great Doom. Nobody held Cricket's hand, of course, but he had an extra protection from the ritual Angeline had already performed over him, and he barked an encouragement every few steps.

We found Lazlo Dunes and his newfound followers at the burned-down meeting pole, the Book of Names just a pile of windblown ashes now, all those words dust for the desert. They all were on their knees in the dirt, banging their metal plates, mostly the derelict and disregarded of the village, the ones with no other families, who had left or lost everything and turned to Lazlo. Blue fire danced over their clothes as they wept and moaned, begging for forgiveness, weird guilty angel beings wandering this cursed endless night. In a world of cowering folks hidden away behind sacred candles, praying to the One Who Listens for some kind of deliverance, Lazlo Dunes lay pleading with the Great Doom itself, repenting in the dust. Lazlo looked up at me, his face streaked with mud.

"Gussy," he said. "Have you come to join us? To renounce your crooked old ways?"

"The Rites aren't crooked," I said. "They're the only thing that's kept us safe."

"You call this safe?" he said. "The old ways are over, Gussy. They have failed."

Just then one of Lazlo's followers, a woman named Cassius Norwood, let loose a cry unhinged enough to send shivers all over me. It seemed to echo through all the dark places in the village, like the shadows were weeping along with her. For some reason the Great Doom hadn't infected any of them, it hadn't taken them over. I wondered why they seemed to be protected. They hadn't performed any rituals and they didn't carry any saints' bones. What was it about them that kept them safe? I felt like I was in a world that had switched places with its own shadow, the dark opposite of everything I'd known and loved and sworn to protect.

Cricket tensed his back and growled. I turned to Angeline.

"This was a mistake," I said. "He's not going to tell us anything."

"Let me talk to him," said Connor.

"Why you?" I said.

"Because I used to practice my act on him and the guys in the street," said Connor. "Everyone just ignores them, you know? But they were the best audience I ever had."

Connor walked past me and hollered out.

"Hey, Lazlo," said Connor. "You got any words for me?"

Lazlo Dunes squinted at Connor in the burning firelight, like he barely recognized him. Then his eyes went wide, and some of that crazed quality seemed to leave him for a minute, and he slumped a little, looking tired all of a sudden.

"Well, if it isn't the young magician himself," said Lazlo. "Have you come to grovel with us?"

"Don't see much good that's doing," said Connor.

"If we beg for forgiveness, the Great Doom might spare some of us. We've been sowing the seeds of our own destruction for ages and ages, since the founding of this very town."

"You saying it's my dad's own fault he got possessed and had to crawl all over the ceiling?"

Lazlo took in a deep breath and sighed. Little flames of blue wisped about his face, circling his scraggly bald head like a crown of lightning.

"You were always a good one, Connor," said Lazlo Dunes, "and I'm sorry about what happened to your daddy. But none of us are innocent. Don't you know that yet? Every one of us who has set foot in this desert is guilty, in one way or another. The whole place is corrupt, and anyone who has participated has a price to pay."

"These people are all just doing their best to live a good life," I said. "To make a living and to get by. They aren't guilty of anything, any more than you are."

"I think you're missing the point," said Angeline.

"Ah, the little witch," said Lazlo. "I've been wanting to hear from you."

"I . . . I guess I am a witch," said Angeline. "No one's ever called me that before, not even my aunt."

"It's no insult," said Lazlo. "Many of my only friends are witches. Though some mean more harm than others." He motioned to the swirling gyre beyond the gates.

"You mean Lucinda Withern?" said Angeline.

"Aye," said Lazlo. "Though I don't suspect there's much of her left anymore. The Great Doom has chosen its instrument, and it has chosen fiercely."

"But what does it want?" said Connor. "Why does the Great Doom want to hurt the village so bad?"

Lazlo Dunes shook his head at us. "Children, I'll let you in on a little secret. The Great Doom is just the spirit of this land turned angry. It only wants back what was stolen from it."

Lazlo Dunes pointed at the Benningsley mansion.

"You mean the Valley's Heart," I said.

Lazlo nodded. "The land was cursed when McGregor

Benningsley removed the Heart, something that people for generations and generations had known best to leave alone. That's why no one ever lived here before this town, and why no one will live here after. The sand scoured itself black with the sickness. Because that gem wasn't any old precious stone of immense monetary worth. No, it was the desert's own soul, and it was stolen. McGregor Benningsley sold a small piece of it—barely the size of his thumb—for enough coin to set him up for life. He used his newfound fortune to build the village, and the promise of the village drew us all here."

"But this is our home," I said. "McGregor Benningsley is the only reason we have a place to live."

"That may be true," said Lazlo Dunes, "but the way he built it was wrong. There are consequences, children. What is forged in the ground over millions of years can be stolen in an instant, but oh, it takes a million years to replace. The land is angry, and it seeks its revenge."

"Then why doesn't the Great Doom just take it back?" I said. "Why doesn't it just blow down the Benningsley mansion and make off with it already?"

"You might want to ask your Grandpa Widow about that," said Lazlo Dunes.

"What in the world is that supposed to mean?" I said.

Lightning struck the ground outside the village, the twister becoming huge, wilder, burning bright with fire.

"I already told you too much," said Lazlo Dunes. "I'll

have to repent of that to stay in the avenger's graces. You kids scatter now, and whatever might happen, take care. The avenger comes, and woe to all who fall in her path."

A great winged darkness swooped over us again, and I heard a woman's voice cry out from the shadows.

"It's Lucinda Withern," said Angeline.

"We better get out of here," said Connor.

"And I know just where we're headed," I said.

"Where's that?" said Angeline.

I pointed past the rubble of the meeting pole.

"It's time to pay a visit to the Benningsleys."

20

I WALKED MYSELF ACROSS THE VILLAGE square and right up to the Benningsley mansion, my pals following behind me in the terror of the night. I balled my fist and banged as hard as I could on those gargantuan wooden doors.

"Open up," I said. "It's Head Protector Gustavina M. Pearl, and I demand entrance!"

Nothing happened. The door was still, silence from inside. Lazlo's followers cackled at me. I noticed eyes shining in the shadows, figures gathered in the places of the deepest dark. The villagers, my friends, the people I was supposed to protect, were now infected, fully under the control of the Great Doom, nothing but puppets. They stood eerily still, watching me, and I could feel their eyes like little moons bearing down on me.

I bit my lip and made a fist and banged harder on that Benningsley door.

"I said open up!" I hollered. "This is official business!"

Nothing. Just silence, that door still as a palace guard from some old fairy tale. I didn't know quite what to do.

The sky shuddered above us, and it was like a ceiling had formed over the moon and stars, a darkness so thick as to be touchable, and it was slowly lowering, threating to squish us to the earth.

"Maybe we should go," said Angeline.

"Yeah," said Connor. "It doesn't look like they're going to open up for us."

"I am not about to be shut out by Mayor Benningsley," I said, "and that's just a fact."

This time I kicked the door with my boots. I kicked it so hard I scuffed it, the boom resounding out into the darkness. I heard laughter behind me, but I didn't care.

"Open up this door right now or I swear to you I will get Big Gordo to come and rip it off its hinges, do you hear me?"

The door opened a crack. I saw Mayor Benningsley's beady eye staring out.

"Go away, Gussy," he said. "I have nothing to say to you."

He tried to shut the door on me, but I stuck my boot in and blocked it.

"Well, I have a heck of a lot to say to you," I said. "So open up and let us in."

"I don't think that's a good idea," he said.

"I think it's the only idea," I said. "You have a lot of explaining to do, and as much as I hate to admit it, I don't think we can beat the Great Doom without your help."

"I'm sorry, Gussy, but I can't help you. You're the Protector, it's your job to protect us. From the looks of it, you failed. Grandpa Widow put enough charms on this place to make it a fortress. The Great Doom can't get in here, and lucky for me, neither can you and your little gang here."

"But you can't just abandon your people," said Connor. "You're the Mayor, after all."

Mayor Benningsley looked out into the darkness beyond me, and I could see the fear grow in his eyes.

"They don't much look like my people anymore," he said. "Not to me."

Mayor Benningsley kicked my boot out of the way and slammed the door shut. I heard multiple locks turning, the jangle of keys. There was no way we were getting in now.

"What do we do?" said Angeline.

I turned to Connor and Angeline and Cricket. Lazlo and his followers had dispersed, headed off to some other place, and the crowds of the infected had gathered, standing still as trees, their eyes shimmering with blue fire. To be honest, I didn't know what to tell her. I didn't have a clue what to do. I shut my eyes and said a silent prayer, because the One Who Listens also hears our thoughts and intentions, not just the words we say. That was my hope, anyhow.

I prayed and I prayed and I prayed, hoping something would happen, anything at all.

A window opened on the far side of the house, and a voice cried out from it.

"Hey, Gussy!"

Lulu Benningsley poked her head out the window.

"Don't leave!" she hollered. "I'm coming down!"

Lulu climbed out the window and scuttled down the trellis of her house so quick and nimble it was like she'd done it a thousand times, which come to think of it she probably had. The opal ring flickered yellow like a cat's eye in the darkness. Lulu landed with a thud in the dust and ran toward us.

"I was wondering how long it would take you to come for me," she said.

"Why would we come for you?"

"Because it's all my fault," she said. "All of this. It's because of me."

"Well, this is a story I need to hear, and fast," I said. "But first we got to get out of here, and the Rectory's too far to go."

"How about Old Esmerelda's?" said Angeline.

That seemed about the safest place left, and there was no doubt Old Esmerelda would let us in. It was near impossible to get banned from Old Esmerelda's, unless maybe you actually killed someone inside. Of course, if you could prove it was in self-defense, that was another story altogether. Point is, we weren't getting shut out of there, not on a night like tonight.

"Let's go," I said, and we made our way across the village square.

Old Esmerelda's was mostly empty, save for a few confused out-of-towners huddled in the main room. I walked over to an old woman in gray curlers and a bald man with big spectacles. They were holding hands and quaking at a little round table.

"Don't worry about anything," I told them. "I'm going to have this all cleaned up soon as I can."

They looked at me like I'd lost it. Once again, folks not wanting to trust a kid to do her job. That's okay. I'd show them all, I truly well and good would. Just as soon as I figured out a way to save everybody, of course. That part still needed some working on.

Old Esmerelda walked on out from a doorway in the back. She seemed distraught, her normally perfect hair springing up all over the place, her makeup a little smeared, like she'd been crying.

"Well, Gussy," was all she said.

"I'm on it, ma'am," I said.

"And we're here to help," said Connor.

"That's a relief," said Old Esmerelda, but I could see the doubt settled deep in her eyes. "I burned all the Sigils of Discord and chucked the infected furniture, but I don't know how long we'll be able to hold out."

"Parlor room," I said to my crew. "Now."

We headed on through the swinging doors into the parlor room of Old Esmerelda's just the same as if it was our very own clubhouse. We settled down at the big round table in the center of the room, a single candle for our light. The piano played itself all minor key and ghostly behind us, the tendrils of the Great Doom reaching even into this place.

"We got to hurry," I said. "This place is liable to be full infected at any moment. What have you got for us, Lulu?"

"Well, the village is infected and it's all my fault," said Lulu. "Everything. The shadows, the darkness, all those yellow eyes peering at me from nowhere. I think I saw a giant black bird swooping over our house. It was like a winged demon, something out of a nightmare. All because of something stupid I did."

"Calm down. You're safe," I said. The parlor room walls shuddered and shook, splinters of wood falling from the ceiling. "For now, anyways."

"I don't know what good that's supposed to do me," she

said. "Not after I've put the whole village in danger."

"You knew about Lucinda Withern?" I said.

Lulu scrunched her eyebrows at me. "The famous witch? She's here?"

Now that right there surprised me. I guessed there was a lot more going on this village than even *I* knew about.

"Never mind," I said. "Just tell us your story."

Me and Connor and Angeline and Cricket all leaned closer to listen. Old Esmerelda's was still and quiet, minus the eerie tinkling of the piano playing itself behind me. I had no idea what Lulu was about to tell me, but I hoped it would be one more piece to this puzzle I'd been trying to solve since the moment Grandpa Widow had left me in charge.

"Well, I don't know if you've noticed," said Lulu, "but my brother Chappie's not around much anymore. The truth of the matter is, he's sick, has been since he was born. We've always kept it quiet, a secret. Only my family and Grandpa Widow knew. You know those folks always showing up in carriages, doing business with my father? Those are jewelers. Every month or so, my father cuts off a bit of the Valley's Heart and sells the shards to those men in exchange for special healing herbs for Chappie. Grandpa Widow set the whole thing up years and years ago. He's even the one who found the herbs to keep Chappie alive. What Chappie's got isn't a normal illness, understand? It's something different, a magic sickness, more akin to a curse. That's what Father says, anyhow."

"A curse?" I said. "Why would Chappie be cursed?"

"If you'll shut your mouth a minute, I'll tell you," said Lulu.

Even if she was coming to us for help, she was still kind of a brat.

"Sorry," I said. "Keep going."

"Like I was saying. A few weeks ago, those special healing herbs quit working," said Lulu, "and Chappie got sicker and sicker. That's why that man in the tweed suit came to visit. He took a bigger chunk of the Heart than usual to sell. I was in bed one night when I had a dream. A pretty woman with long brown hair came speaking to me. She told me that she was a good witch who knew all about my brother's sickness, that the secret of it had been revealed to her in a vision. She said the only way my brother would be healed was if I helped her let the Great Doom into the village. She said the Great Doom was the only thing powerful enough to heal my brother, and that it would look kindly on my service. So I dug up the chicken foot and disrupted all your rituals. I even knocked the Book of Names off the meeting pole. I did it with a slingshot, if you were wondering."

"And let me guess, Chappie's not any better, is he?" I said.

"No, he's not," she said. "He's actually gotten worse. That's why I crawled out my window. My parents think

I'm at home in bed. They're so worried about Chappie they probably won't even notice I'm gone."

Right about then Lulu Benningsley burst into tears, slumping over with her face down. Cricket hopped up and put his front paws on the table, giving Lulu's face a lick.

"Stop it," said Lulu, but she wrapped her arms around his neck and cried harder. Sometimes all you need is a sweet creature to let you cry on his fur. That might sound selfish, but it's the truth, and Heaven bless them for it.

"This isn't your fault," I said. "Even if it was pretty awful of you for digging up that chicken foot, I understand why you did it. You dug it up because you love your brother, and there's not a thing wrong with that. But that's not what caused this."

"It's not?" said Lulu, raising her eyes to me.

"Nope," I said. "The person who came to you in the vision was Lucinda Withern. She tricked you, same as she tricked me and Grandpa Widow."

"Are you joking with me?" said Lulu. "It's really not my fault?"

"Not any more than it is mine," I said. "Moping won't fix anything. So hop on up. If we're going to save the village, and your brother too, then we got to get to work."

Lulu stood up and straightened her dress. She took a deep breath and let it out slow, same as I do when I'm flustered.

"Okay," she said. "What do I do?"

I looked Lulu deep in her eyes, the candlelight flickering

on her face, the whoosh and boom of the Great Doom outside, the piano meandering off-key in the corner.

"I'm going to need you to steal the Valley's Heart."

Lulu's eyes got real big and wide and scared a minute. Then she set her eyes to stern and stared me straight in mine.

"Okay," she said. "I can do that. I can try, anyways."

I had to hand it to her. Even if she was a brat, Lulu Benningsley had grit, and that counts for something.

"Then what?" said Connor. "We just give it back? How do we keep the Great Doom from destroying us all?"

"To be honest," I said, "I'm still working on that part of things."

The darkness outside rumbled, and I felt a cold fear crawl across my bones. I could tell the others felt it too. Angeline looked at me, her eyes tired and squinty, but with a new-found sparkle of hope in them.

"Gussy," she said, "we looked through so many Rites tonight."

"And?"

"And, well . . . I don't think any of them will work. Not for a problem this big."

This was excellent news, truly wonderful. Just the kind of thing to get you up and rearing for the hardest fight of our lives. I had had so much hope that if anyone could find the answer, it would be Angeline. But even the oldest books had let us down.

"So what do you suggest we do?" I said. "Just give up?"

"No," said Angeline. "Not at all. I think we have to make a new Rite."

"A new Rite?" I said. "Like our very own?"

"Why not? I mean, someone made up all these Rites and rituals in the first place. They didn't just appear out of nowhere."

"Yeah, but those were the great Protectors and scholars of the ages. We're just kids, you know?"

"When has that ever stopped you before?" said Angeline. "You're a Protector, Gussy, and a good one. You do what's best for the village. And I'm telling you right now, the old Rites won't cut it. We need something new."

"Fine," I said. "Got any ideas?"

"As a matter of fact, I do," she said. "It's going to take me some time to work it all out, though. And we're going to need supplies."

"You mean I have to go back out there?" said Lulu.

"Not if you don't want to," I said. "I think I can handle this one alone."

"Yeah, right," said Connor. "Gussy, you know I'm coming with you."

"If you insist," I said, secretly glad I didn't have to ask him to myself.

Cricket yelped.

"Of course you're coming, Cricket," I said. "I didn't mean to leave you out either."

"What about me?" said Lulu.

"How about you go with Angeline back to the Rectory and help her work out the Rite?" I said.

"Anything's better than sitting around here," she said.

"Here's a list of all I need," said Angeline, and she tossed me a scrap of paper all scribbled on. Her handwriting was this strange loopy swirl, like while she was writing a hurricane blew up on the page and sent the ink a-whirling, like she wrote in windblown raindrops. I loved it a little bit, even if it was kind of hard to read.

I pocketed the list in my robe and made the sign of the Four Winds and spat on the ground. I held the saint's ankle bone and the rabbit's foot and the black dice of Morovan Pewterbelly, a famous gambler from down by the swamplands that Grandpa Widow met once. I had all the good-luck stuff I needed.

"Anything for you?" I said to Connor.

"Not a chance," he said, flashing that gapped grin at me. "I got all the lucky I need right here." He patted his hand on his heart. Boy, that Connor sure was something. I was glad he was coming with me.

Angeline splashed us with blessed water from the canteen and spoke a Mystery over us, and sang the "Holy Starlight

Evensong," one of my favorites.

"How'd you know that one?" I said.

Angeline shrugged. "Heard you play it a dozen times since I got here."

"Figures. I never can keep a good thing to myself."

"Be careful out there," she said, and gave my hand a squeeze. And with that, me and Connor and Cricket set off into the darkness, the Great Doom churning the black clouds above us like the stormy ocean in my dreams.

We slunk around boarded-up houses and down back alleys, avoiding the main streets as best we could. That fire twister outside the gates still burned, a cold flaming whirlwind blowing like winter through the darkness. The infected villagers were gathering at the meeting pole, more and more of them every minute shuffling down dark streets, jaws slack, eyes burning with a blue light. Why were they gathering there, and what was the purpose? In every few houses you could hear screaming, the sound of glasses shattering, homes reduced to rubble. What would be left of the village after this endless night?

But I couldn't think about that, not when I still had a job to do.

"Uh, Gussy?" said Connor. "Look yonder."

I turned around. There stood Cynthia Synderline, one of Lulu's old cronies. She was maybe the second meanest kid in the whole village. Well, since me and Lulu were sort of friends now, I guess Cynthia was officially the number one meanest kid now. I thought about congratulating her, but then I noticed the odd tilt of her head, the slight shimmer of blue in her eyes. Cynthia was infected.

"You are the new Protector," she said. The words came out all garbled and wrong, the voice canyon deep. I realized she was speaking in the voice of the Great Doom, like it had finally learned how to use us to talk. "You are the one now tasked at keeping me out."

"That's a fact," I said.

"It appears that you have failed," she said. "Your predecessor would not have let this happen."

"Yeah, well," I said. "I got a plan."

"As do I, little Protector. As do I."

Cynthia gnashed her teeth at me, stepping stiff legged my way. Saliva dripped from her jaws, and she growled.

"Gussy?" said Connor.

"Yeah?"

"I'm thinking we should run about now."

"And I'm thinking you're right."

We sprinted through the darkness, Cynthia on our heels, snapping her teeth, howling like a wolf. I saw the hatchery looming strange and lopsided in the perpetual dark.

"There it is!" I hollered. "We're going to make it!"

Let me tell you, that's about the worst thing you can ever

say when you're running from something. You might as well just go on and hex yourself right then and there. Because Cynthia got up some kind of extra speed and jumped all stretched out and long, clamping her teeth around my ankle.

I went down, and I went down hard.

Connor tried to pull her off me, and she backhanded him into Cricket, both of them toppling over into the dust.

The door to the hatchery swung open and out stepped Mr. Mayella. He looked positively unhinged, his hair wild all over the place, his face unshaven, and his eyes bloodshot. He waved a purple candle in one hand, and in the other he held what looked like a human rib. He thrust it at Cynthia, and she unclamped her teeth from my ankle, staggered back into the shadows.

"Off with ye!" he hollered. "Flee to the darkness from whence you came!"

Cynthia hissed at him and spat, a great blob flinging onto Mr. Mayella's cheek.

"I said get, and be quick about it!" he yelled, and lunged at her with the rib. Cynthia scampered, howling, into an alley and vanished into the night.

"Up, up, children!" said Mr. Mayella. "Gustavina, can you walk?"

I stood. It hurt a little, but I'd be fine.

"Yeah," I said, "I got it."

"Well, hurry, hurry!" he said. "Before something worse than Miss Synderline comes along."

It was cold and dark inside the hatchery. A few candles burned in the waiting room, illuminating Mr. Mayella's strange and magical collection, but in the darkness of the Great Doom, not even Mr. Mayella's candles could do much good. He still held the bone tight in his fist as he ushered us inside.

"What is that anyway?" said Connor.

"It's a rib bone from Saint Petunia herself," said Mr. Mayella. "Took me decades to track it down. I had to trade a pint of hellhounds' blood for it, and I still barely escaped with my life."

"Gross," said Connor.

"Are you kidding me?" I said. "Saint Petunia is one of the first great Protectors. The Rites we use today are based on her systems." I looked up at Mr. Mayella. "Can I hold it?"

"Of course you may," he said, and handed me the rib bone. It was slender, fragile feeling, almost like I could snap it in half like a twig. But it radiated a power that rushed through me, prickling every hair on my head. It was like the world grew brighter in that moment, even with the Great Doom all around, like I could feel the power of Protectors long gone sparkling inside me.

"Very good, Gustavina," said Mr. Mayella. "Very good indeed."

I handed the rib back to Mr. Mayella, and when it left my hand I felt dizzy a little, exhausted, like I'd just run a mile. I guess that's what it's like when power leaves you, when you fall back into your old self.

"We've come for supplies," said Connor.

I handed Mr. Mayella the list. He read through it by the dim candlelight, his eyebrows raised.

"What an odd assortment," he said. "No one has asked me for salamander tongues in ages."

"It's for something new," I said.

Mr. Mayella frowned at me.

"New is often dangerous, Gustavina," he said. "Are you sure you know what you're doing?"

"Nope," I said. "But I don't think we have any other choice."

"I suppose you're right," he said. "Well, I shall fill this order to the best of my ability. My birds are frightened and shedding feathers at a rate faster than I can preserve them, so you'll have to make do."

"That's fine," I said. I watched as he riffled through drawers and mason jars, digging out all the oddments Angeline had requested. When it was time to gather the cardinal feathers, Mr. Mayella opened the big wooden door to the hatchery.

"Mr. Mayella, can I come into the vault with you?" I said.

Mr. Mayella sighed.

"Might as well," he said. "It will be a night of firsts, rules meant to be broken."

We walked in and shut the door. I was astonished anew at the cardinals all gazing down at me like bloodred angels, the tan-greenish females dotted among them like leaves. So secret, those, and yet so essential, so often unnoticed.

"Do you want to know something?" he said. "Most folks use the male feathers, because of the commanding red color. But the female birds' feathers are actually more potent in their power. It's not that the male feathers are decidedly lesser magic, not in the slightest. But the effects are different, tamer, easier to control. It is the subtler colors in which the loveliest magic lies. Would you like some of the gray-gold feathers?"

I nodded. "I think, Mr. Mayella, that yes, I would, very much."

"Then they are yours."

The birds watched me, their black eyes shining, calm and unworried. They seemed wise to me, stately and regal, as if their concerns were beyond this world, like they were focused on something higher. I wondered if they minded living their lives in the hatchery, even among the gold and finery. I wondered if they wouldn't rather be free, flitting around some forest somewhere, their magic belonging to no one but themselves.

I knew I needed to ask the question I was thinking, but I didn't much want to, not after Mr. Mayella had saved my life. Still, I was a Protector, and asking tough questions was my job.

"Mr. Mayella," I said, "what were you doing the night Grandpa Widow left the village?"

"What was I doing?" he said, his back still to me, gathering up feathers. "I told you already. Minding my birds."

"But I saw you," I said, "outside in the dark. You were walking somewhere. Where were you going?"

His shoulders slumped. It was like he was a blown-up pig's bladder and I'd just deflated him.

"Fine, Gussy. Yes, you saw me," he said. "And I suppose you've found out about the Valley's Heart as well, what it does, what it's for?"

"I know that it shouldn't belong to anyone but the desert itself," I said. "That it doesn't belong to any person, not really."

"That," said Mr. Mayella, whirling around to face me, "is patently false. It must not belong to a cretin, a man incapable of appreciating the Heart's more peculiar qualities."

"What are you saying, Mr. Mayella?"

"The stone is the most powerful source of magic in this

entire desert," he said, "and it is being wasted, sold chip by chip to jewel mongers in cities. It is a disgrace, Gustavina, the shame of the age."

He got right up in my face, peering down at me, his eyes gone strange and flickery, almost blue-like in the hatchery gloom. I was frightened, but I wasn't about to back down now.

"Did you help let the Great Doom into the village, Mr. Mayella?" I said.

"So what if I did?" he screamed. "It was only to serve as a distraction, to break the flimsy defenses I, along with your precious Grandpa Widow, helped erect for the Benningsley mansion. I figured if it broke through, then I could stroll in, immune and ceremonially protected, and snatch the stone for myself. How do you think Lucinda Withern was allowed to sneak by Grandpa Widow undetected? It was because I blinded him, and you too, Gussy. I tricked the both of you, in hopes of keeping the stone for myself."

Mr. Mayella's eyes burned a flame-bright blue. He thrust his hands out at me and wrapped his long fingers around my neck. I fought him, but he held on tight, his fingers like talons. The birds watched us calmly from above, unbothered, as if we were just some puppet show being put on for their entertainment. I couldn't breathe, and I couldn't pry Mr. Mayella's fingers from my throat. I tried to holler for

Cricket and Connor, but I couldn't get the air to do more than croak a little.

"Because I deserve the Heart, do you understand?" said Mr. Mayella. "I am the one who knows it best, who can appreciate its powers, who can use it for the betterment of mankind. I deserve the Valley's Heart, Gustavina. I have *earned* it."

"Mr. . . . Mayella . . . ," I whispered, my vision going black. "Please."

Suddenly his eyes lost their blue flame. Mr. Mayella let go of my throat, his face aghast. I dropped to the floor, sucking in the fetid hatchery air as hard as I could. My throat ached and my head was all swimmy, but I would be okay.

"Oh, Gussy," said Mr. Mayella, burying his face in his hands. "My god. How did this happen?"

"It looks like the Great Doom got to you too," I said.

"Only because I let it," said Mr. Mayella. He kept staring at his hands, like they weren't his own, like they belonged to some kind of stranger. "This whole village is corrupt, Gussy, and it has corrupted me as well. I want the Valley's Heart, I always have. I thought if I sabotaged the Rites, I'd be able to steal it for myself before the village fell. But when I saw the terror of what the Great Doom brought, I couldn't do it. I realized I've failed in my duties. I've failed myself and your Grandpa Widow. Now all I want is to get my birds to safety."

All of a sudden Mr. Mayella fell to shaking, like there was

a tiny earthquake going on inside him. His fingers opened and closed themselves and he shivered all over like a dog shaking water off himself, his eyes all big and red rimmed and bulging, his teeth clacking together like the saints' bones in my pocket.

"Gussy," he said. "It's coming. Not even the hatchery's magic can keep it away."

The ground began to shake, the birds all rising up in flight, their wings barely flapping, like they were levitating. Mr. Mayella grabbed the fringes of his hair and pulled it down over his ears, as if to block out some awful music I couldn't even hear. I snatched up the bag of feathers and flung the door open to the waiting room.

"Let's get out of here," I said, my voice a scratchy wheeze from being choked.

"You okay, Gussy?" said Connor.

"Been better," I said. "But we got to go, and now."

Mr. Mayella came stumbling out of the hatchery vault, big clumps of his own hair in his hands, muttering to himself.

"What about him?" said Connor.

"There's not a thing we can do for him," I said. "Not right now, anyways."

Mr. Mayella stood in the doorway, his finger pointed at the ceiling.

A great rushing sound came, like a twister descending

down into the village. The roof of the hatchery was ripped off easy as wrapping paper and sucked upward into the black sky. The clouds whipped and churned above us as each one of those cardinals rose like a magic trick, vanishing like little drops of blood skyward.

"Run, children!" hollered Mr. Mayella. "Flee for your lives!"

The tower of fire twisted outside the gates, the sky opening red above it like a wound. It came crashing down in a single whoosh, flames rising like a cardinal's wings high above the city.

Connor yanked open the door and we stumbled out into the darkness, my windpipe aching, my bloody Cynthia-bit leg dragging a little behind me, Cricket yipping ahead of us. I knew we needed to hurry, that we had to hustle back to the Rectory if there was any chance of saving the village. But I had to take a look, I had to see for myself. I hobbled over to the main road and took a peek around the side of Bartleby Bonnard's cabin.

There stood the Rider, the witch Lucinda Withern herself. Giant wings of fire sprang from her shoulders like a great red cape, and her skin crackled with blue flames. As she walked her way through the town square, a line of fire burned the dust in her wake. The infected villagers gathered around her, a blank-faced, mind-controlled army.

"Gussy," said Connor.

"I know, I know," I said. "We got to hurry."

"No," he said, "that's not what I meant."

Lucinda Withern strolled through the village streets like the queen of demons, a blue-fire crown flickering above her head, the infected villagers trailing her like a shadow, hollering out in a voice that crackled and boomed, half Lucinda, half something else.

"I know what you meant," I said. "And yes, we still got a chance."

But I was lying. I knew our gizzard was cooked. There wasn't any chance we could beat an army like that. Not me, nor Grandpa Widow either.

It was just a fact. We had no hope left.

"Come on," I said. "Let's hustle back to the Rectory."

21

WE MADE IT BACK WITHOUT TOO MUCH trouble, seeing as how all the infected folks were so focused on Lucinda Withern, who so far as I could tell was a walking, talking Great Doom incarnate. I had no idea what was left of the secret witch who'd posed as the Rider, who'd set all of this in motion. I wished I could ask her what she was thinking, letting a power like that inside these gates—if it was just a desire for the Valley's Heart or if there was some secret grudge she had against Grandpa Widow or the Benningsleys or the village itself, I just did not know. I could have spent all night wondering about it, but it wouldn't have helped much. I had to do what Grandpa Widow always said to do.

"Don't worry yourself with explanations, with the billion

what-ifs that come parading through your brain at all hours of the day," he'd tell me. "Focus on what's right in front of you, the problem at hand. Once you solve that, you can get to worrying about the rest."

So right now, our problem was that we had an infected village and a witch filled to the brim with the Great Doom, a half-human fireball making her way through the streets, presumably on the way to the Benningsley mansion to take the Valley's Heart. I had every intention of getting the Valley's Heart back where it belonged—in the Hidden Mines, deep underground, never to be touched by a human hand again. Thing was, I couldn't just leave it at that. What if the Great Doom decided it liked waltzing around in Lucinda Withern's body, controlling each and every person who set foot in this village? What if its plan was eternal nighttime forever, all of us living in a fog of darkness without a brain of our very own?

No, what we needed was a way out, a means to bargain for the very lives of every last soul in the village.

First things first, though. We had to get our hands on the Valley's Heart. If Mayor Benningsley wouldn't hand it over—and at this point, in that Rite-protected mansion of his, he'd have very little reason to, all safe and sound in there—our only hope was Lulu.

"How's that Rite coming?" I asked Angeline.

She frowned at me. "Almost got it, I think. I mean, it's a

doozy, and no one's tried anything of this magnitude since the time of the Four Roaming Magicians."

"That's reassuring."

"I'm doing my best."

I was worried, I truly was. Angeline had powerful skills, and that was a fact. But what if her homemade magic wasn't the stuff of the Rites? What if it was too hardscrabble for something like the Great Doom to respect? The Rites had to be performed perfectly if they were to work, everyone knew that. But didn't they have to be designed perfectly to work too? Was Angeline—not even a trained Protector, just a runaway witch who had showed up at my doorstep—really able to make something precise enough to work as a Rite?

I didn't know, but judging from the rumbling and screaming outside, there wasn't much time to figure it out.

"Your best will have to do, I guess."

If it won't, I wanted to say, *it doesn't much matter, because the Great Doom will just swoop in and take us over and that will be that.*

Of course, that's not the kind of thing you say if you're a Protector. You just got to keep your head up and give it your all, and whatever came next would be our fate.

Still, it was a marvel watching Angeline work. Singeing those cardinal feathers (her delight in the gray ones was clear, and it made me smile despite myself), whispering the Mysteries over the saints' bones, the amphibian tongues, the six-sided dice, and one of Conner Carnivolly's red aces, for luck. Sketching the words of the Rite all slapdash across page after page, Lulu and Connor copying them down fast as they could, so that we all had a copy, so that we could all do the Rite together.

For my part, I was hobbling around on my ankle-bit leg, my voice still scraggled, blessing each and every one of us with every bit of ritual and Rite I could muster.

Still, I wasn't sure if it would be enough. We had never faced anything like this. I'm not sure anyone in history ever had. And as I looked around the Rectory, we didn't seem like much in the face of the Great Doom. Just an orphan, a runaway, a brat, a street magician, and a foundling mutt. How were we supposed to save a whole village?

At the same time, was there anybody I'd rather be doing this with? Well, apart from Grandpa Widow, of course. But hadn't he been part of the reason we were in this mess to begin with? I guessed it didn't matter now. You don't get to choose who you save the world with, but I was plenty glad with the crew the One Who Listens had given me.

"It's almost ready," said Angeline. "I just need one more thing to protect us."

"And what's that?" I said.

Angeline pointed to Lulu. "I need her ring."

"What? Not my grandma's ring," said Lulu. She clutched her hand to her chest. "Why would you need that?"

"Because your grandfather was the one who took the Valley's Heart," said Angeline. "And nothing could be more powerful for this Rite than the family of the one who transgressed."

"But it's the only thing I have left of her," said Lucy, clutching her ring to her chest. "It was Grammy's gift to me, the most precious thing she owned."

"If there was another way," said Angeline, "I promise you we'd choose it. But the spell won't work without giving something up. Unless you have anything better to offer."

Lulu sighed. "No, I guess I don't," she said. "I guess if my family's the one that committed the first crime, then my family ought to be the ones to fix it too." She fidgeted the ring off her finger, and it glimmered a million colors at once, the whole night sky in a simple tiny stone.

Angeline took the ring and placed it on Grandpa Widow's table, onto a little plate of iron he used for grinding ingredients. She whispered a Mystery over the stone, and quick as a batwing's flap, she slammed Grandpa Widow's hammer down onto it. The opal crumbled under the hammer, nothing but a shimmery pile of dust among the mangled metal of the ring. Angeline swept the dust into the little black mixing bowl of Grandpa Widow's.

Suddenly a feeling of peace shivered over the room, flickering the candle flames. Good magic was like that sometimes, a notion that cut like a blade of sunlight through a darkened room, illuminating everything, if only for a moment.

Angeline smiled. "I guess that's it then."

So far, the Rite was working, at least the part that was supposed to protect us from getting infected. As for what would drive the Great Doom out and cure everybody else, that was another thing altogether.

"So what's the plan?" said Connor.

I laid it out for them as best as I could.

"The plan is we anoint ourselves, purifying us as much as we possibly can to protect us from the Great Doom. Then we march through the village, performing this Rite, reclaiming what we can for our own. Mostly that will be to let the uninfected know we're out here, so folks don't give up hope. It's like Grandpa Widow used to say: 'I've seen some powerful magic in my day, Gussy, but nothing quite compares to hope, and that's a fact.' Once we've got the Great Doom's attention, we'll make our way to the meeting pole and demand an audience. Then we bargain."

"What are we bargaining with?" said Connor Carnivolly.

"Why, the Valley's Heart, of course," I said.

"But my dad will never give up the Heart," said Lulu. "Not willingly. And what if my brother can't get his medicine anymore? What if he dies?"

"I guarantee you, I will find a way to get your brother his medicine," I said. "We aren't going to let anything happen to him."

How I was actually going to do that, I didn't have a clue. My hope was that since the Great Doom had supposedly caused Chappie's sickness, the Great Doom could heal it too. That would be part of the bargain. Truth was, I had no idea if the Great Doom would take the bargain or not. I needed the village out from under the Great Doom more than anything, and I was willing to do anything to make that happen. Did that mean I was lying to Lulu? Yeah, a little bit. But you better believe me when I tell you that if the Great Doom wasn't willing to take that hex off Chappie, the second all this was over I was going to make it my life's work to get Chappie healed. You don't have to believe me, but it's the truth, I swear to you on the honor of the One Who Listens and my dog Cricket both, and that means something.

Outside there sounded a great boom, like a thunderclap loud enough to rattle my rib bones. I came running to the window and opened it a hair and stuck my head out. Big blue flashes of lightning arced across the sky, the thunder banging loud enough to make even angels cover their ears. Sparks shot up like high wild laughter, scattering in the wind. Lightning was striking the Benningsley mansion, there was no doubt about it. I wasn't sure just how strong the protections Grandpa Widow and Mr. Mayella had put on that house were, but I didn't figure much of anything could withstand lightning strikes. But that wasn't immediately what was worrying me. No, it was the sparks flying around everywhere, little gremlin flames ready to attach themselves onto wood and get burning.

I don't have to tell you that a fire is disastrous in a village like ours. First off, everything's made of wood, so fire catches quick and spreads even quicker. Second, it's not like there's a big river or something nearby we can just shuttle water to and from. Nope, we got to use the few wells we have in town, and we have to fight that fire with buckets passed down a chain of hearty villagers ready to dump that water on the fire. As it stood right now, if something big caught, the whole village would be burned down in minutes, and unless the infected villagers suddenly pitched in and got a nice bucket chain going, there wasn't much hope of stopping a fire.

"There's no time," I said. "We've got to go now."

"But I haven't finished copying out the Rite," said Connor. "I only have one copy for me and Lulu."

"That's fine," I said. "I don't like to sing the words anyhow. If you can teach me the melody real quick, I'll play that on my fiddle and it'll be enough."

"I don't have to teach it to you," said Angeline. "You already know it."

"What's that supposed to mean?" I said.

"Listen," she said, and she began to sing.

Yeah, I knew that melody all right. It was the exact one me and her had written a few nights ago in this very room, the music we had improvised all on our own. It was our song, and she had made a hymn out of it.

"Do you think that'll work?" I said. "Like, is it powerful enough? I mean, it was just you and me fooling around."

"No," said Angeline, "it was you and me singing our hearts out. There's something magic about this melody, and that's the truth. So long as we sing it with our best and fullest intentions, I don't see any reason why it won't be the strongest Rite this world has ever known."

"But the older Rites are perfect, based on traditions passed down from the great Protectors of the ages," I said. "I just don't know if a little song we wrote could ever be that powerful."

"You don't have to know," she said, "because I do know it, and I believe it with all my heart. Now let's hurry, before the Great Doom gets us all."

Lightning boomed outside, and the ground shook. A great wind blew through the village, and in the distance I heard screaming. There wasn't any more time to waste. We had to act, and we had to act now.

I anointed us with the potion Angeline had made, sprinkling drops of it on our foreheads, speaking a Mystery over each one of us, Cricket included. When it came time for me, I asked Angeline to do the honors.

"But Gussy," she said. "I'm not a Protector. I haven't trained properly."

"Oh, come on," I said. "You know the Rites better than anybody, even me. Besides, we're in a crisis. I hereby deputize you, or whatever the Protector version of that is. Now get to it. We got a village to save."

"Thank you, Gussy," she said, and for a minute I thought she was going to cry. She anointed me just right, whispering the Mystery in High Speak, as lovely as could be. I thought about how much she had changed from the terrified, hail-battered girl conked out at the gates. Now she was a Protector, in my eyes anyway. I was proud of her, I really was, and so happy I'd let her in.

"All right, everybody," I said. "Remember, no matter what, keep singing, and keep a steady intention in your heart. If you're afraid, that's fine, let that fear pass right by you. If you're nervous, that's fine too. Remember, keep your mind focused, and if any bad thoughts pop up, just let them drift on by. Got it?"

"I guess," said Lulu.

"Well, that's good enough, I suppose," I said. "Now let's go save the village."

And off we went, into the greatest darkness of our lives.

22

WE MARCHED OUT INTO THE RUINED village, wrecked like some colossal twister had whipped through and ravaged everything. Houses lay leveled, businesses destroyed, the gloom thick enough you could breathe it right into your lungs, leaving you coughing afterward. We marched into a darkness so complete the stars had vanished, the moon swallowed up, the sky a sunken rooftop pressing down onto us. We marched into the smell of burning, the smoldering ruins of lightning-struck buildings, houses of folks I knew, each one a monument to my own failure. Yeah, I'd failed at protecting this village from infection, but I wasn't going to fail at curing it.

And that's where the Rite came in. First, we were to walk widdershins inside the village, right up against the walls, as opposed to outside of it. That's because this was a Cleansing Rite, the likes of which no one had ever tried before, not in the whole history of Protectors. We were to cleanse the village from the inside out. I walked up front, head Protector that I was, my fiddle lifted high, my notes precise. Beside me was Cricket, of course, howling along, the purest harmony you ever heard. Behind me came Angeline, holding the script for our Rite, singing the words so sweetly in her high birdsong voice. Connor came behind her, hollering out in his deep lovely voice, banging a little ceremonial drum Angeline had found for him in the Rectory, something that belonged to Grandpa Widow from years and years ago. We marched to his tempo, his voice rising high above all the rest of us, singing the words Angeline had written with a purity and a goodness that made me feel like maybe they were holy, maybe this Rite was a real Rite after all. I realized that the words weren't nearly so important as the spirit you brought to them, as the power of a human voice crying out in the bleakest of all times. That really is something, I tell you right now. Connor seemed to make all of this real somehow, his faith and heart and courage. I was proud he was my friend.

Last of all came Lulu, hollering along all tone-deaf but sincere, singing the song of the wrongs her own ancestors had wrought. She was brave, I'll give her that, to face the truth without shrinking away from it, to try and make things right. I guess it was the least she could do, but it still counted for something.

After we'd finished walking widdershins, we took to the streets, threading our way down boulevard and alleyway, brightening the grim with our music. The village was mostly a darkened rubble, and lightning crashed all around us. The ungathered infected shouted insults at us, curses, as we passed by. But never did one of us walk astray, never did we sing with less than our highest intentions. Our hymn echoed through the streets, rising above the hecklers and naysayers, a song lifted up to everyone still left in the village and beyond, past the gloom and to the hidden moon and stars, all the way up to the One Who Listens itself. I hoped it heard us, wherever it was. I hoped it was marching right along with us, lending its own holy silent voice to all we did.

I started to feel good even, a little bit. It's hard not to feel good when you're playing a song you helped write, something beautiful and true you made with your friends, and you're belting it out into the world, no matter how dark that world is. In fact, it might be the best feeling there is. To this day I've never found a better one, if you want me to be honest about it.

But just as we were passing by the Rectory again, something bad happened.

I mean, real bad.

The neck of my fiddle snapped, the head dangling by the

strings. I don't know if it was the Great Doom, or the drastic change in temperature, or my own negligence. One of the strings snapped and whipped me right across the face, cutting my cheek. My own blood streamed down my face, and it stung like a mutant bee sting. My beautiful fiddle, the one I'd had since I was just a kid. What was I supposed to do now?

"Are you okay?" said Angeline.

"I'm fine," I said, though it still hurt. "Don't stop, whatever you do. Don't stop singing."

I held my busted fiddle in my hand, and I marched with them, but I knew that wasn't enough. I knew I needed to participate, that my voice was important too somehow. But I hated my singing voice, I hated it so much. I hated the croaky way it sounded, the wild unwieldiness of it. Just to hear myself sing was enough to set me cringing. But these weren't times when embarrassment counted. I had to speak up, and I had to holler as best as I could. All of our lives—yes, even the lives of my friends—counted on it.

So I took a deep breath and let it out slow, and I held my head high, and I hollered out the words of the hymn (I'd learned it by now, a whole walk through the village), I sang them with all of my heart.

Did I sound great? Probably not. More than likely I sounded like a bullfrog choking on a horsefly. But I sang anyway, and I sang with every bit of my intention. And you know what? It felt wonderful. It was the best feeling I ever had in my whole life.

And somehow, impossibly, I felt the gloom lift, just a little bit, like the Great Doom's grip on the village was loosening.

On that second swoop through the village, I heard another voice tailing us, a lovely vibrato-filled voice, pretty as a swallow's song. It was Big Gordo, come striding out of his hut, a bandage on his head. He carried a torch, a bright burning beacon in the darkness. I could tell he was hurting, and he was afraid, but he walked tall behind us, his voice like the sun rising over our heads. It was a boon, an encouragement, and there was no doubt about that. Soon we heard other voices, other villagers left uninfected, and they joined our procession, singing the refrains as they learned them, marching in place behind us.

More and more uninfected villagers crawled out from the rubble, opening their locked doors and latched shutters, stepping out from the shadows and walking with us, their voices sounding out into the night, growing stronger every moment. There was Mr. Coldcuts the taxidermist, Millard Dinkens the blacksmith, and Marjorie Willoughby the bull rider. There was Sam Pinkston, the tallest kid in the village, and Lily Kim, the girl who was scared of nothing. There was Lucille Downing and Horace Romanov and Binky Jacobs and Madame Golescu, her voice deep and rich and loud enough to shake the shingles off a roof. There was Martina the locksmith and Donald Dithery and Leonidas Tucker and Old Esmerelda herself and Petey Kinkler and the Abakar twins and Marceline Chatlani and even mean old Sylvana Plainclothes. There were so many more, all my beautiful villagers, the ones I had sworn to protect, the ones I loved with all my heart. I realized in that moment how much they all meant to me, how connected we all were, even if they did drive me nuts half the time. That's what it means to be a part of something bigger than yourself, the whole of us singing together, our joy beating back the darkness together. We did three laps around the village like that, and it was wonderful.

As good as all that made me feel, I was still terrified to go to the center of the village, where the meeting pole had been. For one, it wasn't far from the Benningsley mansion, where Lucinda Withern and her minions waited. I knew we were protected, the five of us at least, but I didn't know how strong Angeline's ritual would hold up against a power like that. I was half afraid the Great Doom would zap us with lightning bolts the first chance it got. But I knew that the plan wouldn't work unless we could get its attention focused on us. One thing was for certain—if we were all going to burn alive, at least we would do it together. I took some comfort in that.

When we came to the charred embers of the meeting pole, our gang had grown from four kids and a dog to nearly forty people, scared and wounded villagers stronger and braver now with all of us singing the same song together. I could see Lucinda Withern standing in front of the Benningsley mansion, her crown of blue fire, those burning wings tucked behind her back, the Great Doom filling her with a power greater than anything I'd ever known. She seemed to be watching us, curious, a little smirk on her face, like maybe this was all a big joke to her. It scared me a little bit. Heck, it scared me a lot bit. I didn't know what the Great Doom had up its sleeve. I only hoped our plan would work, that I hadn't just doomed us all.

As we sang, the sky seemed to crackle and burn, ripping itself open like a letter, and for just a moment I could see the stars impossibly far away like angels off in the distance, just a glimmer, waving goodbye. Then the clouds closed themselves, and from the darkness fell a great blue flame, ball lightning flung from the sky, headed straight for us. Angeline gripped my hand, and I held Connor's, all down the line.

"Do not stop singing," I told Angeline, and she nodded.

Closer and closer came the burning thing, like a god's eyeball loosed from its socket, hurtling through the sky toward us.

Just as it neared, the uninfected villagers screamed, dropping to their knees, covering their heads. I figured we were probably toast, that there wasn't any hope left in us at all. But I didn't stop singing, no sir, and neither did Angeline or Connor or Lulu or Cricket or Big Gordo. And just as the fireball was about to smash into us, cooking us all into dust, it dissipated right above our heads, scattering in a barrage of blue sparks. The Great Doom couldn't touch us while we sang.

Slowly the uninfected villagers rose from the dust, and our song only grew louder as Angeline drew a great big ritual circle around all of us, anointing the villagers with blessed water from her canteen, shaking the tan cardinal feathers over them for protection. She made a sign of three with the feathers, burying them in the four corners of our gathering. She clacked saints' bones in a bag and shook them over our heads. She scattered the dust of the desert in her left hand and dirt from the grave of Grand Master Orinoco, the Wise Priestess of the Fourteenth Age, in her right. I watched in awe as the wind picked up the priestess's dust and it burned away like something scattered from a star.

The Rite worked, is what I'm saying. Angeline's Rite worked every bit as well as Grandpa Widow's had, and better. She was a true Protector, down to her bones, and my heart nearly burst with joy watching her perform her work.

Once the ritual was complete, Angeline made a motion for the song to stop.

Silence fell over the village, a crackle of dying flames, the wind whistling through debris. Faint thunder rumbled in the distance, but there were no voices heard, everyone watching Lucinda Withern under the sway of the Great Doom, waiting for what she might say.

The voice came out scratchy and broken, like a pile of rocks sliding slipshod down a hill.

"I like your song," she said. "It is a very pretty song."

Well, I wasn't expecting that. It didn't sound like Lucinda Withern at all anymore. No, she had changed, become something else.

"Um, thanks," was all I said.

Lucinda Withern's arms were raised high, the great red wings lifting behind her, a cursed angel from the bowels of the earth.

"Never before have I had a voice," said the Great Doom. "A human voice, that is. Never have I had a body powerful enough to contain the fullness of me. Not until this witch came to me."

"It's just you now, isn't it?" I said. "The Great Doom. There's no Lucinda Withern left, is there?"

"The witch put up a fight, it's true," said the Great Doom. "But only a fool would think she could control me for long."

"I'm not sure if that's a good thing or not," I said. "But to be honest, I sure would appreciate it if you'd leave our village now."

"Your village?" said the Great Doom. She made a sound like an old man coughing up a lung. I'm pretty sure she was laughing. "Your village is a mistake, an infraction, a blight upon my blank beautiful desert. I am before you and I will be long after your kind pass from the land. This village is no more yours than this dust is yours. Your kind may play your part in the great cycle of things, but you matter no more to me than the life of the briefest desert flower. Perhaps even less."

"Good to know," I said. "So what can we do to get you to leave us alone?"

"Return what was stolen from me," she said.

"I'm working on that. If I give you the Valley's Heart, will you let go of my people? Release their minds, all that?"

The Great Doom smiled at me, twirling her fingers in the air, writing fire-blue words in the darkness, symbols I couldn't read.

"If you wish. Though I suppose they would be happier controlled by me. I can feel their insides, their horrid grasping thoughts, their worries and fears. You are not a happy people, and I pity you. The peace that I grant them is a peace beyond death. They are connected to me, connected to what lies beneath their feet. The squiggle of worms and the heartbeats of snakes, the toad buried under the mud, the wolf howling on high, the pull of the moon upon the world, the fire burning deep in the earth's belly. They are a part of all that now, experiencing eternity. Would you deny them this fate?"

"Yes," I said, "I surely would. People deserve to make their own choices, and then to live with those consequences, be they good or bad."

"But do they deserve to ruin what is not theirs?"

"That's a whole other argument," I said. "And to be honest, I don't quite know how to answer that question. But I think we can live better and be better, if only you'll give us another chance."

Her eyes burned with a blue so blisteringly bright I had to turn my face. The light from her made me sweat all over in my robes, like I was standing next to an actual star come swooping down to earth, something ancient and elemental and true. I knew I was in the presence of something older than people, something that would outlast us all too. It was like the ocean in my dreams, you know? Something unknowable and unfathomable. It reminded me that, at best, we were all just guests on this earth, not belonging anywhere, not destined for any particular thing, like raindrops falling everywhere at random from the sky.

The Great Doom seemed to understand what I was thinking, and she dimmed her brightness for me so I could look into her eyes again. I saw compassion there, sure, but a kind of exasperated indifference too. I wondered if sending that blue fireball to burn us up was the worst she could do. Probably not. She was probably going easy on me. Truth was, I bet she could open the earth up right now and have it swallow me whole if she so desired. It was tough, trying to negotiate a deal with someone so powerful. Dangerous business, this, and I had better keep my head.

"You are bargaining with something that is not yours," she said. "You and your miserable kind, who have stolen so much from me and used little human tricks to keep me out. Your Grandpa Widow, that scoundrel Mayella—their names I have only just learned. From the minds of these, no secrets are hid from me. Even you, Gussy. I know where you come from, the tragedy that brought you here."

"Wait, you know about me?" I said. "You can tell me about my parents?"

Right about then, Lulu and Connor Carnivolly came bursting out of the Benningsley mansion's front door, lugging something heavy in a bedsheet between them. They'd stolen it, the Valley's Heart. Mayor Benningsley came running out after them but stopped at his doorframe, afraid to cross the threshold into the world of the rest of us.

"Lulu, get back here!" he screamed. "You're risking your brother's life!"

"No," she said, "you already did that, Dad. I'm trying to save him."

The Great Doom watched all this with a curious expression on her face, like she was reading some strange-lessoned story, a parable of a bunch of unknowable creatures, ornery in their ways, their reasons unfathomable to her.

"So you have come to return to me what is mine, little girl?" she said.

"Yes, we have." I took a deep breath and let it out slow.

This was the tricky part. "On one condition. Actually, a couple conditions, if I'm being truthful about it."

"I could destroy you now, you know," she said. "I could set fire to your blood and boil you inside out."

"Respectfully, ma'am, no, you can't," I said. "Not while we're in this circle."

"Do you honestly think your little rituals can hold me back?"

"They have for over sixty years," I said. "I figure they'll hold another few minutes."

I could be wrong, but I swear the Great Doom grinned a little at that.

"Very well," she said. "State your terms."

"I need you to let all these folks free of your control," I said. "And I need you to leave the village."

I held my breath for a second. This last request was the scariest of all.

"And I need you to take your curse off Chappie Benningsley."

Fire danced across her face, flickering like a second tongue from her mouth, and I shivered despite the heat.

"He is the Benningsley heir, is he not?" she said. "Does he not deserve to be cursed for what his family has done?"

"Well, I'm not real clear on deserving," I said. "That's a strange word to me. Hard to know who deserves what. You'd probably have to be the One Who Listens to know something like that, to be able to see into people's hearts and minds, to know the actions behind the actions, you know? But, to be perfectly honest with you, I don't think Chappie deserves to die. It's his granddaddy who stole from you, after all."

"And his father that chipped and sold what was most precious to me," she said. "In truth, the punishment isn't the son's. It's the father's. The boy will pass into the world, in peace and bliss, at one with everything. It is his father who will have to live with the guilt for what he's done, an agony that can never be diminished or taken from him."

At that, Mayor Benningsley stomped on his front parlor floor and screamed.

"I will not allow you to do this!" hollered Mayor Benningsley. "It isn't right!"

There were big tears in his eyes, and his face was all red. I'd never seen Mayor Benningsley more afraid in my life. It made me hurt for him. It also made me understand him a little bit better, why he'd done the things he had. I'd do anything to protect the ones I love too.

"It's okay, Dad," said a scratchy little voice, coming up behind him. It was Chappie Benningsley, all pale and sickly in his pajamas. He looked so frail that the slightest wind through the village would have toppled him over, but his eyes were brave. He stepped past his father and into the village square, unprotected. "Go ahead and give her the Heart,

Gussy. I'm tired of living like this, and I don't want everyone to get hurt because of me."

"Get back inside!" said Mayor Benningsley.

"Let him talk, Dad," said Lulu, her eyes bright with tears. "Let Chappie say what he wants. You're always trying to control us, always telling us what to do. Why don't you listen to somebody else for once?"

"But . . . ," said Mayor Benningsley.

"Shut up, dear," said Lucretia Benningsley. She walked outside the house, past the circle, and knelt before the Great Doom. "Will you please let my boy live? We will do everything we can to help make this right, I promise you that, no matter what it takes. And we will never bother you or anyone else again. I know we don't deserve another chance, but I'm begging you for your grace."

The Great Doom glowered at her, red wings of flame blistering the air.

"Please?" said Mrs. Benningsley. "From a mother to a mother." She looked up at her. "You are a mother, aren't you? Of all that is here, in the desert?"

The Great Doom frowned, the fire sparking in her eyes. "Very well," she said. "The boy will live. But someone has to die. Someone has to suffer for what you've done."

I didn't have to think twice about it. I'm serious. I didn't even pause. And I'll be proud of that one fact until the day I die.

"I'll do it," I said.

"But Gussy," said Connor. "You can't."

I shrugged at him. "It's my job."

I turned to Angeline, who wore my old patched Protector robes, the girl who had come to the gates all battered and bruised, the exile, the cleverest and strangest person I'd ever known. I was so lucky she had come to this village, that she'd wound up in the Rectory all these days.

"Angeline," I said, my voice cracking a little, "can you take care of the village for me? When I'm gone, I mean?"

Angeline was crying real hard, I could hear her behind me. "I don't know if I can do it, Gussy. I don't know if I'm worthy."

"Are you kidding me?" I said. "You're the one who made up this whole new Rite by yourself, a Rite so powerful not even the Great Doom could break it. You're a heck of a Protector, Angeline. You're born for it. So will you take care of this village after I'm gone or not?"

She nodded. "I will."

"Then it's settled," I said, and stepped forward out of the ritual circle. I faced the Great Doom as bravely as I could, that fire crown rippling above her head, the flutter of her burning wings. I saw the faces of all the infected villagers standing there dully, blank minded, watching me. I'd never been so scared in my whole life, but I wasn't about to show it. No sir, I was performing the highest service a Protector can ever do. I was sacrificing myself for the village. More than that, I was sacrificing myself for my friends, for the people I loved. For my family. Because it was a fact. The folks standing in this circle with me were my family, my real one. Imperfect as they were, as difficult as they could be, as isolated as I'd felt from them at times in my life. I loved them, each one of them, even Mayor Benningsley. I really truly did. It was an honor to die for them, even if it was scary, even if it would probably hurt. I only wished I could say goodbye to Grandpa Widow before I went. Oh, well. Nothing I could do about that now.

That was when Cricket leaped from the circle and stood next to me, his head held high, fearless as always. I knelt down and rubbed Cricket's head. Dogs know. They always do.

"All right," I said. "Let's get this over with already."

The Great Doom stretched her hand out and laid it on my forehead.

And then, well . . . I don't know what happened.

It was like I blacked out.

It was like I was dreaming.

I saw a skinny, sweet-faced man with a mustache and his round, pretty wife, a flash of mystery in her eyes. They danced out in a forest somewhere, the air so cold you could see their breath, their laughter nothing but smoke coming from their mouths. He twirled her and she spun him and you could tell they were in love, you could feel it. And the sky rained down the light of the stars, and they were beautiful.

Those are my parents, I thought.

Somehow I knew it to be true.

And then there was me. A squawling, screaming little baby, a head full of hair, my fingers and toes all making fists. I saw my mother hold me until I quieted, my father smiling and crying. They loved me, I knew it, I could see it all.

But there was trouble. There is always trouble.

I saw people in uniforms, what looked like soldiers, with swords and knives, kicking in doorways, herding people out into the streets. I saw my parents flee into the woods, clutching me tight. I saw them hide and starve, all of us hungry, lost, and afraid, hiding from men in the woods, cowering from death.

I saw us by the ocean, on a dock. I saw my father on his knees, his hands full of coin, begging. I saw a man with a pink scar on his cheek shake his head and sigh, and then motion them onward. I saw my family board a ship, all three of us, and we were happy and laughing, our bellies full for the first time in weeks. I could feel my own joy, I could feel the joy of my mother and father, I could feel the starlight sing down to us on our first night at sea, the darkness not unlike that desert, stretching forever in both directions. I saw a school of dolphins leap from the water and spin, the moonlight shining off their wet shimmering skin.

And then came the storm.

This I had seen before, I knew what happened next.

In my dreams I wept for my parents, for what happened to them. In my dreams I wept for myself, lost and alone, stranded on a sea-drenched rock, waiting for somebody to come and save me.

And then I saw him, my eyes blinking open—an old man with a sun-burned face, smiling down at me. Grandpa Widow. I looked up into his face, the crinkles around his eyes, his gray beard dangling almost low enough for my little fingers to touch it, and I saw nothing but love for me in his eyes. And in that moment I understood finally that Grandpa Widow was my family—my true family—no matter what.

When I came to, I was crying.

It was like no time had passed at all. Maybe all of that had happened in just a few seconds, but it felt like hours, like weeks even, a whole lifetime. But the Great Doom was just removing her hand from my head, a sad look in her eyes. She bent down and scooped up the Valley's Heart, lifting it as if it weighed as much as a pebble.

The sky opened up, the black clouds swirling, a twister of blue lightning dropping down, striking the ground behind the Great Doom. She held the Valley's Heart up to the sky, and I watched the twister yank it from her hands, carrying it skyward.

"Farewell, Gussy," she said.

And Lucinda Withern's body dropped lifeless to the dust.

The sky cleared suddenly, and it was morning, the sun rising pinkly in the distance. The infected villagers blinked, awake now, back to their old selves. Angeline ran to me, hugging me tight. Cricket leaped up and licked my face, and Connor Carnivolly tackled both of us, knocking us all over. Lulu ran to Chappie Benningsley and hugged him, the boy not so sickly looking anymore, the four Benningsleys holding each other tight on their own front porch.

Everyone was so happy, laughing and hugging each other and singing.

So why was I crying?

23

GRANDPA WIDOW GOT BACK LATE IN the afternoon the next day. He rode up worn out on the back of an even worse-off Miss Ribbit. They both looked ready to keel over, clopping up to the wreck of the village. Grandpa Widow just sat there on horseback, a droop of a human, outside the ruined gates. You should have seen the misery on Grandpa Widow's face. He really did love this village, loved the whole Darkling Valley, despite everything.

After we got him and Miss Ribbit good and watered, he wouldn't hardly say a word. He kept looking around and blinking at everything, like he was in shock. It wasn't very Protector-like of him. In fact, I'd never seen him look so frail, so old, like he could just up and blow away with the tumbleweeds. It broke my heart a little.

Eventually Grandpa Widow sighed.

"You going to tell me what happened or not?" he said.

So I gave it to him. The whole story, every bit of it, even the stuff about Mr. Mayella and the truth about how the village was started. He just looked at me, nodding.

"Well, now you know," he said. "The greatest shame of my life, you know."

Then he walked back to the Rectory and closed the door. I stood there in the noontime heat, halfway between being furious at him and being so overjoyed he was back I wanted to cry. I wasn't quite sure how I was supposed to feel, so I just let myself feel everything, the good and the bad of it.

About ten minutes later Grandpa Widow came out of the Rectory. He'd changed into his best robes, the ones he used only for the finest ceremonies, the solstices or yearly sacrifice or the Feast of the Seven Eggs. Then he walked across the way to Doc Myrtle's place, where the back wall had fallen in. Doc Myrtle wasn't so young anymore, and he wore thick glasses and limped on a bum knee. He sure was having a hard time fixing up that wall. Grandpa Widow grabbed a hammer and nails, and without a word to me he walked over to the aging old doctor with the kindest eyes in the village.

"Hi, Doc," said Grandpa Widow. "How can I help?"

Me and him got to talking around dinnertime, after a long day's work fixing things. Grandpa Widow told Angeline and me and Cricket what had happened. The fake summons of the council that the Rider delivered was a pretty good forgery. I wondered if Mr. Mayella had anything to do with that as well, but there wasn't any way to ask him. He'd fled the village while we were fixing everything. That was okay. We could get a new hatchery, and a new person to run it too. There were always people out there willing to do a good job, if only you looked hard enough.

Once Grandpa Widow figured out he'd been had, he hustled back to the village as quick as he could. But try as he might, he kept getting lost. He figured he'd done about twenty laps around the whole Darkling Valley, passing the same weird rock and the same bleached horse skull and the same sad squat toad stuck in the mud croaking at him over and over again. That was Lucinda Withern again. There'd been a hex on the summons, so it was a good thing Grandpa Widow hadn't let me touch it. I wouldn't have been able to be much good in this crisis if I couldn't get anywhere without taking a thousand wrong turns first.

Over the next few weeks, we kept steady rebuilding the village, everybody doing their part. Mayor Benningsley promised the rest of his leftover fortune to help, and he was good to his word. Lazlo Dunes was out every day keeping everybody accountable, rapping his stick on the ground and hollering all the time. Lord help him, the man couldn't keep his voice down to save his life. Lulu even did her part, lugging materials around, taking care of the sick. She never stopped being a brat though, and she never was quite nice to me. I don't know. I kind of respected her for that.

Grandpa Widow took it upon himself to get Angeline certified as a Protector apprentice, going through all the council channels. You should have seen her face when she got her official notice delivered, all stamped and sealed, with her very own name on it. She just held it in her hands and cried and cried. It was one of the happiest days of my life.

After the ceremony, I told her that since Grandpa Widow was back and things were calming down a little, maybe he could locate her parents for her.

Angeline frowned.

"I don't think that will be necessary," she said. "Eventually my parents will find me on their own, and I'll have to face them then."

"Yeah," I said, "but at least you won't have to do it alone."

Her face brightened a little, and she smiled at me. "Thank you, Gussy."

I got to say, I felt pretty good about that.

Then there was the matter of my file.

It took me ages to work up the courage to ask Grandpa Widow about it. Mostly because I was afraid Grandpa Widow's answer would hurt me. I was right, of course.

"I burned it," he said.

"You burned it?"

"Yeah," he said, all ashamed but still staring me right in the eyes. "About five years ago, I woke up one night terrified you were going to leave, Gussy. That if you found out where you were from, you'd want to go back there. So I stole it out of the courthouse and set it aflame outside the gates. I'm sorry I lied to you about the nature of your duties, and I'm sorry for how I helped this village get started. I'm sorry, and there isn't much more I can say than that. I suspect you don't like me much right now. You got a right to that. I got a lot to repent for, there's no two ways about it."

I *was* pretty mad, if you want me to be honest. That made me madder than just about anything in my life. I didn't talk to Grandpa Widow for nearly a week, excepting for official duty, of course.

But the more I thought about it, the more I realized that even if what he'd done was wrong—and it certainly was wrong—he'd done it out of love, because he loved me. Folks don't always act wisely when they love you. Nope, they can get downright selfish. That's a tough thing about love, how it brings out both the best and the worst in a person, no matter how hard they try. He knew he'd failed me—heck, he'd failed the whole village—and he knew a simple sorry wouldn't cut it. He'd let every last one of us down. That was why he was out there, every day, working his ancient tail off, trying to fix things. Because repentance isn't something you just say, it's something you do. It's putting in the effort. And Grandpa Widow sure as heck was working hard, day and night, hour after hour. There's something to admire in that, no matter how mad you get at a person.

I'm not making any excuses for Grandpa Widow, don't get me wrong. I forgive him, but that doesn't mean it doesn't hurt. I suppose I'll be hurting for a long time. To be honest, I don't think things will ever be quite the same between us, not again. And maybe that's for the best. But I still love Grandpa Widow, and I forgive him too.

It's just what Protectors do.

Besides, it's not like I didn't need forgiving for plenty of things myself. You could make a list of my mistakes longer than the Book of Names, no doubt about it. I might not have even opened the gates for Angeline if Cricket hadn't half forced me to, I was so dead set on following the rules. That's something that I'm still more than a little bit ashamed of. I suppose everybody has something they need to be forgiven for. Everybody except Cricket, of course. If there was any actual saint to this story, it's Cricket, and that's just the truth.

Anyways, Grandpa Widow had my file memorized, and there wasn't much to it. I had him tell me the whole thing, once I was unmad at him enough to speak to him again. See, I was from a land far off, one I'd never even heard of, the only survivor of a terrible shipwreck. My parents were dead, both of them drowned. But I survived, for some reason, and maybe I had some family across the ocean. Part of me wanted to hop on Miss Ribbit right then and ride on to the nearest seaport and take the first ship that would have me. I could be a sailor, I knew that. I still remembered the way the salt air tasted in my dreams. I wanted to see where I came from. I wanted to meet whatever family I had left. I wanted to know everything about the land of my ancestors, what clothes they wore and what kind of food they ate and what my actual birth name might be, because nobody knew, it wasn't even in the file.

But you know what? Even if I wasn't from the Darkling Valley, it was still my home. I'd been raised here, and I had people who loved me. More than that, I had a whole community that still counted on me, that was still rebuilding. I was needed, is what I'm saying. My home needed me. I couldn't just up and bail on it yet, not when I still had all these responsibilities.

So you know what I decided? One day I'll take that journey. One day I'll board a ship and sail myself past the moonrise, find the land of my ancestors. I'll eat their food and hug the necks of any cousins I got left. I'll track down every scrap of information on my family I can find, and I'll love doing it, even if it's all sad news. That's what I'm going to do, I swear my life on it.

Just, you know, not today. And I can live with that.

Besides, Grandpa Widow left the drafting of the new Rites up to me and Angeline. He said it was long past time for a new generation to try things their way. We talked to all the folks in the village, every last one of them, about the kind of place they wanted to live in, about what sort of Rites would help them the most. Figured it was best to start from there, you know? Build everything around taking care of everybody's needs as best as we could. We're part of a long line of Protectors, me and Angeline, trying our best to honor those who came before us, and to keep safe those still here. We build on the past and try to make it better. Sure, we were going to make mistakes, same as previous Protectors had. There just wasn't any way to get it all right, to do everything perfect. There would always be a better way to do things, a better way to fashion the Rites and rituals that govern a village, one we hadn't the vision or knowledge or know-how to get right yet. That's what next generations are for. But we were going to do our darnedest, no doubt about that. Me and Angeline and Cricket were going to give it our best.

Not sure there's much more you can ask of a body than that.

It's been two months since the Great Doom broke into the village and the Valley's Heart was returned.

I'm lying down in my bed now, listening to Grandpa Widow snoring like a fiend, Cricket sniffling in his dreams, the pages turning in Angeline's books as she tries to read by candlelight. Outside, coyotes yelp, and the wind scatters the starlight through the desert darkness. It's not a dark that scares me anymore. In fact, I find it wonderful, inviting almost. It's the kind of dark that calls to you, that won't let you stay inside and ignore it, not on a night like tonight.

So I wait until Angeline snuffs her candle out, tucks her book under her pillow. Soon she's snoozing just like all the rest of them. Quiet as I can, I slip out of my cot and ease myself into the night, just to see.

Outside the Rectory, the moonlight shines itself over my still wrecked and ruined village, every splintered board and broken glass dear to me, precious somehow. I think about all the people sleeping inside, all that they've lost, how hard the last couple months have been, and how much harder the next ones will be. I think about all of them lying soundly in their beds, maybe a few tossing nervously with nightmares from the weeks before, but hopefully nothing too bad, and I love them. I love all of them, even the ones I don't like. It's almost overwhelming, this feeling, a total gratitude, a gift so grand it could only come from the One Who Listens.

I look out on the walls of the village, now gateless, as they will remain forever. We don't have any need of gates, not anymore. I look out over the desert, the world beyond, all starlit and blue-black night, stretching on endlessly every-where I turn my head. It's not too hard to imagine myself on a boat, sailing out for lands unknown, the dark ocean all around me, not a speck of dry ground as far as the eye can see.

In time, I think, *in time.*

I sneak my way back into the Rectory, into my bed that's grown a little cool in the nighttime. I pull the covers up and shut my eyes and pray for good dreams, for sweet sleep. Because I'm going to need my strength tomorrow, that's for sure.

After all, I still have work to do.

ACKNOWLEDGMENTS

Thanks to Jess Regel, Andrew Eliopulos, Courtney Stevenson, Louisa Whitfield-Smith, and Yuta Onoda. Thanks to Mom, Dad, and Chris. Thank you.